PIPER DAVENPORT

Road To PEACE

DOGS OF FIRE BOOK #6

Happy reading!
Piper Davenport

DOGS OF FIRE

Cover Art & Model
Jack Davenport

TRIXIE
PUBLISHING

ISBN-13: 9781711897097

ACKNOWLEDGEMENTS

Jack:
Thank you for all your hard work on the covers. I couldn't do this without you!

Brandy:
Thank you for keeping the characters and timelines right!

Mary H.:
Thanks for the multiple read throughs!!!

Gail:
Thank you for your eagle eye!!! You're amazing!

Lila Rose:
You have been a wonderful source of fun and distraction! Love your MC boys, and I greatly appreciate your support of mine! Love you!

Harper Sloan:
Thank you for your love of all things alpha and your support for my Dogs! Love you!

Liz Kelly:
Thanks again. Your insight is always so spot on! You keep this up, you're going to be on my permanent BETA list. You're welcome!

PRAISE

Get ready to fall head over heels! Road to Peace is another page turner of alpha brilliance from Davenport. I fell in love with every single page and spent the last few wishing the book would never end! ~ Harper Sloan, NY Times & USA Today Bestselling Author

Piper Davenport can write one hell of a sexy biker! I can't get enough of the Dogs of Fire MC series ~ Geri Glenn, author of the Kings of Korruption MC Series

Road to Peace sinfully hot, creatively captivating, and I loved every second of reading as the pieces of Hatch & Maisie's lives and hearts intertwined. Piper Davenport paints the most beautiful pictures of love with her words. I'm in awe. Felicia Lynn, Contemporary Romance Author

All it took was one page and I was immediately hooked on Piper Davenport's writing. Her books contain 100% Alpha and the perfect amount of angst to keep me reading until the wee hours of the morning. I absolutely love each and every one of her fabulous stories. ~ Anna Brooks, Contemporary Romance Author

ROAD TO PEACE was an incredible, page turning ride! If you're looking for a take-charge alpha hero who'll protect his heroine at any cost, then you HAVE to read Hatch and Maisie's story! I was swooning from the moment that badass biker stepped on the page! ~ Sybil Bartel, Author of the Uncompromising Series

This is one series I will most definitely be reading!! Great job Ms. Davenport!! I am in love!! ~ Tabitha, Amazeballs Book Addicts

Hey, T.M.

I won't "out" you to the masses, but never leave a fellow woman stranded, and never do it to an author...you'll end up in a book!

ONE

Maisie

I WALKED OUT of Lonnie's salon and into the blaring heat of an unusually hot Pacific Northwest April. Squinting against the brightness, I slid my sunglasses on and headed to the Chinese restaurant next door to pick up my takeout order. Ten minutes later, food in hand, I was ready to go home and soak in the tub. It had been a long day and I needed a little down time. Only, when I climbed into my car and pushed the start button, nothing happened.

"What the—?" I tried again, but still nothing, so I climbed out and looked around. Lonnie's lights were off, the closed sign hung on the door, and the parking lot was all but empty. "Just great," I said, and groaned.

I considered going back into the Chinese restaurant for help, but I'd had to repeat my order three times, so I had little faith they'd be able to understand my request for a jump. I grabbed my cell and called Triple A.

"Roadside Assistance, how may I help you?"

"Well, I'm in Orchards and I have a dead battery," I said.

"No problem, we can send someone out. What's the address?"

I rattled off my location, gave her my card number and other pertinent information.

"We can have someone out to you in about an hour."

"Really? Nothing sooner?"

"No, sorry. We're really busy today."

"Okay," I said. "Thanks."

I sighed and hung up, turning to find Lonnie walking out of her shop. "Hey, Maisie. You're still here?"

"I have a dead battery. I called Triple A, but if you have a minute, would you mind giving me a jump, please?"

"No, sorry, I actually have to be somewhere."

I stared at her, so shocked by her unwillingness to help me I couldn't even form a response. It would take maybe five minutes to jump my battery. I'd been loyal to her for more than ten years, even following her to this crappy part of town, and she couldn't take five minutes to help me? I think my mouth was still slightly agape as I watched her climb into her car and drive off, smiling and waving at me as she passed.

God! I'd just given her a thirty-percent tip. Not to mention, I always sent her a Christmas card, even though she *never* reciprocated, and even sent her a gift on her birthday. Not cool!

I sighed and leaned against my car, scanning the area. I lived and worked in downtown Portland and only ever came up here for my hair needs. But there had to be someone around who could help me so I wouldn't be stuck here for another hour.

I walked a few feet away from my car and looked around. *Bingo.* A little hole-in-the wall mechanic's garage was across the busy street and three doors down. Concerned they wouldn't be open, or would be manned by grease monkeys who liked to take advantage of women in need of automotive services, I shuddered, but trudged toward the shop anyway. If they were open, I figured they'd probably be able to help me, but if they weren't willing, then I'd give them a nasty Yelp review. I should probably do that to Lonnie, but wasn't entirely sure I was quite that brave. It took me years to find her.

* * *

Hatch

I dumped an armload of parts onto the front counter of Bruce's Specialty Auto Services and pulled out my phone to check them off. My buddy's shop was one of several I'd made deliveries to today, but luckily it was the last and the least amount... it meant I'd been able to carry everything in the saddlebags of my Harley Fat Boy. The day was too nice to be locked in a cage. I'd needed to ride. And now I wanted beer and pussy, not necessarily in that order, but I had to wait 'til I got back to the compound to enjoy either.

"Hatch!"

"Yeah?" I called back, still making notes in my phone.

"Hot one comin'."

I glanced up to see a woman navigating the intersection and heading toward us. She wore a fitted light-blue blouse, tight, white jeans that hugged her shapely legs, and heels that looked like they cost more than my bike. Her long, blonde hair hung in straight sheets, but as a gust of wind caught her locks, she had to fight to keep the strands out of her face. She slid her sunglasses on top of her head, pulling her hair away from her face and my breath left my body. She was like the first ray of sunshine after the rain. Damn, she was a knockout.

She walked into the tiny customer area and gave me a tentative smile. "Hi," she breathed out. "My battery's dead and Triple-A's going to be a while. Is there someone here who'd be willing to give me a jump?"

My dick took notice of her sweet, British accent.

"Yeah, sweetheart, I'll jump you. Anytime, anyplace," Bruce said, and I watched her step back slightly, her face a little paler than before. For whatever reason, Bruce's dirty innuendo made me want to beat the shit out of my old friend.

"Piss off, Bruce," I ordered quietly, then turned to face her. I was shocked by a sudden need to protect her, but I planned to help her and get her the hell out of my space. I needed a woman to protect as much as I needed a hole in the head, but I did have a sister and I'd never leave a woman stranded. "I'll get you goin' again. Where are you parked?"

She pointed to the parking lot across the street. "Just over there."

"Bruce, where's your portable jump pack?"

Bruce grabbed it from the back room and handed it to me. I smiled at the woman and nodded. "I'll follow you."

"Thank you."

"Be back, Bruce." I nodded to the clipboard on the desk. "Sign off on the delivery so I can get out of here, yeah?"

"No problem, Hatch."

I followed the woman to her car, and she popped the hood, sliding inside the car to start it. After hooking up the jumper cables, I called out, "Okay, push the button."

After several tries, we were still unable to get the Mercedes going. She joined me at the front of the car with a sigh. "It's not the battery, is it?"

"Nope." I dipped my head further inside and checked all the cables before checking the fuses. "Your ignition fuse is blown."

"Crap," she said. "Please tell me you have one in the shop."

"It's my buddy's shop, so I'm not sure, but give me a minute and I'll find out."

She nodded, and I called Bruce. "Hey man, you bang her yet?"

I turned away from the woman with a scowl. "Shut the fuck up, asshole. She's got a blown fuse. You got one over there or not?"

"Depends on what car."

"Ma'am?" I asked. "Your car's new, right?"

"Maisie."

"Sorry?"

She smiled. "My name's Maisie. I'd rather that than 'ma'am,' and yes, my car's new."

I forced myself not to react to the fuckin' sexy ass name

4

attached to the fuckin' sexy ass woman as I rattled off the information to Bruce. But hell, if I wouldn't be conjurin' up her image as I fucked some other pussy later on that night, wishin' her sexy-ass voice was callin' my name as she came.

"Yeah, I think I got one," Bruce said. "Let me find it and I'll bring it by."

I hung up and slid my phone in my pocket. I closed the hood of the car and turned to Maisie. "Bruce is lookin' for your part and then we'll get you on your way."

"Thank you." She smiled, but it didn't quite reach her eyes. Despite her obvious politeness and confidence, there was a sadness about her. "You've kind of been my knight in shining armor today, I must say. I'll just give Triple-A a ring and cancel."

I nodded, and she pulled out her cell phone, canceling the truck just as Bruce jogged over, part in hand. I replaced the fuse and Maisie's car started without issue.

"You're all set," I said. "You should call the dealership on Monday and let them know what happened. Fuses don't typically fail this quickly."

"I will. Thank you. How much do I owe you?"

"Sixt—" Bruce started to say.

"Nothin'," I interrupted.

"You deserve to be paid for your time," Maisie countered.

"It's all good," I said. "Just drive carefully."

"Well, thank you, Mr. Hatch… and, ah, Bruce is it?" she said.

Bruce's head bobbed up and down like the douchebag he was, but Maisie didn't seem to notice, her million-dollar smile back on her face. "Thank you again."

She climbed in her car and took off, giving us a sexy little wave as she headed toward the freeway.

"Fuck me, that woman was fine," Bruce sang out.

"Shut the hell up, Bruce," I ground out.

"You gonna pay for that part?"

"Yeah, man, I'll pay for the fucking part."

We headed back to the shop where I grabbed my shit, climbed on my Harley, and headed for the only place I knew I could get the beautiful woman out of my head.

* * *

Maisie

"I'm sorry?" Alison, my best friend and business partner, snapped over the speaker. "She just left you there?"

"Um, yes," I said, and guided my car onto the freeway. Alison had called just as I hit I-5 and was now on hands-free.

"Who does that?" she continued. "It's woman code, bitch. Never leave your sister behind."

"I know! And I gave her a thirty-percent tip!"

"Did you annihilate her and then tell her you were never coming back?"

"No," I admitted. "I was so in shock I lost my words for a period of time."

"Your British politeness was a hindrance wasn't it?"

I smiled. "You may have a point."

"Why didn't you call me?"

"Because it would have taken you an hour just to get over the bridge. I figured Triple A would be faster and in the end, the nice but scruffy man who helped me was even faster."

"Mmmm, scruffy good or scruffy bad?"

I thought about that question for a second. Mr. Hatch had long, dark hair, pulled back into a partial ponytail, which was sexy as heck, and his beard was full and slightly peppered with grey, but not out of control. He obviously manscaped, which a woman like me appreciated. "Scruffy good." I nodded. "Definitely good."

Ali giggled. "Only *you* would meet some hot guy after blowing a fuse."

"No doubt." I smiled. "How's Poppy?"

Ali was watching my twelve-year-old daughter while I took some time for me.

"She's good."

"Hi Mummy," she called in the background.

"Hi Poppet." I smiled. God, I loved that girl. "I should be there in about twenty minutes."

"Okay, we'll see you then," Ali said.

Ali hung up and I continued down the freeway. My thoughts turned to Mr. Hatch, then almost as quickly to my very dead husband, Niall. It had been nine years, but I was still quite miffed with him for leaving me. We'd been in the States for about five years when he got cancer and beat it into remission twice.

Unfortunately, third time was the charm in the form of a nail in his literal coffin, and he was gone. We thought we had more time. We didn't. If Ali and her cop husband, Ryan, hadn't been there, not only would I have crumbled, the business Niall and I had built together would have as well. Much to my family's disappointment, I had no intention of going back to England and had sent my brother home alone despite his pleas for me to join him. Even my sister Kenna, whom I was closest to, couldn't convince me to go back. I'd needed the distance.

I could only thank God that Poppy was too young to remember, because truly, I think it would have broken her. It took me a good two years and two visits a week to a therapist to get to the point where I could get out of bed in the morning on my own. Currently, I was down to one visit a month for "maintenance."

I was now somewhat in control of my insanity and no one could be happier than me. Or maybe Poppy. Or Ali. I sighed. Now I was even rambling in my head. Maybe I wasn't in control after all.

I pulled up to Ali's home and climbed out of the car, rushing up to the front door and letting myself in. "Mummy's home," I called.

Their golden doodle, Curly, barked as he ran to greet me.

"Hello, gorgeous," I crooned, stroking his head as I headed further into the house.

"Kitchen," Ali returned.

I headed through the large great room and into the newly renovated kitchen, where my daughter wrapped her arms around my waist and squeezed. "Can I stay a little longer, Mum? Please?"

"Sure, darling. Fifteen minutes, okay?"

She let out a little girl squeal and went to find Ali's daughter, her best friend, Grace. Ryan and Ali also had a fourteen-year-old son, Merrick, who was probably laying in wait to torture his sister. I hugged Ali briefly, then pried off my heels and sat at her island.

"You hungry?" she asked, pulling open the fridge and grabbing me a bottled water.

"No, I have Chinese waiting in the car. Have you eaten?"

"No. Kids did, but I'll wait for Ryan. I did feed Poppy, hope that's okay."

"You can feed my kid anytime," I said with a chuckle. "She likes your food better than mine anyway... although, tonight it's takeout. More for me."

She grinned. "Did you snap a photo of the hottie mechanic?"

I shook my head. "I probably should have, eh? God, lovey, the more I think about him..." I sighed. "He was edible. Rollo from Vikings edible."

Ali joined me at the island. "So... not your type."

"How do you figure?"

"Bad boy, sexy, edible."

"You may have a point." I sighed. "It doesn't matter. I'll never see him again. I've had my great love, so he'd only be a dalliance anyway."

"Which you would never do. You're a one-man woman... and only do long-term."

I'd met Niall in kindergarten, and it was love at first sight. He'd moved from Scotland into my neighborhood and, when we were old enough to walk alone, he started walking with me to and from school. We'd been inseparable ever since. I'd been so blessed to have a best friend who protected me with all of his being and loved me just as much. He was my first, my last, and everything in between.

"You're probably right." I smiled and slid off the stool. "I should get the Poppet home. The bathtub is calling my name." I stepped to the mouth of the hallway and called, "Poppy, love, we're going."

"Are you still good if I come in late tomorrow?" Ali asked. "Ryan's taking me to a few doctor appointments I've been putting off."

"Of course," I said. "Anytime, you know that. I still have the gremlins this weekend, right?"

"Yes." Ali grinned. "Ryan and I need some sexy sexual time."

I giggled. "I think that's a bit too much information, darling."

"In our business?" she scoffed. "There's no such thing."

"You might be right."

"Are you sure you're okay with staying here?" Ali asked. "The kids *can* come to you."

"No, it's fine. I love your home."

"I know, but I want you to be comfortable."

I smiled. "It'll be less upheaval for your kids and Poppy loves staying over, so it's perfect. As long as I have internet and can get some work done, I don't mind where I am."

"This is one of the many reasons I love you," Ali said, and hugged me again.

"Ready!" Poppy announced, Gracie on her heels. Grace looked so much like Ali it was like they were cloned. They had the same long, dark hair and tall, lanky build. Her big blue eyes were the only difference. Ali's were more of a periwinkle, whereas Grace's were darker.

"Thanks, love," I said, and Poppy and I headed home.

I left Poppy to watch a movie while I soaked in my tub, then after our bedtime ritual of reading a chapter from a favorite book (her choice tonight), I fell asleep dreaming of the scruffy Mr. Hatch.

TWO

Hatch

I WALKED INTO the Dogs of Fire compound and stalled.
My sister sat at the makeshift bar by the pool table, her
hair falling around her face, and a shot glass in front of
her. I did my best to control my irritation, considering we'd
agreed she wouldn't come here without me. "Cricket? Why
are you here?"

She raised her head and I saw red. Her bottom lip was cut,
and she held a bloody washcloth against her mouth. Her eye
was also black and swollen.

"What the fuck happened to your face?" I bellowed.

"First, you should see the other guy," she quipped.

"Not funny," I growled.

One of my soldiers, Flea, walked out of the kitchen and

handed Cricket a bag of ice.

"Thanks, Flea," she said, settling the ice against her mouth.

Flea smiled. "No problem, babe."

I growled and stalked to her side. "Cricket."

She sighed. "It's okay, Con."

"You're beaten to shit, Christina, it is *not* okay!" I snapped. "Now tell me what the fuck happened."

"I was walking into work and Matt jumped me… and not in the good way."

"Are you shittin' me?" I growled. "Where the fuck was Pug? Or Mack?"

She grimaced. "Mack's off tonight and I hadn't gotten to Pug yet. I didn't see Matt as I was walking in—"

I raised my hand to stop her from giving me some shitty excuse as I pulled out my phone just as it rang. *Booker calling.*

"Have you seen my sister's face?" I demanded.

"Yeah, brother." Booker sighed. "I take it she's at the compound?"

"Yeah." I dragged a hand through my hair. "Her ex was layin' in wait."

"We know," Booker said. "She doin' okay? Dani's worried about her…Cricket was pretty freaked when she left here."

"Seems to be."

"Okay, good."

"She's done, Book," I continued. "No more workin' at Blush."

Cricket gasped. "You can't do that!"

"Yeah, I'm okay with that, brother. I'm gonna have guys tendin' bar for a while, anyway," Booker said. "We got the asshole here. You okay with us takin' care of him for good now, at least until you get here?"

I had given my sister a long lead to deal with Matt, but now it was the Dogs turn to take care of the problem once and for all. I glared at her. "Yeah, man. Take him the fuck down. I'll swing by when Cricket's sorted."

"On it."

Booker hung up and I slid my phone back into my pocket.

"You can*not* dictate my life like that, Connor," she snapped. "I moved out for that very reason. I need that job to pay my rent. And since I'm going to school during the day, bartending means I can take care of it all. You also promised you'd let me deal with Matt."

My blood boiled. "And he fuckin' hit you. Again. We're done, Cricket. It's our turn to deal with him."

"What you failed to ask was what happened to *him*! I nailed him, Con. Took him to the ground, just the way you taught me! Yes, he got a couple hits in, but I really did make him hurt worse. His balls are probably the size of watermelons right now. You can't just arbitrarily run my life like that! Aren't you sick of meddling in my life? Don't you think you've done enough?"

She was referring to my interference several years ago when one of her infatuations got a little too close. I'd dealt with him for her protection, but it would appear she was still holding a grudge. I shook my head. "Not up for discussion."

"You're worse than having an overprotective father," she complained.

I was the oldest of five kids. Our mother was dead and our father in jail by the time I was twenty, and since we had no living relatives, I'd taken on the responsibility of raising my siblings, rather than letting them end up in foster care. Cricket was the baby…and the only girl. At twenty-four, she was seventeen years younger than me, but she acted like she ran the family. She'd recently moved into Knight's old lady's condo.

Knight was a soldier in the Dogs of Fire MC, probably my closest friend…if I had friends. Knight's wife, Kim, was loaded and had made Cricket an offer she couldn't refuse. I hated the idea, but I'd conceded because it was a secure building with a doorman, and Knight had reinforced the security system not so long ago.

I shook my head. "You can come work at the shop until you find something else."

"*Hello.* School. Daytime," she snapped.

"Hello. Summer break. Soon," I retorted.

She groaned. "I don't want to work in a dirty shop, Con. I want a real job."

"It *is* a real job. A real payin' one. And we need the help. You know it helps to have a woman working the front counter. Makes other women feel more comfortable."

She sighed. "Well, I guess I don't really have a choice now that you've blown up the one good job I've had in a while."

"You ever gonna *not* be fuckin' drama?"

"You ever gonna stop messin' with my life?" she countered, and then smiled. "Not every woman's drama, Con."

"Yeah, 'cause you're proof o' that," I droned sarcastically.

"I'm *hardly* drama," she countered.

I raised my eyes to the ceiling and shook my head. I did *not* want to have this conversation with my sister... again.

"Jana was a bitch, granted. But you're too good of a guy—"

"Time to go," I said, interrupting her grumbling.

She sighed. "Katie's meeting me here to check me over. We can't leave yet."

Katie Jameson was Flea's sister and a registered nurse. She was also Cricket's best friend. The two of them were trouble alone, but when they got together, might as well prepare for something to burn down.

I dropped my head back and stared at the ceiling again. "Fuck me."

"Have a drink, big brother," Cricket ordered with a snarky grin. "I can make you something."

"You stay put." Resigned to the fate of a sexless, shitty night, especially now that I had to deal with Cricket's ex, I nodded at Flea. "Whiskey's good."

Flea handed me the bottle and a shot glass.

I ran my knuckles gently down my sister's face. "Booker said you were freaked."

She nodded, leaning into my hand. "I'm okay, Con."

"You sure?"

Cricket smiled. "Why do you think I'm here? My big brother always makes everything okay."

I pulled her close and kissed the top of her head and then sat beside her. "Yeah."

Two of the club women walked our way, Lila breaking away to sidle up to me. "Hey, honey."

"Hey, babe." I took a shot as Cricket slid off the stool and walked over to the pool table.

"You got some time?" Lila asked.

"Not tonight."

I'd slept with Lila a handful of times. She was good... up for anything, but I could tell she wanted more and I wasn't interested in that, so I'd backed off in a big way.

She leaned against the bar. "It's sweet how you take care of your sister, Hatch."

"Yeah?"

"Yeah. But you've been kinda distant with me lately."

"Been busy," I said, and poured another drink.

"You brushin' me off?" she asked.

I cocked my head. "Didn't make promises, Lila."

She tapped her fingers on the bar. "Got it."

"Good."

She walked away, and my sister sent me a questioning look before talking to Lila for a minute. She then headed back to me and sat back on the stool.

"What was that all about?" she asked.

I leaned forward to study my sister's lip. "Get the ice back on that."

"You're not going to tell me?" She huffed. "Really?"

"Ice, Cricket."

She lifted the baggie to her mouth. "I don't want to give up my job at Blush, Connor."

"I heard you."

"Will you at least reconsider?"

I frowned. "We'll talk about it on Sunday."

We'd made a pact as kids that no matter what, no matter where, Sundays would be our days. We'd never missed a day

14

to debrief about the week and even when we moved up from San Diego, we came as a group. Even though my brothers didn't agree with my decision to leave, no one chose to stay in Southern California.

"That's a no," she grumbled.

"It's a, we'll talk about it on Sunday."

"Why are two of my favorite people glaring at each other?" Katie asked as she breezed into the main room of the compound. Cricket faced her, and Katie gasped. "Holy shit. Are you going to finally let the club deal with that shithead?"

"Yes, she is," I answered for her, then took another shot of whiskey.

"*I* took care of him," Cricket said.

"Not fast enough, apparently," Katie said, as she checked Cricket over and smiled. "Ibuprofen and ice. Nothing feels broken, but if the swelling and pain aren't better in the next day or two, you're getting x-rays."

"Yes, Mom," Cricket quipped.

"Okay, I'm gonna grab a beer. Can I get you anything?" Katie asked.

We shook our heads.

"Sorry if I cock-blocked you," Cricket said, and I groaned.

"Fuck me, Cricket, I'd rather not talk about my cock with my sister. Or anyone."

"Why are you so easy to mess with?"

I dragged my hands down my face. "How about I drop you home?"

"I have my car."

"You drove?" I snapped.

"*No*," she said slowly. "Flea brought me here, Buzz drove my car."

I relaxed… sort of. "How about I follow you home, then?"

"Or I could stay and have another drink."

I chuckled without mirth. "You're funny."

She sighed. "Fine. I'll see if Katie wants to come over."

"Great plan," I said.

"You're kind of a pain in the ass, Con."

"Backatya, sis."

With my need to make sure my sister was okay, my plans were effectively shot to hell, so I followed Cricket home, then headed to Blush. I couldn't help my mind from turning to the class act I'd helped earlier as I rode. Fuck, she was gorgeous. I wondered if she'd made it home okay and if she was having any other issues with her car. Not that I could do anything about it, unless I was willing to cross over to the stalking line and have Booker do a background check. I had her license plate, it would be easy.

I shook my head. No, I wouldn't do it. She was far too classy to be anything but high-maintenance, and the last thing I was lookin' for was more drama. I'd done that once before and suffered the cost. Never again.

I walked into Blush and Booker led me downstairs to where Matt was handcuffed to a metal chair, his mouth duct taped closed.

Matt's eyes darted between Pug and Train, two of the scariest individuals on the planet, but, then again, Matt hadn't seen what I could do.

"Hey, Hatch," Train said, and stepped away from Matt.

I gave him a chin lift and then turned my attention to Matt. "You remember who I am?"

Matt nodded.

"So, you also remember how you and I had a nice little talk about how you needed to treat my sister right?"

Matt nodded again.

"And remember how I told you that if you didn't, there'd be consequences?"

Matt scowled in response.

"So, we seem to have a little problem here, because my sister has some bruises and a bloody lip. Blush cameras got a real good look at the person who put those bruises there... and it's you; in case you were gonna try to deny it, so I'm real disappointed that you didn't listen to my warning." I cracked my knuckles, then crossed my arms. "Do you know why they call me Hatch?"

Matt shook his head.

"It's short for the Hatchet Man. I take care of people who get in the way and I do it without blowback. You have just become one of those people who got in the way, Matthew, and I'm going to take care of you."

* * *

Maisie

Saturday afternoon, the kids were bouncing off the walls and I was ready for a break. The rain had stopped, so I decided it was time to take a little walk to the neighborhood park and see if I couldn't get them to run off some of their energy.

Don't get me wrong, I loved watching Ryan and Ali's kids, but three on one was a lot more work than just Poppy. She and I had a symbiotic thing going on, plus I could theoretically beat her since she was my own.

"Right, loves. Let's go," I called down the hall.

"Can I bring my skateboard, Auntie?" Merrick asked.

"Yes, as long as you wear your helmet."

We leashed Curly, donned rain jackets (just in case), and piled out of the house. I loved the rain, which, in a roundabout way, was how we ended up in Portland. I couldn't fathom the thought of leaving London and going somewhere perpetually sunny. I craved the rain like most people craved the sunshine, so when Niall had been offered his dream job and discovered they had an office in Portland, we jumped at the chance. I smiled at the memory, the grip on my heart easing as I took a few deep breaths of the clean air. The smell of the ground after a downpour was always so peaceful... and peace was something I longed for more often than not.

Arriving at the park, I wasn't surprised to find other parents with their children enjoying the sunshine, brief as it might be. A beautiful young woman who was quite pregnant sat on a bench and had her gaze fixed protectively on a little girl heading for the ladder to the playhouse. "Cambry, careful baby."

"I *am*, Mama," she sassed.

"Hi," I said.

The woman sighed and smiled at me. "Hi."

"Is this seat taken?" I asked.

"Nope. It's all yours. I'm Kim."

"Maisie," I said, sitting on the damp seat and securing Curly to the bench.

"Are those all of yours?" Kim asked.

I chuckled. "No. I'm watching my bestie's kids. Mine's the blonde one. Poppy."

"She's gorgeous."

"I'd have to agree with you." I smiled as I watched Poppy and Grace help Cambry up the ladder. "How old's your little one?"

"Cambry's three going on sixteen."

I chuckled. "They do that, don't they?"

"Yes, they do. She also has her daddy wrapped around her little finger."

"Well, that's also their job." From the second Poppy was born, she'd bonded to Niall. They were inseparable.

"This is so true." Kim ran her hands over her belly. "Do you and your husband have other kids?"

I shook my head. "He died before we could."

"Oh, I'm sorry."

"It's fine, love. It was a long time ago."

"I haven't seen you here before. I take it you don't live in the area?"

"No. I'm watching the kids at my friends' place. Easier for them." I smiled. "Poppy and I actually live in the Pearl... not that you needed to know that."

"It's all good." Kim smiled. "I love the Pearl. I have a condo there, although, I rent it out now. It's not really condu-cive to equine pets."

I laughed. "No, I don't suppose it would be. I had horses as a girl. Gosh, I miss them. I'd love for Poppy to learn to ride." I sighed. "One day."

Kim rummaged in her purse and pulled out a card, hand-ing it to me. "We have a training facility with some amazing instructors. Give us a call and we'll find Poppy a lovely horse to ride."

I focused back on my daughter.

"Daddy!"

Kim and I turned toward Cambry's squeal, and I saw a tall man (very tall) walking toward the play structure, catching his little girl as she threw herself into his arms. He had dark, longish hair and wore jeans, motorcycle boots and a leather vest over a long-sleeved thermal.

"See?" Kim said. "She has daddy radar. She'll know he's around even when she can't see him."

"Hard not to see him," I pointed out.

"I know. He is rather large." She licked her lips as he approached, then added, "And delicious."

"Hey, sugar." He leaned down and kissed Kim.

"Hey, honey. Did you come to rescue me so I didn't have to waddle home?"

He chuckled. "Pleadin' the fifth on that one."

"Smart man," I said.

"Knight, this is Maisie," Kim said.

"Nice to meet you," he said.

Cambry snuggled closer to her daddy.

I smiled. "You as well."

"Hatch is back at the house," he said. "We grabbed pizza."

My ears perked up at the name. "Hatch is quite an unusual name."

"Hatch is quite an unusual man," Kim said.

"I met a Mr. Hatch the other day. Probably not the same one, but it's interesting."

"Is he tall, in his early forties, long hair usually manbunned?" Kim asked.

"Yes, that sounds just like him," I said, my heart suddenly racing.

"His name's just Hatch." Kim glanced up at Knight. "What's his real name, honey?"

"Connor," Knight said, kissing his daughter's neck. Cambry squealed and leaned in for more.

"Right," she said. "No one uses their real names. Well,

the wives do when we're pissed at them, but otherwise..."

"You're funny, sugar," Knight said.

"I know." She turned to me again. "Where did you meet Hatch?"

"If it's the same man, he got my car started for me." I shared the story of breaking down and Hatch's subsequent assistance.

"What a bit—I mean, what a mean thing to do," Kim said, glancing at her daughter who was suddenly listening to every word her mother said. "Never leave another woman stranded."

I nodded. "My friend said the same thing."

"Hatch helps out with deliveries to a few shops around town," Knight said. "So it sounds like the same guy."

"Small world," I mused, suddenly wanting to see him again.

Strange.

"We should go," Kim said, pushing up from the bench. "But please give me a call. My cell phone's on that card. We'd love to help Poppy out with lessons and perhaps you can get back into riding yourself."

I patted my chest. "Gosh, I'd love that."

"It was so nice to meet you, Maisie." Kim smiled again. "Have a great rest of the weekend."

I waved. "You too, love."

I watched the happy family walk away and I thought how strange it was to have come so close to Hatch again. Serendipity was a strange thing.

* * *

Hatch

I grinned at little Cambry as she rushed up to me. "Unca Hatt."

"Hey, baby girl, how are ya?" I asked, and picked her up.

"Pizza!" she squealed, slapping my face gently.

"Yep, we got pizza."

"Cambry, honey, let's go wash up," Kim said, leaning

down to kiss me on the cheek as she took Cambry from me. "Hey."

"Hey, babe," I said.

"Thanks for waiting on the pizza."

I chuckled. "No problem."

Kim took Cambry to the sink and they washed hands as Knight grabbed beers from the fridge, handing me an open one.

"Did you get hold of Ryder?" Knight asked.

Ryder Carsen was a buddy of our club's, almost a brother, to be honest. He was an ex-biker, and owned a local bar, the Brass Frog. He also owned several buildings around Portland, along with his business partners.

"Yeah. He's got a contact for a supplier."

"Excellent," Knight said.

"If I said the name Maisie, would you know who I was talking about?" Kim asked.

I nearly choked on a swig of beer. "What?"

"I found out we might have a mutual acquaintance."

"Blonde. British, fu—ah" —I stalled, mindful of Cambry—"I mean, real pretty."

Kim giggled, lifting Cambry from the sink and handing her off to Knight. "Yes, that's the one. You helped her with her car?"

"Yeah. How do you know her?" I asked.

"Met her in the park today."

"Yeah?"

"Sugar, leave Hatch alone," Knight ordered.

I chuckled. "She's good, brother."

Typically, I wanted nothing to do with the club old ladies trying to set me up, but at the present time, I wanted to know more about Maisie.

Kim filled me in on the circumstances that left Maisie stranded and I felt my blood run cold. Pissed that she might have been in real trouble if I hadn't been there to help, despite the fact Triple-A had been called, I suddenly wanted to hit the bitch who didn't help her. "No kidding?" I said.

"Sugar," Knight warned again.

"Anyway, her daughter might come take riding lessons."
I raised an eyebrow. "So, she's married."
Kim shook her head. "Widowed."
"Shit, seriously?" Fuck. I didn't expect that, but it explained the sadness.
"Yep." Kim took a bite of pizza.
"Fascinating."
"Isn't it though?" she sang.
I chuckled when Knight dropped his head back and swore at the ceiling, then groaned out, "Babe."
"Okay, okay. I'm done," she promised. "Unless, of course, you want me to get more information."
"Kimmie, stop," Knight snapped.
"I'm good, babe, but thanks," I said.
I could tell Kim was disappointed, and although I thought Maisie was gorgeous, I reminded myself (again) that she wasn't easy pussy and that's all I was looking for. I finished my pizza, begged off staying for another beer, and headed home, my mind swirling with Maisie thoughts.
Fuck. Now I knew I really needed to avoid the bitch at all costs.

THREE

Maisie

MONDAY MORNING ARRIVED far too early for my body; however, my mind had been awake most of the night. I forced myself to get up and face the day, deciding to shower before waking Poppy. I was surprised to find her up and already eating breakfast in the kitchen. She'd even made coffee. "Thank you, Poppet. For some reason, I'm extra tired this morning."

She giggled. "It's Merrick's fault, huh?"

Merrick had been wired for some reason, sneaking reading time when he should have been sleeping. I'd been up and down a few times trying to get him to shut off his light and go to bed. Not that I'd been sleeping. I was battling my own fantasy world.

"Ah, no. It's no one's fault." As if to mock me, a vision of Hatch filled my head. "Just have a lot going on this week."

"Don't forget Grace and I have that dance workshop tonight. You're driving."

"Bloody—" I cut my curse off. "Right, I actually did forget. Thank you for reminding me."

Poppy and Grace had been involved in ballet for a while, but there was a new class being offered once a month for advanced dancers. Grace was amazing. Poppy was good, but she was missing something, and I'd hoped this instructor could assist us in figuring out what it was. My perfectionist daughter tended to berate herself if she didn't excel at everything she did, and I needed to get a handle on it.

"Do you think she'll hate me?" Poppy asked quietly.

"Who?"

"The teacher."

Oh, the joys of hormonal girls. "My love, no one could possibly hate you. Mrs. Quinn may have some important things to say about your technique though, darling, and it's important you don't take those personally. Dancing is not who you are, it's what you do. I love your passion and your need to do your very best, but even if you didn't dance, you'd still be the most amazing young woman I know." I cupped her chin. "I'm proud of you every minute of every day. Don't ever forget that."

She smiled. "Even when I'm angry at you?"

"Well, no, I'm much less proud of you then, and admittedly, I love you conditionally, but only when you're being a strop…when you're not being a strop, I love you unconditionally."

Poppy giggled. "You're ridiculous."

"I know, love." I grinned. "Right, I'll get dressed quickly and drop you at school."

"I love you, Mummy."

I adored it when she called me "Mummy." It wasn't often because my little girl was growing up, but she'd pull that out when she needed me to know just how much she was feeling.

"Love you too, Poppet." I kissed her forehead and headed

to my room to change.

* * *

Four-thirty rolled around faster than expected, so I left Ali at the office to handle the final meeting and rushed off to pick up the girls and take them to dance. Glad to find they were ready, we all piled in the car and headed to North Portland. Traffic was hellish, but I'd left in just enough time and we arrived with ten minutes to spare.

"Girls, you go warm up and I'll check you in," I directed, and headed to the desk.

A stunning brunette smiled up at me. "Hi. Welcome."

"Thank you. I have Poppy Mann and Grace Lundy."

"Perfect. You're all set. If you head inside, my daughter will show you where you can watch the class."

I smiled and headed through the doors. Poppy and Grace were already at the barre stretching along with several other girls.

"Ma'am?"

I turned to the young woman smiling. "Yes."

"If you'll please come with me, I'll take you to the viewing room for parents."

"Thanks, love." I followed where she directed and joined several of the other parents. They had coffee and bottled waters set up on a table against the back wall, along with a few snacky-type things, which I deeply appreciated since I was starving. I'd promised the girls dinner afterwards, but I grabbed a couple of crackers to tide me over.

Small talk ensued amongst a few of us as we waited for the class to begin, but once the door was closed and our only access to our children was through the looking glass so to speak, the room went silent.

The young woman who'd showed me into the room served as the example dancing before the class and her technique was flawless. Her petite curvy build seemed to lengthen with each limber move, and as she broke into a pirouette, little wisps of blonde hair escaped from the loose bun piled on top of her head. She moved like water through a graceful stream.

"Lily," Mrs. Quinn instructed. "When you go into the petits jetés, point your toes a bit harder."

Lily nodded and did a little jog, then went straight into the jump, her feet arched perfectly (as far as I knew, anyway).

"Beautiful, honey," Mrs. Quinn said. "Now, who'd like to try that?"

I smiled to see both Poppy and Grace raise their hands immediately. Grace went first and she was lovely (as I suspected she would be), then it was Poppy's turn and my heart was in my throat. She did well, but I could tell by her face she wasn't happy.

The class moved on and I sighed as I watched Poppy's countenance change. It was slight, and I knew that only I, as her mother, would notice, but it was enough to put a stone in my gut. She watched Grace with suspicion and a little jealousy, but would quickly force a smile. I knew she wanted to be supportive, but I think all girls fight the tendency to be mean on occasion, even to our best friends. Something was going on with my girl and I couldn't put my finger on it.

Before I knew it, the hour was up and the girls began to disperse. Mrs. Quinn pulled Grace aside and Poppy watched, her expression pained. Grace beamed as the instructor spoke to her and I wasn't surprised she'd been noticed. She truly was a gifted dancer.

Class was officially dismissed, and Mrs. Quinn sought me out. "Are you Grace's mother?"

I shook my head. "No, I'm Poppy's."

"Oh, they're both such lovely dancers." She reached out her hand. "I'm Cassidy, by the way."

"Maisie," I said, shaking her hand.

"Would you please let Grace's mom know I'll call her later this week?" she asked.

"I'd be happy to."

The girls walked to where their bags were and began to remove their toe shoes.

"I can see Poppy works very hard."

"You have no idea," I said.

Cassidy smiled. "I think I do. Is this something she's passionate about? And I mean, does she breathe ballet?"

I thought about that question for a few seconds. "No, actually. I don't think she does. Not like Grace, anyway. Gracie is constantly dancing or watching videos. She pulls socks over her pointe shoes and dances around the house. It drives her mother nuts." I chuckled. "Poppy loves ballet, but breathes it? No. Though it doesn't minimize her commitment," I rushed to say.

Cassidy shook her head. "No, and it really shouldn't. I did notice she gets frustrated if she does something wrong. I have always felt dance should be a release... a way to work through my emotions. I've noticed the most gifted dancers can't live without it, but with Poppy, I see a bit of an internal fight. Don't get me wrong, she's a beautiful dancer, but I think if she could figure out what she's fighting against, she'd be able to relax a bit more."

I hummed in thought. "That's an interesting observation. I'll have to ask her about it."

"They're both at a crossroads and I believe they could go quite far, but it's time for them to start making some choices in order to set them up for the future." Cassidy smiled. "I'd love to speak with you further, but why don't you talk to Poppy first and find out what she wants?"

"I'll do that."

"Great." Cassidy said goodbye to each girl individually and then we started out to the parking lot.

I wasn't fully prepared for the next few minutes. As we walked through the foyer, I stalled. Hatch stood with a group of gruff looking men, all in jeans, boots, and leather vests or jackets, and one of them had his arm around Lily as he kissed the brunette who'd checked us in. A teenage boy stood with his arms crossed watching Lily as he spoke with a man who I assumed was his father since they looked alike.

My heart raced, and I felt tingling in places I had convinced myself were dead. Hatch looked my way and I averted my eyes, sure he wouldn't remember me, hoping to escape.

"Let me get you my number," Cassidy said, reminding me

I had unfinished business.

I forced a smile. "Right."

"Are you okay?" Cassidy asked.

"Yes, fine."

She chuckled. "Please don't let them scare you. They look rougher than they are. They're here to help tear down."

"They don't scare me," I said. "Not in the slightest."

She didn't look convinced as she handed me a card with a number jotted down on the back. "This is my cell. Call me this week and we'll have a chat about options for Poppy."

"Great, thank you," I said, and turned to gather Grace and Poppy who were speaking with a few of the other students.

I glanced down to put the card in my purse and when I raised my head I nearly ran into a wall of muscle. I gasped.

"Sorry, babe," Hatch said. "Didn't mean to scare you."

I swallowed. "That's okay." I met his eyes and shivered.

"Maisie, right?"

God, he remembered my name. I nodded, unable to find my voice.

"Hatch," he said.

"I… yes. Hello," I managed.

"You takin' a dance class?" he joked.

I chuckled. "My daughter is."

"Yeah?" He glanced over his shoulder to where I was staring, then focused back on me with a smile. "She looks like you."

I nodded, again unable to speak. I didn't seem to have this problem when he rescued me. Maybe it was because he was standing close and he smelled incredible. Soap, leather, and all man. I was rendered useless when he ran his hand over his beard. I wanted to do it, so bad in fact, I fisted my hand at my side to keep myself from touching him.

He smiled. "I'll let you go."

No. No, don't, please.

"I really appreciate you coming to my rescue the other week if I didn't mention it before," I rushed to say.

"Glad you got home safe. Did you call the dealership?"

I nodded. "I'm taking my car down next week."

"Good."

I bit my lip and took a silent breath. I needed to get myself together, but I felt like time stood still. It was just me and Hatch standing in the foyer of an old building in Northeast, the rest of the world had ceased to exist.

"Mum?"

I was startled out of my trance by Poppy and I forced my gaze from Hatch's. "Are you ready, honey?"

She stared up at Hatch, a curious expression on her face. "Hi."

"Hey," he said.

"I'm Poppy."

I drew my eyebrows together in confusion. Poppy didn't introduce herself to strangers... well, adults, anyway, but she had no hesitation talking to Hatch.

He smiled. "Hatch."

"Cool name," she said.

"Thanks."

"Are you a friend of my mom's?"

"He's the man who helped me when my car broke down," I provided.

She frowned at me. "Oh, you mean when that lady left you stranded?"

I shook my head.

"I mean, who does that?" she continued.

"Who indeed," Hatch said, his voice gruff.

"Let's give Lonnie a break," I said. "Sometimes people make mistakes."

Poppy rolled her eyes and then asked, "Can we have pizza?"

I wrinkled my nose. Gross.

"Before you say you hate pizza," Poppy rushed to say, "there's a place around the corner that has other stuff as well."

"Vincenzo's," Hatch said. "It's good."

"You should come with us," Poppy said.

"Poppy," I admonished. "Mr. Hatch is busy, honey."

"Just Hatch," he said.

"Right. Well, we should go. It was good to see you again."

"This won't take long," Hatch said. "I could join you after."

"Really?" I couldn't keep the surprise out of my voice.

"Sure."

"I have to get Poppy's friend Grace home by nine."

"Shouldn't be a problem," he said.

I smiled. "Okay, then. We'll save you a seat."

He nodded and walked away. I slid my arm around Poppy's shoulders and gave her a squeeze. "Let's go, hmm?"

We grabbed Grace and headed to the restaurant around the corner, and I tried to keep myself from losing the few crackers I'd eaten earlier.

* * *

Hatch

There was something seriously wrong with me. When I saw Maisie walk out of the dance studio, I lost my fucking mind. Damn she was stunning. Prettier than I remembered and when she saw me, she smiled shyly, and my dick took notice. I couldn't figure out what it was about this bitch that made me want more of her.

I knew she remembered me, but she couldn't seem to make eye contact and it was fuckin' cute how nervous she was. I could read every emotion on her face and I liked that a little too much.

After helping tear down Ace's old lady's rented space, I headed to the restaurant later than I wanted, but glad to see Maisie was still there. We had less time, but maybe that was a good thing.

She met my eyes as I approached, and I forced myself not to smile at the sight of her cheeks pinkening. But when she licked her lips, I imagined her mouth wrapped around my cock and I had to take a second to think about something else.

"Hey," I said, stopping at the table.

"Hi," she whispered.

"You came!" Poppy exclaimed with a smile.

"I did."

Maisie scooted further to the wall and I took it as an invitation to sit beside her.

"This is Grace," Poppy said. "She's my best friend."

I gave her a quick nod. "Hey."

Grace smiled. "Hi."

"Help yourself," Maisie said finding her voice. "We ordered a bit too much."

"Can we go play a game, please?" Poppy asked.

"Sure, love. We have to be out of here in twenty minutes, though." Maisie handed her daughter some money and the girls flitted off to the arcade area.

"You live around here?" I asked as I grabbed a slice of pepperoni and took a bite.

She shook her head. "Pearl. You?"

"Beaverton."

"Are you a mechanic?"

"Yeah. You?"

"CEO."

"No shit?"

She blushed again. "My husband and I started the company fifteen years ago. So, I suppose CEO's really a fancy title for buck stopper."

"Makes sense." I took another bite.

"He's dead now," she said so quietly I almost didn't hear it.

"Sorry to hear that."

She leaned her elbow on the table and settled her cheek in her palm. "What about you?"

"Divorced."

"Sorry to hear that," she mimicked.

"Don't be. Shoulda never married her," I said. "Your car runnin' okay?"

"Like a champ," she said. "I didn't even know there *were* fuses that would affect the starter. It would have been the last thing I checked."

"Your hair girl leave you stranded?"

31

Maisie rolled her eyes. "Technically, yes, she did."

"You wanna fill me in?"

"Not really." She sighed. "It's no big deal. She was busy, and you were there to help, so it's all good."

"What happened, Maisie?"

After a few seconds of hesitation, she filled me in, and I scowled. "Bitch."

"Yes, it wasn't very nice," Maisie agreed.

I dropped it and focused on her again. "Feel free to call me if you have any other problems with your car again. I'll be happy to have a look at it."

"That's kind of you, Hatch, but I don't have your number."

I chuckled as I wiped my hands and then held one out. "Give me your phone."

She handed it to me, and I loaded my contact information in it, sending myself a text so I'd have hers.

"Now you have my number."

She glanced at the screen. "And you have mine it would seem."

I grinned. "Weird."

Maisie chuckled. "Isn't it, though?"

Her phone buzzed in her hand and she sighed, firing off a text to someone. "I need to get Gracie home."

"I'll get you a couple boxes," I offered.

"No, it's okay." She shook her head. "We won't eat it, honestly. It'll just end up in the rubbish. Will you take it?"

"I'll take it if you're gonna chuck it."

"I really will chuck it. Pizza's not my thing and I don't want Poppy eating it on a regular basis."

I slid out of the booth and Maisie followed. She waved to Poppy whose face fell, but she tugged on Grace's arm and they finished up their game.

"My treat next time," I said.

Uncertainty covered her face as she studied me, but then she nodded, and I realized I'd been holding my breath just a little.

I smiled. "I'll call you."

"Okay," she said, her voice husky, quiet, and sexy as hell. Poppy and Grace arrived, and Maisie gathered their coats.

"Bye Hatch," Poppy said, and I gave her a chin lift, then watched them walk out the door.

FOUR

Maisie

"**M**AISIE?" GRACE ASKED in a worried voice as I pulled up to her house.

"Yes, love?"

"Daddy's not home."

I turned to face her from the front seat. "I know, love. But Mum is."

"I know, but she's been acting a little weird again."

"Really?" I asked. Grace nodded, so I gave her a bolstering smile. "Okay. We'll go in and have a look, eh? If she's bad, you'll grab some things and come to my house. Poppy will stay here for now."

Grace nodded again, and we headed inside. Alison had had issues with bi-polar disorder most of her life, but had been managing it beautifully with medication for years. She'd occasionally go a little off-kilter and her meds would need to be adjusted, but all would be well again. However, there had been a few times when it had taken longer to get the right "chemical balance" and she'd scared the children, but those were the times that Niall, Ryan, and I would step in for extra support. It was why she'd been at the doctor the week before… she'd needed to adjust her meds again.

She was covered. Always.

Stepping inside, I kept Grace behind me as we walked through the foyer. "We're home!" I called.

"Kitchen," Ali called back. She sounded fine, but I knew that could be a smoke screen.

We walked up to the island and I studied Alison who was emptying the dishwasher. "How did it go?"

"Really well," I said. "Cassidy Quinn said she's going to call you this week to talk about options for Grace. She thinks she's ready for the next step."

"Wow, honey," Ali exclaimed and hugged Grace. "That's amazing!"

"Thanks, Mom."

When Alison turned back to the dishwasher, Grace gave me an "all clear" nod, so I said my goodbyes and headed back to the car.

As Poppy and I drove home, my thoughts were consumed by Hatch. I felt like a teenager with her first crush again. Or maybe more accurately for the first time. I'm sure I felt that way with Niall; I just couldn't remember… we'd been together forever. Hatch set me on edge. And on fire. And ice cold. Plus, he made me flutter. God, I really was ridiculous.

"Mum? What did Mrs. Quinn say after class?" Poppy asked as we walked into our condo.

"Pajamas then I'll fill you in."

She frowned. "That sounds bad."

"It's not bad, Poppet." I smiled. "Not at all."

I could tell she didn't really believe me, but she rushed off to get ready for bed and I changed into yoga pants and a T-shirt. I was just happy to get my bra and heels off for the day.

Poppy returned, and we curled up in Niall's chair. It was the place we went when we needed to feel safe.

"Mrs. Quinn asked me how you felt about ballet," I said.

"I love it," she said emphatically.

"I know, darling. But she wanted to know what your motivation is, I suppose for a better term. Not just if you enjoy it but if you could live without it."

"I have to dance," she whispered.

"Have to because your soul has to?"

She shook her head.

"Why do you have to dance, Poppet?" She was quiet as I stroked her hair, but I could hear her quiet sniffles. "What's this now?" I lifted her face. "Why are you crying, darling?"

"I have to dance because Daddy wanted me to dance."

"He did?"

She nodded, the tears streaming now. "I found a picture he'd drawn of me. I was dancing and he'd made a little note about how much he loved me and how happy he was when I danced. I don't want Daddy to be sad in heaven."

"Oh, my sweet, sweet girl." I pulled her close and rubbed her back as the floodgates opened and she sobbed into my chest.

Bloody hell.

I hoped that whatever words came out of my useless mouth were the right ones. "Your daddy loved you and he probably drew that picture because you were two and the cutest little ballerina in the world... and he loved to draw. Just like you do. You know he doodled *all* the time. But you'd have been the cutest little bull rider if that's what you were doing at two... not that bull riding's on the table, love... just to be clear." She let out a giggle snort and I kissed her head. "It doesn't matter what you do, darling, he'll always love you. If you want to dance, do it because it feeds your soul and you can't live without it. Or you can do it just because. There's no pressure."

"Is that what Mrs. Quinn said?"

"She said she could tell you weren't into it quite like Gracie. You know how much she bleeds ballet."

"Totally," Poppy agreed.

"So she said you had a choice to make, because you're getting older and if you really want to take this all the way, it would be a good idea to plan."

She turned her watery gaze on me. "So she doesn't think I suck?"

I smiled. "Not even close. You work *far* too hard to suck."

She bit her lip and sighed. "I like ballet, but I don't know if I love it like Gracie."

"I don't know that anyone *could* love it like Gracie, love."

"If I stop dancing, will you be mad at me?" she asked. "Will Daddy?"

I shook my head. "No way."

"Am I allowed to do something else?"

There was my little negotiator. "Like what? The chorus?"

"No one wants to hear me sing, Mummy."

"Yes, there is always that, dear heart." I smiled. "Um, what about piano?"

She shook her head.

"Hmm... well, what do you have in mind?"

"Could I start taking riding lessons instead?" she asked, hopefully.

"I can certainly look into that, yes. But you've committed to finish out the ballet session, so you need to keep that commitment, then we'll look at something else if you'd like to."

She nodded as she snuggled closer and I stroked her hair.

"I wish I could remember him," she whispered.

"I know, love. Is it time for popcorn and old movies?"

She gasped. "Tonight?"

I chuckled. "No, it's a bit late for a school night, but we can do it tomorrow after tea."

"Okay," she whispered.

We sat like this for a while. She was growing up so fast, but I still remembered the tiny baby feeding at my breast.

"I like Hatch," Poppy whispered.

"You do?"

"Yeah. He's nice. And he thinks you're pretty."

I craned my head. "What?"

"His eyes get soft when he looks at you," she said. "Like how Uncle Ryan looks at Auntie Ali."

I squeezed my eyes shut. See? Twelve going on... whatever. Too old. She was far too observant for her own good. "Well, I'm not sure we can go that far, sweetheart. Uncle Ryan loves Ali like your daddy loved me. That takes time."

She shrugged. "Well, I like him."

"I like him too," I admitted after a minute. "Time for bed, I think."

Poppy sat up, but didn't climb off the chair. "Thanks for always letting me talk about Daddy."

"Why wouldn't I, love?"

"Because it makes you sad sometimes, and I don't want to make you sad."

I felt my nose burn, but I staved off the tears. "Well, it *was* sad that Daddy died, but talking about it helps, so never stop okay?"

She nodded, kissed me, and then skipped off to her room. I held myself together until she was in bed and then I melted into my own and sobbed for Poppy and her huge heart to think her dad would be sad in heaven if she stopped dancing. Sobbed because talking of Niall did still hurt a bit, the loss ever present, the alone feeling always in the back of my mind... and then I sobbed myself into exhaustion, and finally sleep.

* * *

Hatch

My phone burned in my pocket. It had been twenty-four hours since I'd left Maisie and I wanted to call her. Had wanted to call her all day, but I'd stopped myself.

Shit. This could *not* happen.

I stared up at the car I was working on and tried to put her out of my mind.

"Hatch!" Buzz called out. "Where you at?"

"Down here, brother." I climbed the stairs and met Buzz

at one of the rolling doors of the shop. "What's up?"

"Prez needs ya," Buzz said. "He's on the phone."

Crow was the Club's president and he didn't call a whole lot. Usually topics were discussed and resolved at church on Wednesdays, so if the Prez was calling something was up.

"Why didn't he call my cell?" I asked.

"He said he did."

"Shit. Okay, let me wash up." I tore off my gloves, washed my hands, and pulled my cell from my pocket. It was dead. I headed into the office, found my charger and plugged in, before grabbing the shop phone. "Prez?"

"Hey, Hatch. Got time to take some parts up to Abe's shop?"

I shook my head. Abe's shop was in the Pearl. Fuckin' fate.

* * *

Maisie

I left the conference room, Ali following quickly behind me. "Then what?" she demanded.

"Shh, hold on," I ordered, and led her into my office, closing the door behind me. "He showed up."

"He joined you for dinner?" Ali squeaked.

"For about ten minutes, love," I said, and sat at my desk.

"Ohmigod, had I known the happiness of your vagina was at stake, I would have picked up both girls and taken them back to my house."

I didn't fill her in on any of this the night before considering Grace was with me and we were making sure all was good. I rolled my eyes. "Let's not rush any of this, Alison. Good lord, he's just a nice man who offered to pay me back for dinner."

"By taking you *out!*" She grinned. "He wants into your panties."

"*Alison*," I admonished. "You know how I hate that word."

Alison flopped into the chair across from me with a

39

groan. "You run one of the largest sex toy businesses in the United States! How is it you get all squirrely at the word 'panties'?"

I shuddered. "Because it's gross."

"Moist panties."

"Gah! You're disgusting."

Alison laughed like she couldn't stop, and I rolled my eyes. When she got on a tear, there was no stopping her. As Alison continued to giggle (having to grab for a tissue because her nose was running), my phone rang, and I fished it out of my purse. "Bloody hell," I whispered.

"What?" Alison asked wiping her nose.

I jabbed a finger toward my phone. "It's *him*."

"Don't answer it. Be cool."

My stomach roiled. "But I'm not cool."

"I know, babe, but *he* doesn't need to know that."

This was very, very true. I set the phone on my desk and let it go to voicemail. "What if he doesn't leave a message?"

"Then you wait for him to call again."

I bit my lip. "Shouldn't I call him back?"

"No. Let him chase you."

"I don't want him to chase me."

"Yes, you do," Ali argued.

I shook my head, the panic really setting in now. "No. I don't."

My phone buzzed on the desk and I jumped with a squeak. Raising my head to meet Alison's dancing eyes; I grimaced and whispered, "He left a voicemail."

"I see that." She grinned. "Listen to it."

"I can't."

"I'll do it." She snatched the phone off my desk and dialed the voicemail, putting it on speaker.

"Hey, Maisie, it's Hatch. I'm in the area. Thought I'd see if you wanted to grab dinner. I'll be here for another half-hour or so, so let me know."

Then he hung up, as did Alison. "Sexy voice," Alison said.

"What do I do?" I asked.

"You call him back."

"I have a daughter. I can't just go to dinner with someone on a whim."

"*I* can take care of Poppy." She waved her finger toward me in a circular motion. "You need to take care of your vagina."

"Stop with the vagina talk!" I snapped. "I'm not having sex with him. Or anyone. Ever again."

"We'll see." She smirked. "Call him back."

"No."

"Niall has been dead for almost ten years, Maisie. Ten. That's a long time. If you want to move on, it's okay."

I blinked back tears. "I don't want to move on."

"Well, you should." She rose to her feet and walked to my side of the desk where she sat on the edge facing me. "I have never seen you this affected by a man. And not to diminish the memory of Niall, but let's be honest, you didn't even react to him like this."

"That's not true."

"Honey, it *is* true. You loved him fiercely, I'm not saying you didn't, but he didn't make you nervous and fluttery like this Hatch person does."

"You just didn't see us at the beginning." Although, admittedly, I'd never been fluttery to this degree with Niall.

"You're right. I didn't." She smiled gently. "But men have been falling at your feet forever, Maisie. Long before Niall passed away, honey, and even as recently as last week—"

"What? Who?"

"Jeremy."

"Marville?" I squeaked.

"Yes."

I let out a rather inelegant snort. "He's a client, Alison. He is *not* interested in me."

"He's *totally* gagging for you."

I blushed again. Alison loved to make me squirm. "Ali," I rasped.

"Sorry. Sometimes it's just too easy." She giggled. "Anyway. Jeremy sends flowers, he's asked you out several times, but this Hatch guy is the first one you've showed any interest in. Have a little fun."

"Ali, I have a daughter to think about. I can't just 'have a little fun.'" I shook my head. "I don't think it's a good idea. I'm going to decline."

She frowned and snatched my phone off the desk, jumping away from me before I could grab her.

"What are you doing?" I snapped.

"I just accepted his invitation." She handed the phone back to me. "You're welcome."

I saw she'd texted him and I scowled. "Why would you *do* that?"

"Because you need this. I'll take care of Poppy and you can pick her up from my place later. Or tomorrow."

"He's probably a serial killer."

"Well, then stay to public areas and you'll be good."

"Why are you not concerned I might be super murdered by a serial killer?" I challenged.

She shrugged. "Because you need *some* kind of adventure in your life."

My phone buzzed in my hand, startling me again. It was a text from Hatch, and I bit my lip, my heart racing as I read it. *The Q? How does an hour sound?*

"He wants to meet me at the Q."

"Hmm, one of your favorites. Definitely a serial killer," Ali retorted.

"You suck."

She pointed to my phone. "Tell him yes."

"God," I whispered.

"God's not going to text him, Maisie. So, you do it, or I will."

She started toward me and I stepped behind my desk again.

"Don't you dare. I'll do it myself." I fired off my acceptance and then lowered myself into my chair, dropping my forehead to my desk. "What did I just do?"

"You just opened the pages of a new chapter, honey. I'm

proud of you."

I wasn't so sure this was true, but I sent my assistant home early and texted Poppy to let her know she'd be hanging out with Grace for a few hours.

After taking several cleansing breaths (which didn't really help), I refreshed my makeup and brushed my teeth, then ran a comb through my hair and headed downstairs. Our offices weren't far from the Q, and even closer to my condo, which was beckoning me. I *could* just blow this guy off and go home. Have some me time, take a bath, drink a bottle of wine.

I groaned aloud and continued toward the restaurant. My word was my bond and I rarely lied unless it was to spare someone's feelings, so my fate was sealed... at least for the moment.

FIVE

Maisie

SINCE PARKING WAS a crapshoot, I took a rideshare and the driver dropped me off at the side of the restaurant. I climbed out of the car and made my way to the front on shaky legs, still wanting to run the other way.

What the bloody hell am I doing?

I squared my shoulders and took a deep breath, forcing my feet forward just as I heard, "Hey, Sunshine."

I turned to see Hatch walking toward me, and my breath hitched. It was warm, but he still had a leather jacket on over a tight black T-shirt, dark jeans and boots. God, he was gorgeous. And what the hell was up with all this "Sunshine" business? I willed my undies to stay exactly where they were, because if he kept saying things like that to me, I was done

44

for.

I slid my sunglasses onto the top of my head and smiled. "Hi."

After closing the distance between us, he wrapped an arm around my waist, and kissed my cheek. "You look beautiful."

"Thank you." I closed my eyes for a second, relishing his touch. He also smelled delicious. Holy crap, I was in trouble.

His gaze scanned my body. "You wear this to work?"

"Yes."

He let out a quiet grunt.

"Is that weird?" I wore a sleeveless, pencil sheath dress. The top was a herringbone pattern, while the skirt was black and it was finished off with a thin silver belt. I had on a pair of black Louboutin sling-backs and the outfit was all me as far as style went.

"No, babe, it's sexy."

I sighed. Well, that certainly wasn't helping the undies stay put.

We headed inside and, although he let me precede him, his hand stayed put on my lower back as he spoke with the hostess and she showed us to our table. I felt a little bereft when he had to remove his touch in order for me to take my seat.

He shrugged off his jacket and settled it over his chair, revealing his muscular arms bulging out of his tight, black T-shirt.

"I'm surprised you could make it," he said.

"Me too," I admitted, setting my menu down so I could look at him. "My friend is taking care of Poppy for the evening."

"She could have come."

"My friend?" I joked.

Hatch chuckled. "Sure. More the merrier."

"I'm not ready for Poppy to be privy to me potentially dating again," I admitted. "Regardless if this is considered a date or not, it's just… well..."

"I get it." He focused back on his menu. "And this is just two people in the same place gettin' a bite to eat. Not a date."

I felt deflated in a weird way. It was painfully evident to me that I wasn't hip to all the nuances of the dating world, and I probably didn't want to be. I'd always believed when a man invited you to dinner alone, it was considered a date... but what did I know? Maybe now, everything was casual and a date was something olde tyme people did when they got bored pushing the hoop with a stick down the dirt street. The server arrived and we gave him our drink and dinner orders and then we were left blissfully alone again.

"I met Kim at the park the other day," I began, trying to break the awkward silence.

"Yeah, she told me."

Interesting. They'd talked about me. I liked that. I actually liked that a lot. Maybe this wasn't so bad.

"How do you two know each other?" I asked.

"Her old man and I are in the same club."

"What kind of a club?" I asked, and took a sip of water.

"Motorcycle club."

"Oh, so you show off your motorcycles and ride them together?" I'd seen clusters of motorcycles on the freeway during the summers sometimes and everyone always looked like they were having a blast.

He smirked. "Sure, we'll go with that."

I smiled. "That sounds fun... if not a bit dangerous."

Our server returned with our drinks, so I never really got clarification on the dangerous part. But regardless, motorcycles scared me. Especially the thought of folks riding them in such a rainy climate.

"What's the name of your club?" I asked.

"Dogs of Fire."

"Oh, interesting." I didn't really know what to say. The name was a little silly in my opinion, but I doubted Hatch had much to do with it. I heard his low chuckle and heat crept into my cheeks. "Sorry."

"It's okay, Sunshine." He smiled. "I like it."

"My inability to hide my thoughts?"

Hatch nodded. "Nice change."

"People hide things from you often?"

"They try."

"Oh." I bit my lip. "I'm sorry."

"How was work?" he asked, changing the subject.

"Good." I smiled. "Uneventful."

"What bucks do you stop?"

I pressed my lips into a thin line.

"Too personal?" he asked.

I shook my head. "No. I'm just never sure what people will think when they find out."

He raised an eyebrow, sitting back slightly. "Oh, yeah?"

I didn't tell people what I did. My company had a boring and vague name, *Mann Industries*, and until I really got to know someone, they just thought we did imports and exports. Which we did... our imports and exports just happened to be of a sexual nature. For whatever reason, I felt comfortable with Hatch and I figured if he was going to run, it would be now and it would be good to get it over with. Taking a deep breath, I leaned forward and whispered, "I run a sex toy business."

"Shut the fuck up," he said.

I sat back and nodded, my face on fire.

He grinned. "That's the best thing I've ever heard."

I laid my palms against my cheeks, trying to cool them. Now I felt weird... well, weirder than I had previously. I shouldn't have told him. He was probably just another pervert who would assume I was a slut because of the business I was in. God, I needed to get out of there.

"Don't, Sunshine," he said, his hand snaking out to pull mine from my face. "You're okay. This isn't gonna get creepy."

I gasped. "How did you know that's what I was thinking?"

"As a beautiful woman in a position of power, you probably attract some assholes, but in the business you're in, those assholes probably have some proclivities that make it difficult for you to trust them. I get it."

God, he *did* get it. "Proclivities is the exact right word," I confirmed.

"Word o' the day calendar," he retorted, and released my hand. "I'm lookin' forward to hearin' more about your company, but let's shelve it for tonight, yeah?"

I nodded; glad to be off the hook. "Thank you."

Our food arrived and I had a few minutes to gather myself.

"What about you? Do you like being a mechanic?"

He shrugged. "Sure. We moved up here from San Diego and I worked a few of the shops the Dogs own until about six years ago. I bought a place of my own and my brothers work it with me when they're not workin' construction. I also help out with deliveries. It was a good way to get to know the area. Now I just like gettin' out of the shop."

"How many brothers do you have?"

"Three. And a sister. My nephew's currently livin' with me too."

"Wow, that's a big family," I said. "How often do you work together?"

"Cullen and Cameron usually work Cade's construction company unless the weather's bad," he said. "But, my baby sister works for just me typically… when she's not drivin' me nuts."

"So, you only let her work for you depending on the level of nut driving?" I gasped as soon as the words were out of my mouth. "Sorry, that just sounded very, very wrong."

"I love it." Hatch laughed. "Fuck, you're refreshing."

I took a large sip of wine.

"Cricket's always been a bit of a wild card," he said, giving me time to compose myself. "She's goin' to school and payin' her own way. She's been workin' for a club downtown, but it's not the safest gig, and she's got issues with an ex stalkin' her, so I needed to shut that down for a bit. Keep an eye out."

"It's good she has you."

"I'd love it if you'd tell her that. Right now she hates me."

"How old is she?"

"Twenty-four."

"So, old enough to be an adult, but still young enough to

get into trouble."

He nodded.

I smiled gently. I remember feeling like her. "Are you close to your parents?"

"Story for another day," he said.

"Oh," I whispered. "Sorry."

"Don't be sorry. I'll tell you about it one day," he promised. "Just havin' a good time and don't want to ruin it."

That didn't really make me feel any less like a heel, but I let it go.

"Shit," he hissed and fished his phone out of his pocket, scowling at the screen. "Sorry. Somethin's up. I'll be right back."

I nodded and he stepped outside. I watched out the window as he paced, his phone to his ear. When he pinched the bridge of his nose, I could tell something was definitely up and our night was probably coming to an end. I waved the server over and asked for the check.

We'd both finished our meals so there was nothing to box up, which helped. I took a final sip of my wine just as Hatch walked back to the table. "Gotta head out. Emergency with my sister." He pulled out his wallet and slid a hundred and twenty into the leather folder.

"Oh, okay." I rose to my feet and grabbed my purse. "I just need to hit the ladies' room, so I'll say goodbye here."

He shook his head. "Got time to walk you to your car, Sunshine. I'll wait."

"I actually took a car."

"I'll wait with you."

My mind whirled as I rushed to the loo and met him back at the side door of the restaurant.

"You order the car?" he asked.

I nodded, rubbing my arms as we walked outside, the early evening suddenly chilly. Without saying anything, Hatch shrugged off his leather jacket and slid it over my shoulders. I pulled it tighter around me. "Thank you."

His hand found its way to my back and I wrestled with the feeling of uncertainty and comfort at the same time. In that moment, I realized this man would be a danger to my heart and I needed to shut him down.

We waited around the side of the restaurant until the car arrived, far too soon for my liking.

"Thanks for a lovely dinner," I said, my heart breaking a little as I knew this would be the last time I saw him. I slid off his jacket and handed it to him.

"We'll do it again."

"Hmm-mm," I murmured, biting the inside of my cheek to keep from saying too much.

He drew his eyebrows together, but his phone rang and I could tell he wasn't happy to be interrupted. He kissed my cheek and waited for me to slide into the car. The car dropped me back at work where I jumped into my Mercedes and headed straight to Ali's.

I pushed open the front door and Ali met me in the foyer, opening her arms and pulling me in for a motherly hug. I fell against her, keeping my tears at bay, but feeling pretty pathetic all the same.

"That bad, huh?" she asked, rubbing my back.

"I'm just glad it's over and I never have to see him again," I admitted.

"Come inside. You look like you could use a drink. Want a Screwdriver?"

I gasped, my heart racing. "Ali, you're not supposed to be mixing alcohol with your meds. I thought you promised Ryan you'd get rid of everything."

Alison and alcohol never mixed, but Alison and alcohol and meds were a lethal combination. She'd had a couple of scary incidents in the last fifteen years. So much so that Ryan carried sedatives with him in case he had to control her. She'd been stable for five years, but her offering me Vodka and orange juice was not a good sign. Maybe her new meds weren't working.

She gave me her million-watt smile and pulled out a flat-head screwdriver. "Totally just messin' with ya, honey. I don't have alcohol in the house. I'll make you a cup of tea."

"Oh, yes, please." I relaxed. The last time I'd been in

London, six years ago, actually, I'd loaded each of our homes with enough "proper" tea to last a while. "I'll just say hi to Poppy, then I'll fill you in."

After getting a half-hearted hug from my daughter who was clearly miffed I'd interrupted her and Grace, but loved me enough to fake affection for a second, I headed back out to the kitchen where I sat on a stool at the island and dropped my head to the granite.

"It can't be that bad," Ali said, pouring water into a teacup.

"It's worse." I sat up and filled her in on the evening, her sarcastic smile making me realize she probably wasn't going to be on my side. "What?" I demanded.

She chuckled. "It sounds like he's protective. Something happened with his sister and he didn't really want to cut the night short, but he did it because he loves his sister."

"*No,* that's not at all what it was!"

"Oh? Well, enlighten me, then."

"I just *did*," I ground out. "When I asked about his parents he shut down and gave me vague answers."

"What if it's bad, Maisie?" Ali leaned across the island. "What if he really likes you and wants to ease into stories about the tragedy of his childhood, or whatever? What if his parents were criminals or something and he doesn't want to scare you off?"

I frowned. "Even if his parents were, it doesn't mean he is."

"I know that, you know that, but people judge." She smiled gently. "The motorcycle club concerns me a bit, but otherwise, he sounds like a decent guy."

"Why does the motorcycle club concern you?"

"Because most of them are outlaw clubs. Like mafia or glorified gangs." She slapped her hands on the island. "I'm gonna have Ryan do a background check on him."

"No you are not." I grabbed her hands. "I'm not going to see him again, so it's a moot point."

"Maisie," she admonished. "Don't jump to conclusions, honey. I get that you're feeling jittery and uncertain, but please recognize this as normal and relax. Don't stop seeing him because he makes you feel too much. Try to enjoy it."

"Don't talk to me like you know me."

"Okay." She smiled. "Lecture over."

"Thank you."

I heard the front door click closed and Ryan walked in, a smile on his face. "How are my two favorite ladies?"

Ryan stood about five-foot-eleven and had short, dark hair and piercing green eyes. He was muscular, not like Hatch, but definitely more than Niall, and was an all-around great guy.

He kissed my cheek, then pulled Ali in for a make-out session a little too in-depth for my comfort, but I'd gotten used to it since neither of them seemed to mind an audience to their affection. I stared at my tea until they finished their X-rated moment.

Merrick came bounding in, followed closely by Grace and Poppy. "Hey Dad," Merrick said, and Ryan pulled him in for a hug, then Grace, then Poppy.

I loved how Ryan treated Poppy like one of his own; lessening the blow of losing Niall by providing a father figure she could look up to.

"We need to get going, Poppet," I said, and slipped off the stool.

Washing out my cup and saucer, I set it to dry next to the sink, gathered up my daughter, and then we headed home.

As soon as we got home, Poppy and I did our nightly reading ritual. Once Poppy was settled, I curled up in Niall's chair and thought about Hatch. He was everything Niall wasn't. Niall had a nerdy confidence and I thought he was handsome and sexy, but in a different way than Hatch. Niall was certainly the smartest person I knew, but it was a brain smarts kind of thing. Ryan used to joke that if we got jumped somewhere in Portland, I'd probably be the one to fight our way out... Niall would be screwed.

Hatch, on the other hand, would probably take on several assailants at one time. The man was big... tall *and* muscular... and commanded a room when he walked in it. Where

Niall was clean cut and the type to bring home to your parents, Hatch had long hair and a scruffy beard, and he used the f-word in regular conversation. It was sexy as hell. It shouldn't be. In my circle, it would be offensive, but for me, it made me want to strip down to nothing and offer myself up as a sacrifice.

I shook my head. *What the hell is wrong with me?*

I couldn't get involved with a man like that. I couldn't get involved with any man, really. I had a daughter to think about, and I needed to make good choices so she'd grow up and make good choices. I needed to steer clear of the sexy as hell Hatch. And this was what I told myself as I climbed into bed.

I awoke the next day feeling groggy, but still resolved to my decision. I had no business chasing after a man who ran in totally different circles than me. He was gorgeous, yes. He was sexy… oh, hell, yes. He seemed like he took care of his family, yes. But I reminded myself I was a single mum and I needed to focus on my daughter and my business. I didn't have time to date, and a man like Hatch was a distraction I couldn't afford. Even if he would be a lovely distraction.

I leaned into the hallway. "Poppy, time to rise and shine. We're a bit late."

"I'm up, Mum," she called from her bathroom.

"Will you hit the button for the coffee while I shower, please?"

"Sure."

"Thanks, love."

I lost a little resolve when Hatch left a voicemail later that day, and I really lost my resolve when he left another one two days later, but I finally felt like I could relax when two days after that, his third voicemail said, *Hey, babe. It's all good. Won't be callin' you again. Have a nice life.*

I was sad, but at least I could move on.

SIX

Hatch

SUNDAY AFTERNOON, CRICKET walked into the kitchen with a case of beer and a box of cupcakes. I grinned, taking the beer from her and setting it in the fridge. "Just a case, huh?"

"Well, since you blew up my job prospects, I can no longer afford more than that," she quipped.

"Nice, sis." Cade grinned, pulling her in for a hug. Cade was thirty-nine, divorced with one kid, and an Army vet. As soon as he'd turned eighteen, he'd headed for war... it was a hell of a lot calmer than home at the time. He and Cullen worked construction, helping out at my shop when the weather was bad. "How's my favorite sister?"

"I'm jobless."

"Yeah, we get it, Cricket," I ground out. "Not gonna

54

change, so off the subject."

"So, you didn't think more about the Blush thing," she accused.

"Thought about it, the answer's still 'no.' Like it was last week."

"Kinda harsh," Cullen said. Cullen was thirty-five and had married his high-school sweetheart as soon as she turned eighteen. She'd died two years later.

"His jaw's tickin', Cull," Cameron pointed out. "Maybe drop the subject." Cameron was thirty and fucked anything with a skirt. The only problem with that was Cam wasn't good at figuring out sane pussy from crazy, and I was pretty sure crazy was acomin'.

"Maybe you three could back me up once in a while," Cricket countered.

"Maybe we don't like your ex beatin' the shit out of you." Cameron hugged her gently, ending it with a noogie, which, in turn, earned him a punch to the gut. "Fuck, Cricket! Did ya have to hit me that hard?"

"Next time, I'll aim for your junk, big brother." Cricket fixed her hair.

Cullen slapped the back of Cameron's head. "I can't believe you're still pulling that high-school bullshit, Cam."

Cameron went to retaliate with a jab, only he missed because Cullen dodged, causing Cameron to fall against the refrigerator.

"Enough!" I bellowed. "Get the fuck out."

"Where's Devon?" Cricket asked, ignoring my order to leave the kitchen.

Cade nodded toward the family room. "Call of Duty."

Cade's ex, Diana, was off on her honeymoon with her third husband, so Devon was staying with them for the next few months. I had a feeling shit was going down, however, considering Diana was a bitch and only wanted Devon for leverage (and child support). Cade was getting fed up with this arrangement, and now that he'd landed somewhere permanent, he had more of a chance of getting his son full-time.

"So, what's up with this English chick?" Cricket asked.

My body locked. Fuckin' Kim.

My brothers turned to me, all eyes focused and alert, waiting for an answer.

"What English chick?" Cameron demanded.

"Connor helped her with her car," Cricket provided. "Kim says she's gorgeous and her name's Maisie. Isn't that so sweet?"

"She's no one," I said, grabbing the plate of steaks and heading for the deck. My family followed.

Cricket greeted Devon as she walked past the sofa and out onto the deck with me, handing me the tongs. "Con met up with her and her daughter at Vincenzo's after Cassidy's dance thing."

"Shut the hell up, Cricket," I snapped.

"Hold up," Cullen said. "She's got a kid and you still met up with her?"

I scowled, but didn't comment as I threw the steaks on the grill.

Cricket nodded. "Kim said—"

"Kim needs to mind her own fuckin' business," I ground out. "I'm done with this conversation."

"She's got money," Cricket continued. "Top of the line Mercedes. Wears Louboutin heels, carries a Louis Vuitton handbag, probably wears Perla."

"What's Perla?" Cameron asked.

"Panties that cost like a grand," Cricket said.

Cameron scowled. "Damn, Cricket. Don't wanna be talkin' about panties with my sister."

She grinned in triumph. "Payback's a bitch."

"I thought the punch to the gut was payback."

"That's because you're an idiot." Cricket focused on me again. "Are you gonna call her?"

"Swear to Christ, sis, you don't drop it, you're leavin'," I warned.

She threw her hands up in the air. "Is it so bad that I want my big brother to be happy?"

I took a deep breath and forced a smile. "Go grab the corn

for me."

She studied me for a few seconds before dropping the subject and heading back into the house. Lucky for me, I only had one sister, and my brothers were smart enough to know that if the subject was closed, it was closed, so they backed off.

The rest of family night went without incident.

Cricket headed home around ten, Cameron had a date or a hook-up or whatever, and Cade was takin' Devon to a movie, so Cullen and I headed down to the basement for beer and a game of pool.

"Maisie, huh?" Cullen asked as he racked. "You really not gonna call her?"

"Already called her."

Cullen raised an eyebrow. "And?"

"And, we went out," I said. "Then she ghosted me."

"Fuck, seriously?" Cullen asked.

I nodded and took a swig of beer.

"You don't get ghosted."

I chuckled without mirth. "Yeah, well, now I do."

"Shit, you like her."

"Don't know her, Cull." I shook my head. "Pretty sure she's high-maintenance if she's buyin' thousand-dollar pant-ies."

"You know her enough to like her though, brother." Cullen leaned against his pool cue. "I get you think I'm a dreamer and I'm an idiot because I don't want anyone since I lost Elizabeth. But you're a good guy, Con, and she obviously made an impression, so if she's ghostin' you, I'm sorry. That can't feel good, especially if you put yourself out there after Jana. Even a little."

I stuffed down the emotion with a nod of my head. Cullen knew me, and he was the only one I would ever admit my true feelings to, because Cullen would take anything I shared to the grave, but that didn't mean I was willing to share right now. "Let's play, yeah?"

Cullen smiled. "Okay, big brother. Let's play."

***

Two weeks later, I sat at my desk well past ten, entering a parts order into the computer when my cell phone pealed.

Sunshine calling.

What the fuck? I ignored the call and went back to my task. However, my phone rang again and it was Maisie again.

I debated on whether or not to answer, but I'd missed her, so I gave in. "Hatch here." All I could hear was sobbing and my heart stopped in my chest. "Maisie?"

"No. It's Poppy. I can't wake Mum."

I stood and grabbed my keys, heading out to my truck. "Okay, baby girl, where are you?"

"I... I don't know. The car made this weird noise and then Mum said something was wrong with the brakes and then we were driving through the guardrail. Mummy banged her head on the steering wheel and her arm looks funny. She's got blood all over her face and I can't get her to wake up."

"Did you call 9-1-1?" I asked.

"No."

"Why the hell not?" I snapped.

She sniffled. "Please don't yell at me."

Fuck! I took a deep breath and dragged a hand through my hair. "Baby girl, I need you to call 9-1-1, okay? But don't hang up. Do you have your cell phone?"

"Huh-uh. But Mummy has the emergency button in her car. That's what I was trying to say. The lady said they're coming, and I told her to send an ambulance, but I don't know if they'll find us. We're off the road. I thought because you're a mechanic you could figure out... I don't know... something. I don't really know why I called you. I just thought you could help Mummy."

She started sobbing again, so I put her on speaker and texted Booker to trace Maisie's phone and get him to send Ace with a tow truck.

"Are you still there?" she rasped.

"Yeah, baby girl, I'm here," I said. "Did your airbags go

off?"

"No," she sobbed. "I hit my head too, but I'm okay."

"I'm gonna come get you, okay? Where were you going?"

"We were coming from Ali's. We're near the zoo I think."

"Okay, were you on 26?"

"I think so. I saw the exit for the zoo. I think. It's really dark."

I swore. It was late, and there were a few winding stretches of that freeway with deep embankments, but the only guardrails you could go "through" were on the exits… everything else was concrete. It was doubtful that she could have gone off the road without a single witness.

"Please don't hang up," Poppy whispered. "I'm so scared."

Fuck!

"I'm right here, yeah? I'm coming."

"Don't hang up, Hatch. Please don't hang up."

I sped out of the driveway and toward Portland. "I'm here, baby girl."

"I'm really tired."

"I need you to stay awake, Poppy, can you do that?"

My phone beeped, and I glanced at the screen. Booker had hacked into the Mercedes mbrace system and sent me the exact location of Maisie's car… right along Highway 26.

"Poppy?" She didn't respond, so I bellowed, "Poppy!"

"I'm here," she said.

I heard sirens in the background and my heart calmed a little. "Do you hear that? The ambulance is close now."

"Yeah," she whispered.

"Stay awake," I ordered.

"I'm just resting my eyes like Mum does sometimes."

I had a feeling if she closed her eyes, she'd be out cold in minutes. "The paramedics will have questions about your mom they'll need you to answer. You have to stay awake, so you can help her, okay?"

"Okay, Hatch."

"I mean it, Poppy. They'll need to know if she has any allergies or anything. She needs you to talk to them when they get there. I'm close. I'll be there soon."

"They're here now. I'm gonna hang up."

"No! Don't hang up, Poppy. You can put the phone down, but don't hang up."

"Mummy's really hurt," Poppy said to whoever had just arrived. "Please help her. I can't wake her up. She's allergic to grass and a couple of trees. I don't remember their names."

"Any medicines?" a female voice asked.

"No. Just grass and trees."

"We've got her, honey, but I need you to come with me."

"Hatch?" Poppy asked.

"Still here, baby girl," I assured her.

"Can you tell him where you're taking Mummy, please?" Poppy asked.

"Hello?" the woman said.

"Hey."

"Sir, this is Mary Walls, we're taking them to OHSU."

"Okay. Maisie is the mom and Poppy's the daughter. Last name's Mann. Take good care of them, yeah?"

"We'll take care of your family, sir. You can meet us there."

I spoke to Poppy one more time and then the line went dead. After checking in with Booker and being assured Ace was on his way, I headed to the crash site, right off the side of 26 before the freeway interchanges to I-5 and I-405, finding the ambulances and police cars had the road blocked off.

Pulling my truck off to the shoulder, I rushed into the chaos, my heart in my throat. I was glad to see that Poppy hadn't been entirely correct in her assessment of being alone. A couple of cars had pulled off to the side of the road and called 9-1-1, but one lady had her two young kids in the back, the other car was an older woman, so I really couldn't fault them for not climbing down the embankment.

Before I could get to the ambulance, it took off just as Ace pulled up with a tow truck. I jogged to him. "What's goin' on?"

"Not entirely sure yet," I said. "Looks like she guided her

car off Jefferson where it went through a guard rail and down the embankment."

"Shit," Ace said. "Who?"

"Maisie."

"Maisie?" Ace asked. "Kim's Maisie?"

I shook my head. Cassidy was Ace's old lady, so even though I didn't advertise the fact I'd gone out with Maisie, Cassidy and Kim were sisters now, so they'd probably done their woman thing and over-shared. "Shut up, Ace. Just fuckin' deal with the car, yeah? I wanna get it back to the shop. Her daughter said somethin' was wrong with the brakes."

Once Ace was on task to deal with the car, I took off for the hospital. I lied to the admittance desk, claiming to be family until they reluctantly buzzed me back and showed me to a room. Poppy was sitting on the bed alone, crying.

"Poppy?"

She raised her head and relief covered her face. "You came."

"Yeah, baby girl. Where's your mom?" I pulled a chair up next to her and frowned. Her head was bandaged, and her left eye was starting to purple.

"I don't know. I'm waiting to find out." She licked her lips. "I'm thirsty."

I poured her some water and handed it to her. "Who should we call, Poppy?"

"No one," she said, and took a sip of water. "Auntie Ali's here. She just went to get the nurse." She put her hand to her head with a grimace.

"Are you in pain?"

Poppy nodded.

"Excuse me? Who the hell are you and what are you doing in here?" A petite brunette advanced on me and I raised my hands in surrender.

"It's okay, Ali. This is Hatch," Poppy said.

Ali paused and studied me. "*You're* Hatch?"

I nodded, bolstered by the fact Maisie had obviously mentioned me. Before we could continue introductions, a nurse arrived and squeezed a syringe of morphine into Poppy's arm. "I can only give you a little, honey, because we need you to stay awake. We're going to take you for a scan in a little bit."

"We'll keep her awake," Ali promised. "Any word on Maisie Mann?"

"Not yet. As soon as I know something, I'll let you know." The nurse left the room and I waved Ali to the chair I'd pulled next to Poppy's bed.

Poppy's eyes were drooping, so I squeezed her arm gently. She looked up at me, her pupils pinned. "Hmm?"

"Feeling a little better?" I asked.

She nodded.

I smiled. "I need you to tell me everything you remember, okay?"

"It all happened really fast. Mum said something felt weird, then yelled for me to hold on." She took a deep breath. "There was glass everywhere and my head hurt, but when Mummy didn't answer me, I got really scared. I pushed the Mercedes emergency button and, since she keeps her cell phone in the console, I called you." She gasped. "I left her phone in the car."

"It's okay, honey," Ali assured her. "The last thing she's going to care about is her phone. She'll get another one."

Another nurse walked in with a wheelchair and informed Poppy she could see her mother.

"Can we all come?" Alison asked.

"Yes. You can't stay for long, though. Mrs. Mann's pretty tired."

Poppy was shaky as she tried to slide off the bed, so I lifted her and set her in the wheelchair. The nurse handed Alison Poppy's bag of personal items and then we headed toward the elevator bay.

We arrived at Maisie's room and Poppy let out a frightened squeak. "Mummy!"

"Don't get up, Poppet," Maisie whispered, eyeing me in confusion as a nurse wheeled Poppy into the room.

I hung back and took in Maisie's appearance. Her right arm was in a sling and a bandage was wrapped around her head. She looked like she'd taken a pretty nasty beating. I saw Poppy's eyes widen and her face contort in fear as the nurse guided her to the side of Maisie's bed.

"I'll be right back," the nurse said.

Maisie nodded. "Thanks."

Damn, but I wanted to reach out and touch her. Hold her. Make sure she was really okay.

"Are you...?" Poppy asked, tears streaming down her face. "Are you okay?"

Maisie took her hand. "I'm good, love. I have to have a little surgery on my arm. It's broken pretty bad. But they're going to wait until my concussion clears."

"Poppy has a concussion as well," Ali said. "They just gave her some pain meds."

Maisie gave her a watery smile. "Thanks, Ali."

Poppy moved to stand.

"Don't get up," I ordered, and Poppy sat back down.

Maisie's eyes flew to me and she bit her lip. "How... what are you doing here?"

"I called him," Poppy said.

Another nurse walked in and smiled at Maisie. "I'm here to take Poppy for her scan."

"Do I have to go by myself?" Poppy asked.

"I'll come with you, honey," Ali offered.

"Thanks, Ali." Maisie smiled at her daughter. "It's pretty straight forward, Poppet. Don't be scared."

"Can Hatch come with me?"

I shook my head. "I should really head out, baby girl."

Ali frowned at me, then schooled her features and faced Poppy. "I'll come with you, sweetie. It'll be fine. You'll see."

"Okay, Ali. Thanks."

The nurse wheeled Poppy out and Ali followed.

SEVEN

Maisie

"I'LL CHECK IN on you later," Hatch said, his eyes searching mine.

I swallowed, feeling more than just the pain coursing through my body. God, he looked gorgeous. "I... don't know what to say."

"It's all good, Sunshine. Glad you and Poppy are okay. I've got your car back at my place, so give me a call when you're feelin' better."

"Okay," I said distractedly, but then registered what he said. "Wait. Why do *you* have my car?"

"Maisie, I'm just going to get some vitals," a nurse said, and walked to my bed.

"Oh, sure," I mumbled, and Hatch turned to leave.

"Hatch, wait. I want to know what's going on. Will you hang out for a bit?"

He walked further into the room. "Sure."

I relaxed, but it didn't stop my head from throbbing. My thoughts were foggy, but my body was on alert having Hatch so close.

The nurse slid her stethoscope around her neck and smiled. "I'm going to get a few supplies then I'll help you change. I'll be right back."

"Okay." I was so tired, but Hatch touched my shoulder and my eyes flew to him.

"Don't fall asleep," he ordered.

"Right." I sat up a little straighter, every movement killing me.

He sat on the edge of the bed and I was grateful I didn't have to look up. "What's going on?" I asked.

"Poppy called me from your phone and told me you were unconscious."

"And you answered? Even after I blew you off?"

He gave me a sexy smile. "Thought about ignoring the call, but I like you, Sunshine, so figured I'd see what was up."

I bit my lip. He liked me.

He tapped my knee. "Don't sleep."

"I'm not." I licked my lips. "I'm just resting my eyes."

Hatch nodded. "Had Booker hack into the Mercedes system, got my guys there to deal with your car, then came here to make sure you were okay."

God, he was so nice. I blinked back tears and melted when he slid a thumb gently across my cheek.

"I'm gonna find out why your brakes failed, and your airbags didn't go off. You good with that?" he asked.

"You don't have to do that," I whispered, the tears flowing freely down my face.

"Why are you cryin'?"

"Because."

Hatch caught a tear with his thumb. "Don't cry, baby."

"I can't help it. You're being so nice, and I've been an absolute tosser."

He chuckled. "I don't know what that means, but it sounds pretty bad."

"It *is* bad," I confirmed. "It really is okay for you to go, Hatch. If you can keep the car until I can deal with it, I'll sort it out. Or I can have Ryan do it."

He frowned. "Who's Ryan?"

"Ali's husband."

He relaxed. "You don't quit cryin' baby, you're gonna make your head throb worse."

"I can't help it. Everything hurts and you're being really lovely, and I'm worried about Poppy." He cupped my cheek and I leaned into his touch, which was stupid, because it hurt. "I'm so sorry I didn't ring you back."

"It's okay." He smiled. "But I need you to stop cryin', yeah?"

I nodded, but I couldn't stop. Now that the floodgates were opened, I couldn't seem to stop, the stress of the day covering me like a blanket of doom.

Hatch leaned forward and pulled me to him, cradling me gently against his chest. I was surprised the action didn't hurt me, but all I felt was safe. He was warm and smelled good and he was stroking my hair which felt super, super nice.

"I'm sorry that took so—" the nurse cut off her sentence as Hatch released me. "Are you in pain? I can give you a little something."

"That'd be good," Hatch answered for me.

"I'll be right back." The nurse left again, and I settled back against the mattress.

Just as the nurse returned with pain meds for me, Ali and another nurse also walked in wheeling Poppy, and Hatch stepped away from me.

"Hello, darling, how did it go?" I asked.

Poppy lowered her head and I frowned over at Alison.

"She was a bit claustrophobic," Ali provided. "They're going to see what they can do. Maybe a CT scan instead of an MRI. They have an open one."

"Sorry," Poppy whispered.

"That's okay, Poppet," I assured. "Those machines can be

scary."

"I'm gonna head out," Hatch said.

"Will you come back?" Poppy asked, and I was surprised by the sound of worry in her voice.

"Yeah, baby girl, I'll come back." He pulled a card out of his wallet, found a pen, and scribbled something on it, handing it to her. "Here's my cell phone number, okay? You need me, you call me. Anytime."

Poppy smiled and held the card to her chest. "Thanks, Hatch."

He made his way to me, leaning down to kiss my cheek. "I'm gonna go check on your car. But if you need me, you let me know, yeah?"

I nodded up at him.

"Call me when you know about surgery. If you want me here, I'll be here, okay?"

I nodded again.

He smiled and straightened, turning to my best friend. "Nice to meet you, Ali."

"You too," she said, and then Hatch left.

"What is *up* with that guy?" Ali demanded. "I thought you blew him off."

"I did. But he apparently wants to help."

"I don't know about this, Maisie. I think Ryan should look into him. It's weird that he's showing up here right after you've had an accident."

"Poppy *did* call him, Ali."

"Still…"

"Don't worry about it, love. It's fine. I'll tell him to back off if it gets weird."

Alison's response was a quiet grunt, but she let it go… thank God.

The rest of the night passed in a fog as I was helped into a hospital gown (I was glad Hatch missed *that*), and we had to focus on the status of our concussions and other injuries. By the time Poppy had been cleared to go home, and I was good to sleep, I could barely keep my eyes open, so Alison took Poppy home and I crashed.

Hard.

I awoke with a start, totally confused as to where I was. It took me a little bit to remember I was in the hospital and I relaxed against the pillows.

A nurse rushed in, flooding my room with light. "Are you okay?"

"I think so," I said.

"You were screaming," she said.

"I was?" I sighed. "I'm so sorry."

"Don't apologize, sweetie. Let's make you more comfortable. Are you in pain?"

"A little, but it's manageable."

"From one to ten?"

"Eight."

She smiled. "Manageable, huh?"

I sighed.

"You're a pretty tough cookie." She pushed something through the IV and my pain disappeared. "Better?"

"Much."

"Press this button if you need anything else, okay?"

I nodded and the nurse set the call button by my hand.

"Can I do anything for you before I leave you?"

"Can you please grab me a phone?" I asked. "I need to ring my daughter."

"Of course."

She rolled the table over with the phone and showed me how to turn the light off and on, and then left me to call Poppy.

"Hello?" Ali answered.

"Hey, lovey."

"Oh, Maisie." Ali breathed out a sigh of relief. "How are you?"

"Tired, but good. How's Poppy?"

"She's good. She finally fell asleep about an hour ago. Do you want me to wake her?"

"No," I rushed to say. "Let her sleep. But she can call me even if it's the middle of the night, okay?"

"Definitely. We've got her, honey, okay? You take care

of yourself. We'll be there tomorrow before your surgery."

"Okay, Ali. Thank you for everything. Seriously. I don't think I could do life without you."

"Hey, don't get mushy on me now."

I smiled. "Fair enough. I'll see you tomorrow."

"Love you, honey."

"Love you too." I hung up and relaxed against the pillows again.

For the next half-hour or so, I tried to sleep, but every time I closed my eyes, I'd jump awake, the accident flashing in my dreams. I pulled the phone toward me again, found Hatch's card, and dialed his number, chalking my insanity up to the drugs.

"Yeah?" Hatch answered, his voice gruff with sleep.

"Hi. It's Maisie."

"Hey, Sunshine, you okay?"

I nodded, although, I realized he couldn't see me. "I'm sorry if I woke you. I can't seem to sleep."

"You in pain?"

"No, the nurse took care of that. I keep having nightmares." I sighed. "Poppy's asleep which is good, but I'm here listening to my own thoughts and I see the accident over and over again."

"I bet."

"Anyway, thanks for answering."

He chuckled. "You can wake me anytime, baby."

I bit back a yawn. "I'll let you go. I'm going to try and sleep."

"Okay. You call me if you need to. I'll keep my phone close."

"Thanks." I smiled. "And thanks for everything today. I really appreciate it."

"No problem."

He hung up and I closed my eyes, finally succumbing to sleep again.

* * *

Pain sliced through my arm and I gasped awake.

"Maisie? You okay?"

I frowned and followed the sound of Hatch's voice. "Hatch?"

He was walking toward my bed and I thought I might be dreaming. He smiled down at me. "Hey, Sunshine."

"What are you doing here?"

He stroked my cheek. "Thought it might be easier for you if I was here."

I bit back tears. "That's so nice," I whispered.

"I'll find the nurse and get you some pain killers."

I nodded, and he left the room, returning quickly with a nurse following, syringe in her hand. "I'm Sammi. I'm here for the next six hours, so if you need me, just let me know. You're in pain, huh?"

I nodded.

She smiled. "You made it over four hours. You're a rock star," she said, and pumped more morphine into my system. I felt instant relief.

"How long until surgery?" I asked, forcing back a yawn.

"A few hours," the nurse said. "Try and get some sleep. The doctor will be in soon."

My bladder was screaming at me, but I didn't know if I could move. "I need to…" I pointed toward the restroom.

"I'll step out," Hatch said, and left the room.

Sammi helped me slide my legs over the side of the bed, then walked me into the bathroom. I moved slowly, still weak and sore, but at least my head felt back to normal.

After doing my thing, we headed back toward the bed and I faltered. Sammi pulled a chair toward me quickly and I sat down. "I'll get someone to help."

She pulled open the door and Hatch stepped in. "What's wrong?"

"It's okay. Your wife was just a little dizzy."

"Well do somethin'," he ordered.

"Just need to get her back to bed so she can rest. I'll call an orderly."

"I got it," he said, and stalked inside.

"I'm okay," I countered.

Hatch shook his head. "Loop your left arm around my neck, okay? I'm gonna lift you, but I don't want you to move your right arm."

"I can do it, Hatch."

"Don't argue with me, yeah?"

"I'm too heavy."

"Baby, will you please shut the fuck up? I've got you."

He leaned down and I looped my left arm around him. He lifted me effortlessly and carried me to the bed, setting me gently on the mattress with a smile. "You good?"

"Yes. Thank you."

"Okay, I'll wait outside again."

I gave him a shaky smile. "Thanks."

"Your man is quite the hottie," Sammi said as she wrapped the blood pressure cuff around my good arm.

I smiled. "We actually don't know each other very well."

"Oh, I'm sorry, I thought you were married."

"Nope."

"And he's here taking care of you?" she asked in surprise.

"Yes. Strange, eh?"

"I think it's pretty darn special. Keep that one around if you can."

A sweet kind of warmth filled my heart. "I'll keep that in mind."

Sammi took a few more readings and then smiled. "Want me to send him back in?"

I nodded. After making sure I was comfortable and the call button was close, she left and Hatch walked back in.

"How ya doin'?" he asked.

"Better."

"I found your cell phone in your car." He pulled it out of his pocket and set it on the table. "I charged it up, so it's ready to go."

"Thanks." I stared up at him. "What are you doing?"

"Whaddya mean?"

"I'm just confused as to why you're here."

"Would you rather I go?"

"Honestly? No." I let out a long, frustrated sigh. "Which

confuses me as well."

He chuckled, pulling a chair close to me. "I think there's somethin' here. I don't know what it is, but I can't get you outta my head."

"You look like you ate something nasty."

"Yeah, well, you know I was chained to a woman before, and it didn't go so well. Thought I was done with this shit, but you just keep pullin' me back in."

"I'm not trying to," I whispered.

"I know." He lifted my hand to his mouth and kissed my palm. "Been in a dark place, Maisie. But you've changed that. Can't explain it, but I see you and I feel peace."

"Is that why you call me 'Sunshine'?"

"Yeah, why?"

My breath hitched on a sob. "I thought it was because of my hair, but that's way better."

He chuckled. "Why are you cryin', baby?"

"Because you're being so sweet and I'm having a hard time processing all of these emotions."

"Don't process anything right now, Maisie. Once all of this is over, we'll spend some time together and find out what this is, yeah?"

I nodded, trying to pull myself together. "Do you still have my car?"

"Yeah. My guys are checkin' it out."

"I don't understand why my airbags didn't go off. I service that bloody car on time every few months. The brakes were working fine the day before." I let out a frustrated sigh. "I don't know why any of this happened."

"Me neither," Hatch said. "But we'll figure it out."

"You really don't need to take this on, Hatch. It's a lot for someone you've just met."

He grinned. "I'm doin' it for Poppy."

I let out a quiet snort. "Oh, really? How's that then?"

"She asked me to help you. I gave her my word, Sunshine, and I always keep my word."

I smiled sleepily. "Well, that's good to know."

"Sleep, baby."

I think I was out before he'd finished his sentence.

* * *

Hatch

Maisie had been wheeled into the operating room close to three hours ago. I had managed to catch a few hours of rest before her nine a.m. surgery, but I was still wiped. I shook my head. What the fuck was I doin' with this woman? I should walk away. Leave her to her life. But I knew I never would. She was under my skin now and I felt more for her than I'd ever felt for anyone. As irrational as that might be, it was no less the truth. And now that I knew someone was after her, I was even more on alert. For the moment, she was safe, so I took that comfort and let it settle into my bones.

I'd been at the hospital since two a.m. and I was exhausted, but still couldn't turn off my brain. I was convinced someone messed with Maisie's car, but the cops had cleared it at the scene.

Sipping coffee while I waited with Alison and Poppy, I thumbed my phone on, hoping to see a message from Ace, who'd gotten an early start this morning, pulling the mangled car apart one piece at a time. Ace's brother, FBI agent, Jaxon Quinn, was documenting everything they found and dusting for fingerprints. Even though I wasn't a fan of law enforcement, I had asked Jaxon to assist. Jaxon had backed up the Dogs on several occasions, including his assistance in saving Ace's woman, Cassidy, from a psychopath.

"You're the family of Maisie Mann?" a woman's voice asked.

I turned from the waiting room window as Poppy jumped up from her seat and rushed toward the nurse. "Is she awake?"

"Yep. I can take you back if you like. One at a time, though."

Poppy nodded and walked with the nurse through the double doors. I dragged my hands through my hair and sat in one of the chairs by the window.

"What's your deal?" Alison asked.

I turned my head slowly toward her. "My deal?"

"You know she lost her husband, right?"

"Yeah, babe, I know."

"And that she's never dated another man? Ever? Niall has been her world since she was five," she continued. "She had dinner with you and then didn't call you back for a reason. She didn't want to see you again. Why are you here? Are you some kind of crazy stalker? Because if you are, my cop husband will deal with you."

"You're lookin' out for your girl," I said. "I get it. And I have no intention of doin' anything other than gettin' to know Maisie and sortin' out what happened with her car. But since we don't know each other, nothin' I say's gonna assure you... and it shouldn't. You just gotta get to know me and make up your own mind."

She narrowed her eyes and then let out a sigh. "You're a smart one, aren't you?"

I chuckled. "More smart-ass, but yeah, I'm not an idiot."

"Well, you're on notice. If this goes somewhere, you'll treat her right or I *will* cut you."

I grinned. "Maisie's in safe hands with me."

"We'll see."

"Ali?" a nurse enquired as she walked up.

Alison rose to her feet. "Yes, that's me."

"You can go back if you like." The nurse turned to me. "She's not feeling up to any other visitors just yet. She said she'd text when she was ready."

"No problem," I said. "I'll head out."

Disappointed, but understanding why she needed space, I left the hospital and headed back to my shop rather than go home.

Time for some answers.

EIGHT

Maisie

I AWOKE TO find Alison and Poppy still in my room, talking quietly by the window. They were sitting on the bench seat and had their heads together, focusing on Poppy's phone.

"What are you doing?" I asked.

"Mummy," Poppy said excitedly, and jumped to her feet, rushing to my side. "We were just looking at horse videos. Are you okay?"

I smiled. "Yes, darling? Why?"

"You kept falling asleep in the middle of talking."

"I explained that your body is healing," Ali said.

I smiled and took Poppy's hand. "I'm fine, love. I'm just really sleepy, but that's normal. I'll be home bossing you around in a couple of days, you'll see."

She worried her bottom lip, looking wholly unconvinced. "Can we call Hatch?"

"He's been here most of the night, love."

"But we should call him anyway."

I frowned up at Ali, unsure what to say.

"Your mom needs a little time," Ali said.

"Hatch will keep you safe," she whispered.

"Do you think I'm unsafe, Poppet?" I asked.

She nodded.

"Mama's in the hospital, sweetie," Ali said. "There's no safer place for her to be."

"I'm okay, Poppy," I assured her.

"We should go." Ali wrapped her arm around her and gave her a squeeze. "Let your mom rest."

Poppy shook her head. "I don't want to leave."

"You need to rest, too, Poppet." I reached for her hand again. "Your body's also trying to heal."

"Then I want to stay with you."

"It would be better if you're in a real bed, Poppet," I countered.

"I can't sleep there," she admitted.

"She's having some nightmares," Ali said.

"Honey, why didn't you tell me?"

"Because I didn't want to worry you."

I sighed. "Oh, sweetness, you're safe at Ali's."

"I'm not worried about me, Mummy." Poppy frowned. "Someone could whack you while you sleep."

I snorted out a laugh and regretted it immediately. "Ow."

"No one's going to "whack" your mom, Poppy," Alison promised.

"I'm safe here, love."

"Well, can we call Hatch?" Poppy asked.

I let out a slow breath. "We can't ring Hatch, sweetheart."

"Why not?"

"Because he's busy. I know that some of this is grown-up stuff, but I think you're old enough to understand that you don't ask a person you don't know to take on family responsibilities."

"But he likes us. He told me he does."

I forced back frustrated tears. I loved my daughter, but when she dug her heels in, I had a tough road ahead to change her mind, and right then, I was too tired to argue.

"Poppet, I'm exhausted, so I'm pulling the Mummy card. Hatch doesn't have time, and we don't know him well enough to ask him to fuss over me. He'll come when he can, okay? I'm safe here and you're safe with Auntie Ali, and we're going to keep it to us for the moment."

She nodded, but admittedly, I wavered a little when I saw the silent tears streaming down her face as she leaned forward to kiss my cheek.

"I love you, Poppet."

"I love you too," she whispered.

"I'm gonna talk to your mom for a minute, okay?" Ali asked. "I'll be right out."

Poppy hesitated for a moment before leaving the room. I knew she wanted to "overhear" what Ali and I would talk about, but she finally walked out and closed the door behind her.

"What's that all about?" I asked. "You're not letting her watch mafia movies, are you?"

Alison giggled. "No way!"

"Where the hell did she get "whack" from?"

"No clue." Alison grimaced. "And what's up with Hatch? She adores this man."

"She doesn't know him. *We* don't know him."

"I know, but she trusts him." Alison smiled. "Obviously more than I originally thought."

"Which is weird. Poppy's shy around adults. Kids she can talk to ad nauseam about anything, but when she gets around adults, she's super skittish, especially men. With Hatch, it's like she's known him forever… like he's a knight in shining armor or something." I sighed. "But she needs to understand that we don't need a man. We can handle this ourselves."

Ali giggled. "Does that fall under the British stiff upper lip crap you spout?"

"Absolutely." I smiled. "And, if I'm being honest, I'd love Hatch to be here as well, but I look like a bowl of shite and I'm not ready to let him see me like this."

"You looked like this yesterday as well, hon," Ali pointed out.

"Well, yesterday I didn't have a choice, he just showed up."

She rubbed my good arm. "Okay, babe. But don't be a hero. Poppy's right. Hatch *does* like you. Call him if you want to."

"Weren't you just warning me away from him?"

"I had to see where this guy stood," she countered. "But he seems genuine, so if he can help, then great. Ryan's going to check him out which will make me feel better. So, again, don't be a hero. Got it?"

"I won't be a hero," I promised.

Alison leaned down and kissed my cheek then took Poppy home.

I slept for several more hours, waking to find a text from Hatch.

Checking in. Doing ok?

I wasn't doing okay actually. I was in pain, but I wanted to think for a minute before I loaded myself up with drugs.

Tired. A little pain. But overall good, I think, I texted back.

You due for drugs?

Yes. Trying to wait a little, though.

I jumped when my phone buzzed in my hand. Hatch was calling me now. "Hello?"

"Babe, if you're in pain, hit your pump," he demanded.

"Okay, okay." I hit the button on my pump and sighed as the pain washed away.

"Better?"

"Much," I whispered. "Did I wake you?"

"I texted you, Sunshine."

I giggled. "Oh, right. I forgot."

"Those meds work quick."

"Yes, they do," I agreed. "Poppy wanted me to ring you

earlier."

"Yeah?" he asked. "Why didn't you?"

"Because."

"Because why?" he challenged.

"Just because."

"Oh, because." He chuckled.

"I haven't showered in almost forty-eight hours and I look like I've been hit by a bus." I yawned. "You don't start a relationship showing the worst of you. You ease into the horror."

"I like hearin' that."

"That I want to ease you into the horror?"

"That we're startin' a relationship."

"Oh," I breathed out. "Are we?"

"Yeah, Maisie, we are."

"Oh," I said again. "Okay."

Hatch laughed. "I like these drugs, baby."

"Mmm, me too." I don't really remember what he said, but I was feeling no pain, so I decided I'd just agree.

"I'm gonna let you go, Maisie. But I'm comin' by later, yeah?"

"Hatch it's late."

"No shit?" he retorted. "Is that your only objection?"

"Yes, I suppose."

"I'll see you later, then. Go back to sleep, Sunshine."

He hung up before I could respond, so I set my phone on the table and let myself fall into oblivion.

I wasn't sure how long I slept, just that I came awake with a start as pain shot through my arm and my bladder screamed for relief.

"I got you," Hatch said, and I felt instant relief as he hit the pain pump button.

"You're here," I breathed out, smacking my lips, my mouth dry.

"I'm here," he said, and handed me a cup of water.

I took a long sip and sighed. "Can you get a nurse, please?"

"You okay?"

"Yep. I just need the nurse."

"Can I help?" he asked.

"No."

"You sure?"

"Hatch," I breathed in frustration, then whispered, "I have to go to the loo."

"And I'm guessin' that's way too much for you if I take you."

I screwed up my face in horror. "You can't be serious."

He chuckled. "I'll get the nurse."

"Thank you."

Hatch left the room and a nurse walked in a few minutes later and helped me do my thing. I don't know if Hatch came back because I fell asleep as soon as I was back in bed.

I didn't wake up again until the sun peeked in through the vertical blinds. Glancing around, I realized I was pain free... and alone. Frowning, I pressed the call button and waited for a nurse, who arrived a few minutes later.

"Hi, Maisie. I'm Sally. I'm here with you all day today." Sally was in her fifties, short dark hair, and kind brown eyes. "Let's get some vitals."

"Do I have time to use the restroom first?" I asked.

"Sure. I'll help you."

"Did Hatch leave?"

"Your husband?" Sally asked.

"Um, sure." It was easier to just agree rather than trying to explain.

"He said he was going to the cafeteria."

"Oh, okay." I was surprisingly glad he didn't leave the hospital, but still wished he'd been there when I woke up.

"I can't believe I didn't wake up during the night in pain. I must be healing faster than I thought," I said, once I was back in bed.

Sally checked the pain pump and smiled. "You got your pain dose every four hours, that's probably why. The night nurse said she showed your husband how to dose you, so he must have set his alarm and taken care of it."

"Really?"

She nodded with a smile. "You've got a good man there."

"Apparently so," I agreed. "Is it possible to get a toothbrush?"

"Oh, sure, hon." She opened a cabinet and pulled down everything I needed, then helped me put paste on the brush. It was tough to clean my teeth with my left hand, but I soldiered on, then I fell back into bed relieved that my teeth were no longer wearing fuzzy jumpers.

Sally went through my vitals and deemed I could eat if I was hungry. My stomach rumbled in response.

"What can I get you?" she asked.

"Pudding would be amazing," I said, my mouth watering.

"Chocolate, vanilla, or butterscotch?"

"Um, all of them?" I asked, hopefully.

Sally chuckled. "Coming right up."

Hatch walked in just as Sally was leaving.

"You're awake," he said, and smiled as he made his way over to me. "How do you feel?"

"Like I need a shower."

He chuckled. "I bet."

"But really well-rested. Thank you for monitoring my pump," I said, and reached for his hand. "Did you get any sleep?"

"Yeah, baby, I slept." He smiled. "But more importantly, I'm glad you did."

"You don't have to stay here all day, Hatch."

"I don't actually plan to."

"Okay, good." I said it, but I was actually disappointed he would be leaving.

"But I'm not leavin' for a while, so get that devastated look off your face, Sunshine."

I gasped, releasing his hand with a frown. "I'm not devastated."

"You look pretty devastated."

"I'm not even a little bit sad."

He chuckled. "Just messin' with you."

"How rude." I straightened my bedding. "Have you forgotten that I'm infirm, sir?"

His smile widened. "You're fuckin' sexy when you're

speakin' all hoity toity," he whispered.

"So I'm sexy all the time, then?" I challenged.

Hatch leaned down and kissed my cheek, whispering, "Yeah, Sunshine. All the fuckin' time."

I shivered, closing my eyes briefly, but our moment was interrupted by Sally returning with pudding cups.

"Behave," I ordered.

"No promises." Hatch sat in the chair next to the bed.

"Which one would you like first?" Sally asked.

"Chocolate, please."

The nurse opened the pudding and handed me a spoon.

"Do you need some help?" she asked.

"No, I'm good, thanks, love."

She nodded and then left the room and I tried to dig into my pudding. Failing miserably. I quickly discovered it was really difficult to eat pudding (well anything, really) when your dominant hand was useless.

Before I managed to dump chocolate all over myself, the cup was taken from me as Hatch sat on the edge of the bed. "Let me help."

I hated being so vulnerable, but the fact I was starving trumped my pride. Hatch lifted the spoon to my mouth, and I wrapped my mouth around it, sighing as I swallowed the sweetness.

"I think I can feed myself, Hatch, if you just hold it for me."

He smiled. "I like this better."

I wrinkled my nose. "This seems like a big jump forward in our getting to know each other."

"Feeling a little exposed?"

"More than a little, yes."

"You've been alone a long time, Maisie. It's gonna take a minute to get used to having a partner again. We'll get there."

I turned my head away from the spoon coming at me. "I don't want to rush things, Hatch. I know nothing about you."

"I get it, Sunshine, and we'll go slow, but the fact you're laid up won't last forever. Plus, this gives me brownie points towards our first fight."

"If you do everything I tell you to do and don't piss me off, we won't fight."

"I'll keep that in mind. Now eat your pudding."

I giggled.

"What now?" he asked.

"Pudding's just a funny word," I admitted.

"Yeah, I guess it is." He grinned and shoved the spoon in my mouth again. "Did they say when you could go home?"

"Tomorrow I think." I pushed his hand away when I'd enough to eat. "Do you need to go?"

"Soon. We're almost done with your car and I'm not likin' what we're findin'."

I frowned. "What are you finding?"

"Can we wait until you're feelin' better?"

"No. I'm fine, Hatch. Just tell me the truth."

"Someone cut your brake lines and disabled your airbags, and this person knew enough about new cars to do it," he said. "I also think someone fucked with your fuse."

"You think this was intentional?"

"Yeah."

"Who on earth would try to hurt me? And Poppy?" I bit back tears. "Who?"

"I don't know, baby. We're workin' on it. Can you think of anyone who might want you out of the way?"

"No."

"Think, Maisie. Has anyone ever made any threats? Given you the creeps? Anything?"

"I'm the CEO of a sex toy company, Hatch. I've had to deal with a few kooks, but I've never had death threats."

He frowned. "How many kooks?"

"Not many. My lawyer handles these things. Stephanie, my assistant, doesn't even show them to me anymore, she just forwards anything like that to him. The only reason I know she gets them is she gives me the weekly kook list tally. Usually, I only have one or two a month, maybe."

"Okay, anyone want into your panties?"

I choked on a cough. "What?"

"Men, Sunshine. Anyone who asked you out and didn't

83

take 'no' for an answer?"

"Alison seems to think a client of ours, Jeremy Marville, wants to date me, but he's a nice man who went through a nasty divorce. We had one lunch and he sent me flowers. I highly doubt he'd do anything like this."

"Gonna check that out," he said.

"Go easy, okay?"

He nodded. "How *did* you start the business? It just doesn't seem like you."

"It's not, really. I had a business degree from Oxford." I sighed. "It was a drunken night out with Niall. I said we should design funny condoms and call them Spiffy Stiffies, then he said we could make stencils for women and call them Posh Pussies."

"You're shittin' me."

"He quit his job, ran with my idea, and here I am today." I shook my head. "It was started as a joke, believe it or not, and there's no one more surprised than me that it went anywhere. I ran the business, he ran the think tank and it worked. Weird, right?"

He chuckled. "It's different."

"I don't know anyone who'd want to hurt me and Poppy, Hatch. Honestly. I'm pretty low-key." I bit my lip. "I don't advertise what I do for a living. I wanted to sell it after Niall died, but honestly, the job kept me distracted."

"Okay, Sunshine. We'll keep diggin'."

"Mummy," Poppy cried, and rushed into the room. "You're awake."

"I had a good night's sleep." I smiled at Hatch over my daughter's shoulder as she gently hugged me.

Alison greeted me and Hatch as Poppy released me and smiled up at him. "Thanks for looking out for Mum."

"You're welcome," he said. "I'm gonna take off."

"Can you stay?" Poppy asked.

"I can't, baby girl. Gotta get back to the shop."

"Hatch has to work, Poppet."

She sighed. "Okay."

He smiled. "As soon as your mom's out of here, we'll all

go somewhere, yeah? Dinner or something."

Her face lit up. "Really?"

Hatch nodded. "Sure."

"Okay."

"I'll see you later, Maisie," he said, and without even a glance back, he left the room.

I spent the next few hours hanging with Poppy while Alison headed off to run errands and grab some things for me from home.

After Poppy and I enjoyed dinner together, Ali picked her back up, and I was able to take a shower. The nurse even helped me wash my hair and by the time I climbed back into bed I felt like a whole new person.

I flipped on the television and settled in for a quiet evening. I didn't typically watch TV, so this was a bit alien for me, but I found myself transfixed by a dating show. The women lived in bungalows and men were flown in on a helicopter for the women to choose… a bit like a lobster in a tank awaiting the pot of boiling water.

Hatch walked in mid-way through the program and leaned down to kiss my cheek. "Hey, Sunshine."

"Hi." I smiled up at him.

"What are you watching?"

"Some dating show. It's like a modern-day Timber."

His eyebrows dropped. "I'm sorry?"

"You know, that dating app? You swipe left or right?"

Hatch cocked his head. "You mean, Tinder?"

"Is it?" I giggled. "I always thought it was Timber."

"Nope. Tinder." He grinned and pulled the chair close to the bed.

I turned my head toward him. "So you've used it, then."

"Hell no. I don't date and I don't need an app to hook up."

I smiled. "No, I don't suppose you would."

"How are you feelin', baby?"

"I managed a shower, so I feel really good."

He chuckled. "Nice."

"They told me I'm being released in the morning."

"Yeah?" Hatch frowned.

"You don't want me to be released in the morning?" I asked.

"How secure is your place?" he asked.

"I live in a building with a doorman and security. You have to have a code to park." I sat up a little. "Are you worried?"

"Yeah, Maisie, I'm worried," he said. "Don't know who tried to kill you, so don't know where they got to you."

I sighed. "Poppy's scared as well."

Hatch leaned forward. "What kinda scared?"

"Scared, scared. She's having a hard time leaving me alone. I get that any kid would feel that way after an accident, but I think her fear goes deeper. Poppy has an amazing sense of people and situations. She's my litmus test. If she doesn't like you, you're probably a pretty awful person." I smiled at Hatch. "She *adores* you."

His eyes softened as he linked his fingers with mine. "She's cool. I like her too."

I held his hand a little tighter. "I'm not this person, Hatch," I whispered. "I'm not the person who has someone trying to kill them. It doesn't make sense."

"I know. We're gonna figure it out." He lifted my hand to his mouth and kissed my palm. "In the meantime, you okay with me drivin' you home tomorrow?"

"Ali's bringing Poppy by early. She said she'd come back and pick me up, but I bet she'd like the break. If you're okay with taking us both, then yes, that would be appreciated."

"Yeah, I'm good." He raised an eyebrow. "You okay with me bein' in your space, though?"

"You mean because we only met five minutes ago and now I'm taking you back to my place?"

He chuckled. "Yeah."

I hit my pain pump and relaxed into my pillows. "Since nothing we've done has followed any sort of a normal time-line rule, I'm good. I trust you, which could be my downfall, because I don't really know you, but I feel like I do. Does that make sense?"

"Complete sense."

"Really?" I cocked my head. "Because I feel like I'm high."

He dropped his head back and laughed. "Damn, baby, you're funny."

"I'm not really. It's the drugs." I smiled. "Are you going to show me all your skeletons now that I seem to be showing mine?"

"Don't think you wanna go there, Sunshine."

"I would very much like to go there." When he tried to pull his hand away, I held tighter. "What happened with your ex-wife, for example?"

He sighed. "Long story short, she told me she couldn't get pregnant."

"So you divorced her?"

He frowned. "Sunshine, she told me she couldn't get pregnant, but what she actually did was have two abortions."

"What?" I gasped.

"We were married for five years. She started steppin' out on me, but she came back cryin' sayin' she loved me, so I took her back. But when I got a call that she'd been rushed to emergency, I arrived to find out she was there with excessive bleeding due to an abortion. It was apparently her second."

"Oh, Hatch, I'm sorry."

"Kicked her ass to the curb and never looked back."

"I don't blame you." I shook my head. "What a bitch."

"I think that's generous."

"Yes, I think you're right." I yawned. "I promise I won't ever have an abortion. I mean, I don't plan on getting pregnant again, but even if I did, I'd never have an abortion."

I don't know if he responded because I fell asleep almost before I got my words out.

NINE

Maisie

I AWOKE THE next morning having slept through the night without pain again. Hatch wasn't in the room, so I called the nurse and she helped me freshen up and then get back into bed. Ali and Poppy would arrive in less than an hour and I was looking forward to heading home, even if it wouldn't be for several more hours. Even though I liked the ease of having the pain pump, I couldn't wait to get rid of my IV so I didn't have to drag it with me everywhere.

I was a little confused as to where Hatch was. Normally my guard dog was close in the morning. I smiled when he walked in just as the thought flitted through my brain.

"Hi," I breathed out, surprised by how relieved I was to see him.

"Mornin', Sunshine," he said, sitting on the edge of my bed. "What time's Poppy comin'?"

"Soon." He looked pensive, so I asked, "What's wrong?"

"Besides someone tryin' to kill you and me not knowin' how to protect you without watchin' you twenty-four-seven?"

"My building's secure, Hatch."

Before he could say anything further, the doctor walked in to determine whether or not I was free to be discharged. Hatch stepped over to the window while the doctor did his thing and then as soon as the doctor left, a nurse walked in with forms for me to sign. "I have your scrips, you can fill them here in the hospital or take them to another pharmacy. I'll give you a dose before you go so you have some time," she said.

She removed my IV and informed me I was essentially released as soon as I signed the paperwork. No sooner had she given me all of my instructions, Alison and Poppy walked in, and Hatch and I never got to loop back to our conversation.

"Why don't I grab your drugs while you change?" Hatch offered.

"Thanks," I said as I signed the release paperwork as best I could with my left hand.

Poppy and Alison helped me dress in regular clothes and I realized there was no way in hell I'd be able to do this alone. Poor Poppy was going to have her work cut out for her over the next few weeks as I healed.

I flopped back onto the bed and closed my eyes.

"Are you okay, Mum?" Poppy asked.

"Just tired, love." I smiled. "It's tough work putting on pants."

She giggled. "Only for old people."

"Yes, darling, I'm so old," I droned sarcastically.

Hatch walked in waving a white paper bag right before a volunteer pushing a wheelchair. "Got your stuff, Sunshine."

"Thanks."

"I'm Jim," the volunteer said. "Are you ready, Mrs. Mann? I'll wheel you down."

"I'll get the truck and meet you out front," Hatch said.

"I've got my car," Alison countered. "We can handle it from here."

"I'm comin' with," Hatch said. His voice was soft, but there was no arguing.

Poppy's face lit up. "You are?"

"Yeah, baby girl." He grabbed my bag by the window.

"You're off the hook, Ali if you want to head home," I said.

"No, I've got time. Nicole's taken over things today so I could make sure you were good."

"I'm still comin'," Hatch said.

Alison rolled her eyes, her back turned to Hatch.

"How about you follow us, Hatch?" I suggested.

He frowned, but Poppy jumped in and said, "I'll come with you, Hatch."

"Poppy, you should probably come with us," Alison countered.

"But Hatch doesn't know where we live," Poppy said. "I can show him."

"Would you both give me and Poppy a minute, please?" I asked.

Hatch and Alison nodded and left the room... Jim the volunteer waited while I patted the mattress next to me. Poppy sat on the bed and I wrapped my arm around her. "I'm not sure about you going with Hatch, Poppet."

"Why not?"

"Because we don't know him well and you're a young woman getting in a car with a man we don't know."

She sighed. "Mummy, if he tries to touch me inappropriately, I will tell you immediately. But he won't. He's not a creep."

"Love—"

"Mummy, please. Let me go with him."

"Are you sure?"

"Yes."

"You know you can tell me if you feel uncomfortable."

"Yes, I know." Poppy smiled. "I like Hatch, Mum, and he will protect you."

"I'm not in danger, love."

"I know... because Hatch is here."

I sighed. "Okay, darling. If you feel safe with him, then I'm good."

She hopped off the bed and rushed to the door. Alison and Hatch walked back in and I settled myself in the wheelchair.

"We'll meet you in the parking garage," Alison said.

Hatch nodded. "Okay. See you in a minute."

"Someone's got a guardian angel, huh?" Alison mused as she drove.

I smiled sleepily. "Seems that way."

"Ryan says he's totally clean. His club's clean too."

"That's good, right?"

"Yes, but you just never know with these motorcycle club types... they're glorified gangs."

I sighed. "So far, he's been nothing but a stand-up guy, so I'm going to take him at face value. I like him... so does Poppy, and that means something."

Alison nodded. "Fair enough."

We drove into my garage and parked, Hatch followed in his truck and pulled into my guest spot. Before I got my door open, Hatch was there, virtually lifting me out of the car.

"I *can* walk on my own, Hatch," I bossed as he wrapped an arm firmly around my waist.

He grinned. "More fun for me, though."

Alison's phone buzzed in the car, so she leaned in and grabbed it. "Alison Lundy. Hi. He did? Hmm. Okay. Either myself or my husband will be there as soon as we can. Thank you." She hung up with a frown. "Merrick got tackled during P.E. He and his buddies were messing around and he did something to his knee."

"I got Maisie if you need to be somewhere," Hatch said.

"You okay with that, hon?" Alison asked me. "Because I'll call Ryan."

"It's fine, Ali. Seriously." I smiled. "You've done so much for us over the past few days. Go take care of your family. I'll call you later."

She hugged me and Poppy and then climbed back into her

car, while Hatch helped me up to my condo.

I settled myself in Niall's chair and closed my eyes while Poppy showed Hatch around. A gentle touch on my cheek had me jumping awake. I didn't realize I'd even fallen asleep.

"Sorry, baby," Hatch said with a smile. "I think you should take some meds."

I nodded. "Probably a good idea."

He opened my prescription bottle and handed me two pills. I took them and closed my eyes again.

"You want me to go?" Hatch asked. "Or stay tonight?"

"Stay," I whispered as I succumbed to sleep again.

* * *

Hatch

I covered Maisie with a blanket just as Poppy walked back into the living room and frowned. "Is Mummy okay?"

I nodded. "The meds make her sleepy. Want to see what we can find to eat?"

"I don't know what we have. Mum doesn't do much cooking."

"Well, it's a good thing I do."

Poppy nodded and led me into the kitchen. "There are a couple of restaurants around the corner. We have them deliver... a *lot*."

She showed me where everything was, and she wasn't exaggerating. There wasn't a whole lot in the way of 'prepareable' food. At least they had milk, cereal, and coffee for the morning, but nothing as far as fresh veggies, fruit, or meat.

"Our housekeeper comes on Fridays and usually picks up groceries on her way. Mum gives her a list on Thursday."

I nodded. "Well, that's a few days away, so I'm going to call Cricket... have her pick up a few things."

"Who's Cricket?"

"My sister."

"Is that her real name?" Poppy asked, her eyes wide.

I shook my head. "Christina. We've just always called her Cricket 'cause she doesn't stop hoppin'."

"That's such a cool name." Poppy sighed. "I wish I had a cool name."

"Beautiful name for a beautiful girl, Poppy," I countered. "Your mom and dad did right by you."

She blushed. "Thanks, Hatch."

"Now, what do you want Cricket to get you?"

"Can she get Pop Tarts?" Poppy asked hopefully.

"Yeah, baby girl. What flavor?"

"S'mores."

"Got it."

Poppy glanced over her shoulder to a sleeping Maisie. "Don't tell Mum. I'm not allowed that much sugar."

"Life ain't worth livin' without sugar."

"Right? I knew I liked you for a reason." She beamed and then helped me make a more substantial list.

"What time do you need to go to bed?" I asked. "I feel like I should make you stick to the schedule your mom set up."

"I'm not going to school this week, so I can stay up until ten."

"Yeah?"

"I think so. I'll check with Mum when she wakes up." She leaned over the kitchen island. "You're gonna keep Mummy safe right?"

"Yeah, baby girl." I smiled. "And you."

"Thanks, Hatch." She pushed away from the island. "I'm gonna go call Grace."

"I'll let you know when Cricket gets here."

She nodded and headed down the hall. I texted a list to my sister, then settled myself on the sofa next to Maisie.

I found the television remote (stuffed in a side table drawer) and hit the power button, making sure to turn the volume down low.

About an hour into the slowest baseball game I'd ever watched, my sister texted that she was in the building lobby with groceries. I headed down the hall and knocked on Poppy's door, pushing it open at her quiet, "Come in."

"Hey, Cricket's here."

"I'll call the front desk," she said.

"Thanks."

Poppy led me out to the kitchen and called down to give Cricket permission to come up.

"Who's here?" Maisie asked sleepily.

"My sister Cricket's bringin' some food, baby. Don't get up," I said.

"I don't think I could if I wanted to," she complained.

Cricket arrived with a doorman who helped her with her bags, and seemed to be eyeing my sister, which I didn't particularly like much.

I grabbed the bags out of the man's hand and nodded. "Thanks. We'll take it from here."

"Thanks, Mark," Cricket said, all flirty and shit. "It was really nice meeting you."

"You too."

"She's gotta go," I said, and closed the door.

"Well, that was rude," Cricket complained. "He was nice."

"He was eyeing you like a Rottweiler eyes a steak," I countered.

"Well, he was a really nice Rottweiler."

Poppy giggled and I glared at my sister, then introduced Maisie and Poppy to Cricket. "Let's get this stuff into the kitchen," I said.

"I'm gonna help Mum," Poppy said.

"Sounds good," I said, and led Cricket into the kitchen.

I watched as Poppy helped Maisie out of her chair. "You okay, Sunshine?"

Maisie smiled. "I'm fine, love."

It was the first time she'd used an endearment with me and I felt it all the way in my dick. I grinned and went back to helping Cricket.

Poppy walked out... alone... about ten minutes later just as I pulled pork chops out of the fridge. "Where's your mom?"

"She's really tired, so she's in bed."

"Harder to watch her if she's not in here, baby girl."

Poppy smiled. "I won't repeat what she said to say if you said that."

I nodded. "I'll go talk to her."

"Why don't you help me with dinner, Poppy?" Cricket suggested.

"You just transfer 'em from the packagin' to the plate, sissy... no tryin' to do anythin' more," I demanded, and headed down the hall. Every time Cricket tried to cook, she burnt something... luckily, she was past the stage of setting things on fire, but since the kitchen was unfamiliar to her, I wasn't taking any chances.

Knocking on Maisie's slightly open bedroom door, I whispered, "Maisie?"

"Unless you're here with chocolate, wine or drugs, I don't want to talk to you."

I pushed the door open wider and found her lying on her back on a huge bed, on top of what looked like fuckin' expensive bedding, her bandaged arm cradled on her stomach. "You in a lot of pain?"

Her head flopped to the side and she raised an eyebrow. "Me? *No*... what would give you that idea?"

I chuckled closing the distance between us, leaning over her with a smile. "I'm gonna make dinner, but let's get you some meds for now, yeah?"

She reached up and stroked my cheek. "You cook?"

Sitting on the edge of the bed, I wrapped an arm around her upturned knees. "Yeah, baby, I cook."

Her eyebrows dipped together in a concerned expression. "Are you a secret serial killer or something, because you seem way too good to be true?"

"If I tell you, it won't be a secret," he whispered.

Maisie giggled, and I couldn't stop myself from kissing her gently. "Love that sound, Sunshine."

"I really like you, Connor."

Fuck. Her saying my real name was like a punch to my gut. "You know my real name?"

"Yes, sorry, is that not okay?" She burst into tears. "Kim's husband mentioned it in the park."

"It's fine."

"Please don't turn into yet another bastard who tries to kill me and my daughter." She sniffed, trying to get her tears under control. "I couldn't deal with it."

"Okay, first," I shifted so I was closer to her, wiping her tears from her cheeks, "I love that you know my real name and you can call me Connor anytime you want. Second, you and Poppy are safe with me. Always. Even if you and I don't work out, you'll still be safe with me. I like you too, Maisie, so how about you worry about getting well and leave the rest to me?"

She sat up and looped her arm around my neck. "I don't know what we'd do without you."

"You don't have to find out, baby, I got you." I slid my hands up her back and pulled her close.

Maisie's lips slid along my neck, then my jawline, finally touching my mouth gently. I stroked her cheek and deepened the kiss, my tongue connecting with hers, the minty taste of toothpaste combining with the gum I'd been chewing earlier. I forced myself to break our connection when she whimpered. I didn't want to hurt her further. "Baby, you need to take something for the pain, yeah?"

"I took Vicodin about twenty minutes ago," she countered. "But this is helping more."

I chuckled. "Yeah?"

She leaned back and nodded. "You're a really good kisser, Hatch. Not that I have much to compare you to, but you really are."

"Back atya, Maisie." I slid her hair away from her face. "Are you hungry?"

"Starved."

"Pork chops okay?"

"Perfect." She pulled me close again. "But can we stay like this for a little while longer?"

"Sure, baby."

After a few more minutes, I slid off the bed, then lifted her and carried her back out into the living room. This time, she had the good sense not to resist...much (there was one minor comment about her legs not being broken, but I ignored it). I settled her into the overstuffed chair she was in before, and went about making dinner with Poppy and Cricket's help.

TEN

Maisie

I WATCHED HATCH as he joked around with Poppy and Cricket, his gentleness with my daughter filling my heart with ooey gooey goodness. It could have been the drugs as well, but I didn't think so. Poppy was enraptured by everything he said, and I got it... learning how to properly season a pork chop was interesting, but learning how to properly season a pork chop by Hatch, was fascinating. And sexy.

I couldn't seem to fight sleep, so I didn't force myself to, but when I felt a tickle on my cheek, I opened my eyes to find Hatch smiling down at me. "Hey."

"Hi," I rasped.

"Hate to wake you, but the chops are done and we've eaten. You should really get some food in you."

My stomach rumbled in response and I chuckled. "My body agrees."

"Okay, I'll grab your plate. Stay put."

This was my life for the next week. Hatch catering to my every need, me growing stronger and healing at record speed (according to the doctor), and Poppy falling in love with my motorcycle man... okay, maybe it was me falling in love with him, but she was close behind, and I couldn't blame her.

Alison was also warming to the idea of me and Hatch. Friday night we'd planned a double date, with Cricket hanging out with Grace and Poppy at my place, while Merrick went to a friend's house. It would be an early one, just a quick meal at the Q, but something to get me out of the house, which I desperately needed, however, Friday afternoon, Ryan called, his tone frantic.

"What's wrong?"

"Ali's missing."

"What do you mean, she's 'missing'?" I demanded.

"She didn't show to pick up Grace from school and no one can get hold of her. We've got a BOLO out, but so far no luck."

"I take it you're tracking her cell phone and car?"

"Her car's here and her phone's off," he said in frustration.

"Have you checked Somer's Place?" I asked, just in case she lied to me about not staying clean and was self-medicating with alcohol again.

"Yeah, the bar's closed."

"What about—"

"I've checked every fucking bar in Portland, Beaverton, Gresham, and Vancouver, Maisie, she's nowhere!" he snapped.

"I'm sorry."

"No, I'm sorry. I just... fuck, I can't find her anywhere."

"As soon as Hatch gets back, we'll go look, okay?"

"Yeah, that'd be great, Maisie, thanks."

He hung up and I called Hatch. "Hey, Sunshine."

"Hey. Am I on speaker?" He was picking up Poppy and I

didn't want her to hear what I had to say.

"You're not now."

"Alison's missing. I'll explain when you get here, but tonight's obviously off."

"Okay. We're two minutes away."

"See you soon."

I set my cell phone on the kitchen island just as someone knocked on my front door. Thinking it was Hatch and Poppy, I pulled open the door... to find a very drunk Alison, half-empty bottle of Vodka, stumbling inside.

"Hey, girrrrl," she slurred, waving the bottle with a giggle.

"Alison!" I closed the door and rushed to her. "Honey, Ryan's worried sick."

"Is he? Whatever." She took a swig from the bottle.

"Ali, love, can I take that Vodka?"

She shook her head. "It makes me feel good."

I took a deep, calming breath. It's not like I could wrestle it from her, I only had one useable arm.

Luckily, Hatch and Poppy walked in a few minutes later and Hatch helped get Alison under control so that I could call Ryan.

Ryan answered immediately. "Hey, Maisie."

"Ali's here. She's really drunk, Ryan, but she's safe."

"I'll be there as soon as I can."

"Okay, love."

I hung up and grabbed Alison some water, walking into the family room and handing it to her. "Where's my Vodka?" she demanded.

"I think this will help better than the Vodka," I said.

"I hate water." She looked like she'd crawled through an Army obstacle course, the front of her shirt and jeans covered with caked-on mud, and her shoes damp.

"I know, love," I crooned. "Where have you been? I think we should get you out of those wet clothes, hmm? Get you something warm and dry to wear?"

"It's raining outside."

"I know, Ali, but you're going to catch a cold."

She shivered. "Okay."

"Come on, we'll use my bathroom."

Before I could get her in the shower, however, Ryan arrived and took over. I left them alone and joined Hatch and Poppy back in the family room. "Is Auntie Ali okay?"

"She will be, Poppet," I said, and pulled her in for a hug. "Uncle Ryan's taking care of her."

"Can I please call Gracie?"

"Sure, love. How about you hang in your room for a bit? We'll let you know when the coast is clear."

Poppy nodded and walked down the hall, and I turned to face Hatch. "Still want to be part of my crazy world?"

He chuckled. "Yeah, Sunshine, I'm good."

"Maisie," Ryan called, and I headed to my bedroom.

Alison was stretched out on my bed, clean and dressed in sweats and a hoodie, she appeared to have passed out.

"I gave her a sedative," he said. "I'm going to take her to the hospital and put her on a psych hold. We need to figure some things out."

"I'm sorry, love."

He dragged his hands down his face. "I don't know what I'm going to do Maisie."

I wrapped an arm around him. "We'll sort it out. Don't worry about work, I'll get someone in. I'll help with the kids. Whatever you need. You know that. Let's just get her well."

"Thanks." He leaned down and kissed my cheek. "I'm going to get out of your hair."

"Okay, love."

He picked Alison up, cradling her gently to him, and carried her out of the condo. I locked up behind them and returned to Hatch.

"So, our night just got blown up. I'm sorry."

Hatch wrapped his arms around me gently and kissed my head. "We can still go out, Sunshine. Cricket's happy to hang with Poppy."

"Yeah?" I asked, hopefully.

Hatch smiled. "Yeah."

"I have an hour before the office closes and I really need

to call HR and then our attorney to deal with some legal stuff. If I get all of that done, then yes, I'd love to get out of this house."

He leaned down to kiss me gently. "I'm gonna grab a beer. Want anything?"

"Can you find Bill Anders's number and ring it, please? It's hard to hold the phone and scroll at the same time."

He took the phone from me, then handed it back and I settled it to my ear. "Hey Maisie, how are you feeling?" Bill asked.

"I've been better."

"Uh-oh. What's going on?"

I filled him in on what I knew so far. Bill was our head company attorney, so I trusted that he would be able to handle the sensitive nature of Alison's situation and how best to relay the information.

"Wow, Maisie," Bill breathed out.

"I know." I glanced at Hatch who sat on the sofa and set his feet on the coffee table. "We're going to need to find someone to take Alison's position temporarily. I think Nicole would be the best fit."

"She's young. What about Myron?"

"Nicole knows Alison's job better than anyone."

"But Myron's got the experience."

"Not in this job he doesn't," I countered. "And I need someone who understands that this is Alison's job. She has it for as long as she wants it."

"I just don't know that Nicole's the right fit."

"Why? Because she's young and cute and a woman?" I snapped. "My company. My call."

Hatch raised an eyebrow as he took a swig of beer.

Bill was silent for a few seconds before saying, "If you think she can handle it, I'll have HR make the changes."

"Thanks. Stephanie has my calendar so—"

"Stephanie quit, Maisie."

"What? Why?"

"According to HR, she was bored and got a better offer," Bill said. "She didn't come back after lunch."

I squeezed my eyes shut and dropped my head back. "Well, shit."

"It's not the end of the world, Maisie."

I scowled. "It's a little difficult for my company to run without me, my personal assistant, *and* the CFO, Bill."

"It's going to be a little confusing for a few weeks, I agree, but you have a well-oiled machine here. It's not going to fall apart any time soon."

I stuffed down my irritation and chose my words carefully. "You're right. I appreciate all your help on this. I'll let you handle the legalities of all of this and check in soon."

"Sounds good. Take care, Maisie."

"Thanks." I hung up and fought the urge to throw my phone across the room. "Bastard."

"You okay?"

"Our lawyer's a male chauvinist arsehole," I snapped. "He speaks to me like I'm the little woman." I groaned. "I need to replace him."

"So replace him."

"It's not that simple, Hatch, but Ali and I were starting the process... well, before. And my assistant quit, which just adds to the stress."

"Okay, baby. We'll figure it out."

"Really, Hatch?" I snapped. "Do you know where I can find a highly organized person who knows every computer program on the planet, who can navigate the world of sex toys and weed out the creepos? Oh, and preferably has an aptitude for numbers, because we now have to hire a CFO and Nicole's gonna need help?"

"Me," Cricket said, as she and Poppy walked into the room.

"Cricket's here," Hatch provided.

I rolled my eyes. "I see that."

"What happened to Stephanie?" Poppy asked.

"She quit," I said with a frustrated sigh.

"Oh, good. She was a bitch."

"Language," I warned.

Poppy dropped her head. "Sorry."

103

I didn't miss Hatch's slight smile as he studied me. He slid his hand to mine and squeezed gently. "We'll figure it out."

"You say that a lot, do you know that?" I ground out.

"Can you realistically do anything right now, Maisie?" he challenged.

"Yes." I raised an eyebrow. "I can make some calls."

"Bill's doing that."

"I need to talk to HR about getting the job posted and then I need to look at résumés."

"Baby, it can wait a few days."

I pulled my hand away. "Don't pretend to understand what I'm up against here, Hatch."

"Seriously." Cricket stepped forward. "I can help. I'm graduating in a few months with a forensic accounting degree and I'm a quick learner. I hate working at the shop, no offense, big brother."

"Some taken," he returned.

"I want a real job. Bartending was a good option... well, until, you know...," she nodded toward Hatch, "...but it's not really what I want to do in the long run and if I can get in as an assistant, maybe I can use my degree."

"Poppy has my email address in her phone. Send me your résumé and a list of references and I'll have a look. If it looks right, I'll forward it on to HR," I said, but realistically, she sounded pretty perfect. And Poppy liked her which gave me a good feeling. My daughter was right, Stephanie was a bitch, but she knew the business so I'd kept her around.

"But that's not gonna happen for a few days," Hatch challenged.

"I have to get this sorted," I argued.

"You don't have to get it sorted today, Sunshine, because your priority is getting well and goin' out with your man." He craned his head to look behind him. "And Cricket's gonna respect that."

I met Cricket's eyes. "Is he always this bossy?"

"Pretty much," she said.

"And you listen to him?" I asked.

She grinned. "Only to his face."

"Well done, love."

Hatch moved so he could block my view of his sister. "You, on the other hand, are going to relax. Get me?"

"There's no reason why I couldn't help out while you're healing," Cricket said. "I can type dictated emails, run errands. I'm happy to sign an NDA or whatever and work as a contractor for the time-being."

"Christina," Hatch said in a warning tone.

"That sounds good, Cricket. Thanks." I focused on Hatch and smiled. "You want to swear right now, don't you?"

"More than you can imagine," he admitted. "But I do like to see you smilin', baby."

"I'm going to freshen up and then we'll go, okay?"

"Sounds good," he said, kissing me quickly, and I headed to my bedroom.

Hatch drove us to the restaurant, only it wasn't the Q.

"Where are we?" I asked, as he parked behind a brick building.

"Friend's place. Don't move," he ordered.

"Where am I going to go?"

He grinned and climbed out of the truck, coming to my side and pulling open the door. "I'm gonna lift you down."

"You are not."

"Babe, just let me do this so you don't fall."

"I can climb out of a bloody car on my own, Hatch," I argued.

I released my belt and turned my legs, but he stopped me, leaning in, eyebrows drawn together. "Don't move."

"Hatch—oh!" His left arm slid around my waist and he tugged me gently forward, lifting me out and setting me on my feet. "Bloody hell, love, you could have thrown your back out."

He frowned. "Don't say shit like that, Maisie."

"Well it's true."

"It's not true, baby." He softened his expression and went into an Eastern European accent as he continued, "I'm strong like bull,"

I chuckled. "Sorry if I made it sound like you're not a big strong man."

"Not about that," he corrected.

My stomach did a few flip-flops and I smiled. "Is that your round-about way of telling me to stop calling myself fat?"

He winked. "You're learnin', Sunshine."

"You're a cheeky buggar, aren't you?"

Kissing me gently, he led me inside, and we commenced our first "official" date.

"Hey, Hatch," a deep voice called as a bouncer checked our IDs.

Hatch gave the man a chin lift and smiled. "Ryder. This is Maisie."

Ryder grinned and I melted a little. Lordy the man was pretty. Shaggy blond hair, blue eyes, and he was tall like Hatch, but clean shaven.

"Nice to meet you," he said.

"You too."

"I got a table open in the VIP section if you want it," he offered. "I've gotta check on a liquor delivery, but I'll come say hi when I'm done."

"Sounds good, brother, thanks," Hatch said, and we followed him to a private table where we were wined and dined and treated like royalty. Hatch had dialed the romance up a notch and the whole evening had rocked.

ELEVEN

Hatch

SATURDAY MORNING, I was at the shop catching up on a few things when my phone buzzed in my pocket. I saw "private number" on the screen and ignored the call, but it buzzed again, so I picked it up. "Hatch here."

"Hey, man, it's Jaxon Quinn."

"Hey."

"We pulled a print off the car that didn't belong to Maisie or her daughter," he said. "Nothing hit in the criminal database, so I had a hunch to check places like volunteer databases."

"And?"

"And, we got a hit."

"Yeah? Who does it belong to?"

"Alison Lundy."

"That's Maisie's best friend. She's cool."

"The print was on the inside of the tire and a partial on the brake line at the cut. Also found a palm print on the steering wheel, which I have a feeling will match hers. She removed the airbag completely."

"Are you sure? What about that Jeremy asshole?"

"Jeremy Marville's got an airtight alibi and he's totally in love with Maisie, Hatch, and not in a weird way. He genuinely respects her. Record's clean. Not a pushover. Ex-wife's a psychopath and he's protectin' his kids. Good guy."

"Shit," I breathed out. Ice infused my veins. This fuckin' crazy bitch could have killed Maisie and Poppy. Could have taken them away from me. I dragged a hand down my face. "How the hell would Alison know how to do that?"

"The internet's flooded with how-to videos on this kind of thing. It wouldn't be hard. She's also got a computer science degree, so she has knowledge around coding."

"You think she hacked into the car's computer?"

"Not sure yet. She physically removed the airbags, so she might have done both."

"Damn it. How do you have *her* prints?"

"She signed up to be a volunteer at her kids' schools."

"Makes sense. Maisie probably did too." I rubbed my forehead. "You can't get to Alison right now. She had a breakdown yesterday, so her husband put her on psychiatric lockdown."

"We know Ryan Lundy. He's a good cop."

"Have to take your word on that," I said. "I don't know what the fuck this is gonna do to Maisie."

"We're gathering evidence, Hatch, but this is a pretty clear case of attempted murder, we just gotta figure out if she was in her right mind when she did it."

"Right. Thanks, man."

I hung up and took a deep breath, then dialed Knight. "Hey, man."

"Hey. You talk to your brother?"

"Yeah."

I filled Knight in on what he didn't know, and we made a game plan going forward of who would watch Poppy, who would watch Maisie when I wasn't around (which would be never), and who would watch Alison. No one was to lose sight of the psychopath. She was to be monitored at all times. I hung up with Knight and called Maisie.

"Hey," she said, on the first ring.

"Hey, Sunshine. You cool if I come over in a bit?"

"Of course. Everything okay?" she asked.

"Gotta talk to you about something."

"Okay. I'll let the lobby know."

"See you soon."

She hung up and I locked up the shop, holstered my gun, and jumped on my bike.

* * *

Maisie

I was trying not to panic. Hard to do when I had no idea why Hatch suddenly needed to come over. I was enjoying a blissful day alone today since Cricket had taken Poppy out to Kim's place to ride. They wouldn't be home for a few more hours, so even though I had to eat with one hand and couldn't really do much, it was quiet and I had no one to answer to. I hadn't had that in a while. A drunk and unstable Alison I could handle... Hatch maybe wanting to break up with me... not so much.

My doorbell rang and I checked the peephole, then pulled the door open and stepped back to let Hatch in. "Hey."

He leaned down and kissed me gently. Well, this was a good start. At least he wasn't dumping me... well, I hoped he wasn't. "What's wrong?" I asked.

"Let's get you somewhere comfortable." He wrapped an arm around me and led me into the family room. "I have to tell you somethin' and I think it's gonna fuckin' kill you."

I frowned. "Are you serious right now, or are you taking the Mickey?"

"Takin' the Mickey?"

"Joking around," I explained.

"Not jokin'." He sat in Niall's chair and pulled me gently onto his lap.

My side hit something hard and I leaned away from him. "What's that?" I gasped. "Are you carrying a gun?"

"I usually do, Maisie."

I tried to scramble off his lap, but he held me still. "Why do you have a gun?"

"I've always had a gun, Sunshine, I've just been leavin' it in my truck so Poppy doesn't freak out. But I think it's time to have a conversation with her, because I'm not good with doin' that anymore."

"Hatch, you're scaring me," I rasped.

"I know. I'm sorry. Just got a call from the forensics guy lookin' over the car. He found something."

"Okay," I said, slowly.

He dragged his hand through his hair. "Shit!"

"Just tell me, Hatch."

"It's Alison."

"What's Alison?"

"The person the FBI believes cut your brake line and re-moved your airbags."

It took a minute, but I snorted as I burst out laughing. "Alison would *never* do this."

"I'm just tellin' you what they found."

"Well, they're wrong." I shook my head. "There's got to be some other kind of explanation."

My phone rang on the coffee table and Hatch kept hold of me as he reached for it and handed it to me. "Hey, Ryan."

"Hey, Maisie. I'm at the hospital. Alison wants to see you. We're discussing options, trying to sort out if the hold is necessary, but she'd really like to see you if you can come by."

"Of course I can. Twenty minutes okay?"

"Sure. See you then."

I hung up. "Alison's—"

"I heard."

"Now we can find out once and for all," I said.

"I really want Jax to be wrong, baby."

"He is," I assured Hatch as I climbed off his lap, and headed to brush my teeth. "Can you just let your sister know what we're doing? I don't want to worry Poppy."

"Sure," he said.

Once I freshened up, Hatch drove me to the hospital. We made our way to the mental health ward and Hatch stayed in the hallway while I walked into Alison's room. "Hey honey."

She gave me a sad smile as I approached. She was in a hospital gown, but she looked as though she'd just come from the spa. Her hair was perfectly styled, her make-up freshly applied, and she didn't have restraints on. All-in-all, she looked perfectly normal. Maybe the doctors felt she didn't require the seventy-two-hour hold.

"We really need to stop meeting this way," I said as I hugged her.

"I know, right?"

"Are you okay?"

Tears slid down her face. "No. I don't think I am, Maisie. My brain is all jumbled again."

"I'm sorry, love."

She grabbed for my hand. "I'm doing bad things."

"Are you?"

She nodded.

"Like what?" I asked.

"Bad bad things," she whispered. "You know, you've lost your English accent."

Whoa, where did that come from?

"What, love?"

"Niall never lost his Scottish one," she continued.

"You don't think?"

Alison shook her head. "And he always wore my favorite shirt."

"I'm sorry?"

"The blue one with the paisley collar."

God, I hated that shirt. He wore it the sum-total of twice. Once out to a double date with Ryan and Alison and once to their house, but only because it was ugly shirt night and that was the ugliest shirt he owned. It was put in the donate bin after that.

She sighed. "He wore it just for me. I know he did."

"I don't understand Alison."

"You had to have it all," she whispered. "Why didn't you just die?"

"The police said they found your fingerprints, Alison." My heart raced; fear flooding me that Jaxon might be right.

"If he'd just left you!" Alison ranted.

"Who?" I asked.

"You should have died, Maisie."

"Honey, did you cut my brake lines?"

I moved to stand, but she grabbed my healing arm and twisted. I cried out in pain.

"Niall was mine!" she screamed.

Hatch stormed into the room, the door slamming against the wall. Ryan was close behind.

"I will snap her arm in two," Alison threatened.

Hatch drew his gun, but despite the fact I was in agonizing pain, I snapped, "No! She's sick. You can't hurt her."

"Lower your gun," Ryan ordered, aiming his own at Hatch.

"Both of you, put your guns away!" I begged. "Hatch, please, love."

He scowled, but holstered his and then Ryan did as well.

I focused back on Alison. Her pupils were pinned, but otherwise she seemed normal. This actually scared me more than anything. "Ali, love. Please. Will you tell me what's going on? You're really hurting my arm." This was a total understatement and I was desperately trying not to cry out every time she squeezed my bad arm.

"Get a fuckin' hold on your woman, or I will end her," Hatch snapped.

Ryan rushed over to the bed, but every time he got close Alison wrenched my arm again. "Ryan, just back off," I ordered. "You're making it worse."

"You were supposed to die. Poppy wasn't supposed to be with you. I tried to stop you from taking her! I followed you all the way to the accident site, but forgot to disable your Mercedes emergency call button." She shook her head. "Rookie mistake. Poppy is supposed to live with us! We're supposed to raise her. She's mine."

"I don't understand."

"I want her. Niall said I could have her."

I highly doubted Niall would have told her that, considering we'd always agreed either my siblings or his sister would raise our kids should anything happen to us. "Ali, you know that Niall and I always said Beckett or Kenna... or even Aileen would raise any kids we had until they grew up if anything happened to us."

Her eyebrows dropped and she stared at me in confusion. "I wanted him."

"Who?"

"Niall."

"Lovey, you have Ryan."

"I don't want Ryan!" she screamed, throwing her hands up in frustration.

The second she released my arm, Hatch sprang forward and pulled me away from her. Ryan grabbed Alison from behind and handcuffed her to the bed.

I fell against Hatch, crying out as my arm connected with his chest.

"Fuck, baby, hold on. I got you."

Hatch bellowed orders to nurses, got me in a wheelchair and into emergency where he apparently knew one of the doctors, and made sure I was number one priority to anyone within shouting distance. I was whisked off to X-ray, administered morphine, and ushered into a private room, all within thirty minutes.

As we waited for the X-rays to come back, I melted down and found myself gently guided against Hatch's chest as he climbed onto the bed with me.

"It's okay," he whispered as I sobbed against him.

"I don't understand any of this. Ali's been my best friend for fifteen years. She's had some issues over the years, but she's never indicated any desire to take Poppy... or any de-

sire for Niall. God, we had our babies together." I gasped.
"Poor Ryan! Do you think she's always felt like that? Imagine standing there in the middle of a hospital having your wife yell that she didn't want you. What's he going to do?" Renewed sobbing began and I took the comfort Hatch offered.

"We're gonna figure this out, Sunshine. I promise." He kissed my temple and held me until my sobbing calmed.

"I don't know what I'd do if you weren't here," I whispered.

"I'm not goin' anywhere, baby."

"Thank you." I closed my eyes and we sat quietly for several minutes.

The doctor who'd helped me walked in a few minutes later and pulled up a chair. "I'm Dr. Stone."

"The FBI agent working this case for us works with the doc's brother," Hatch explained.

That explained why I got the star treatment. "It's nice to meet you," I said.

"You too, Maisie. Looks like your arm's in pretty good condition, considering. Your pins and staples stayed put, so that's good. You do have a little more bruising and you'll have some soreness, but I'll give you some more painkillers and that should clear up in a few days. Overall, you were really lucky."

"Thank you," I whispered. "Is Alison okay?"

"I don't know. I can try to find out for you, but honestly, with confidentiality rules, I doubt I'll be able to tell you anything."

"I understand."

"I'll get you your paperwork and get you out of here," he said.

"Thanks, Doc," Hatch said.

"No problem, Hatch."

The doctor left and, once I was cleared, we headed home. I called Ryan's cell to check up on Alison and found out she was forcibly put on a seventy-two-hour hold. As hard as it was to hear my best friend had cut my brake lines and tried to kill me, it was twice as hard telling Poppy.

"Why would she do that?" Poppy asked, sobbing. "Does she hate us?"

"No, Poppet. She's sick. Sometimes people have something chemically wrong in their brains and they can't control things they do. She was having some trouble with her medication, so she tried to compensate with alcohol which made things worse."

"What do you think will happen to Auntie Alison?"

"I'm hoping that now that she's in the hospital they'll be able to get her medication levels right."

"Can I call Gracie?"

"Not tonight," I said. "Let's figure out what's happening with Alison first, okay? We need to let things settle a bit."

Hatch got a call while Poppy and I were talking, so he took it in my office, and I went to find him when I was done giving him privacy. He was still talking.

"Yeah, man. Yeah. I'll let her know. She's not gonna be happy. I get it, but regardless, I don't think she wants—" He cut himself off when he met my eyes. "I'm gonna call you back, brother."

"What's going on?" I asked when he slid his phone into his pocket.

"They've arrested Alison."

"*Who's* arrested Alison?" I crossed my arms, regretting that move immediately and grimacing at the action.

"FBI."

"How?" I snapped. "She's on psychiatric hold."

"I know. Now she's on psychiatric hold, currently under arrest."

I scowled. "Well, they can't. I'm not pressing charges."

"Babe, you don't really have any say in it. People can't just go around trying to commit murder, then drinking and driving, and stealing cars."

"She stole a car?"

"Yeah. That's what she used to get to your place."

"Bloody hell. What a mess."

He closed the distance between us, and I leaned against

him.

"Is she okay?"

"After the shit she pulled, you're askin' that?" he challenged.

"Honey, she's not in her right mind."

"I know." Kissing my temple, he lifted my chin. "If you hear from either Ryan or Alison, I want to know about it, yeah?"

"They're my best friends—"

"Immediately."

"They're not going to do—"

"Fuck me, Maisie, she tried to kill you!" he snapped. "If you minimize this one more time, I'm gonna fuckin' lose my mind."

I burst into tears and he pulled me against him again.

"I'm sorry," I whispered. "You're right. I just... I don't know why she'd do this."

"I know, baby."

"Will you stay tonight?"

"Yeah, Sunshine. I'm stayin' all weekend."

"Okay, thanks."

He held me until I pulled myself together enough to fake it for Poppy, and then we spent the rest of the weekend trying to forget what Alison had done. Epic failure, but we did try.

TWELVE

Maisie

MONDAY MORNING, HATCH left me long enough to pick up breakfast and arrived with both food and his nephew, Devon. Introductions were made and I thought Poppy's head might explode. My confident (with kids her own age), chatty, beautiful young daughter suddenly went all giggly and tongue tied around the boy. Granted, he looked like Zac Ephron's younger brother, but still, Poppy wasn't typically the boy-crazy type. My stomach churned. This was her growing up even faster. Gah!

"Cade's on a job," Hatch explained as he made me a cup of coffee and cheesed me up a bagel. "So, I'll drop Poppy at school, take Dev to his appointment, then to school, and grab lunch. Does that work?"

"Yes, that's fine, love," I said, and sat at my kitchen island. "But I could have figured something else out for Poppy this morning. You don't need to stretch yourself so thin."

Hatch stood in front of me and kissed me gently. "It's all good, Sunshine."

"I have something for you."

"Yeah?" His face showed excitement.

"Nothing fun, I'm afraid. Just practical."

"Practical's good."

I nodded toward the small desk by the window. "There's a spare set of keys and I got you a code to the garage, so that you have your own entry. You can park in my space until I get a new car and then you can park in my guest space. You also don't have to check in at the front desk anymore."

"You sure about this?"

I smiled. "Very sure. I trust you."

He stroked my cheek and nodded. "Okay, baby."

"Okay."

He grinned, leaning down to kiss me again. "Now, eat your breakfast. I'll text you when I drop Dev off... decide what you want for lunch."

"Thanks, darling."

"Like that, Maisie."

"I'll keep that in mind, Connor."

He kissed me once more, then gathered up the kids and headed out. I finished my breakfast and took pain meds before settling in for a quiet morning of catching up on a few business emails.

An hour into my uneventful work time, my doorbell rang. Since the doorman hadn't called up, I assumed Hatch had forgotten he had a key and pulled open the door. Ryan stood in the doorway, looking haggard. He had bags under his eyes and a few days' stubble over his cheeks.

I pulled him in for a hug, holding him tight. "How are you?"

"Not good."

"How's Alison?"

"She's really bad, Maisie. Doctors aren't hopeful. I'll give you the full rundown on what they've said, but can we go somewhere? Grab a coffee, maybe? I feel like I'm running on fumes."

My heart went out to him, but his request made me a little sick to my stomach. "Ryan, I'm sorry, but Hatch is going to freak out if I go somewhere with you, and he really doesn't want you here with me alone."

His eyes narrowed with hurt. "Alone with me? Maisie, you've been alone with me a million times and I've never—"

"Neither did Alison," I pointed out.

His jaw snapped shut. He rubbed the back of his neck. "I get it. I thought after all we've been through... after how much we helped you after you lost Niall..." He stepped back into the hall, shaking his head. "You know what, never mind."

I felt like crap. He was right. He and Alison had done so much for me, and it wasn't like Ryan had a drinking problem. After everything he'd learned over the past couple of days, he had to be devastated. And I couldn't even offer him a shoulder to cry on. "Ryan, wait. I'm sorry."

"It's fine, Maisie. I'll call you in a few days."

He took off and I watched him leave, replaying the conversation in my head and wondering how I could have handled it differently. Ryan was my friend, too, and I should be there for him. But I felt so betrayed and leery after Alison's attack, I knew Hatch was right and I couldn't trust either of them.

Ryan disappeared around the corner and I closed the door and secured the deadbolts. It took several tries because I was shaking so bad, and my left hand kept slipping off the locks. My phone buzzed on the coffee table, but I didn't get to it in time. Picking it up, I saw a missed call from Hatch, but I needed a minute to calm down, so I waited to call him back. Unfortunately, he called again... this time I ignored it. We played the game again, and I answered figuring he wasn't going to stop.

"What's wrong?" he growled.

"Ryan was here."

"Don't move."

He hung up and I dropped my phone on the sofa. I was still shaking, but I couldn't seem to make myself move from my spot on the area rug. The locks turned and Hatch walked inside and pulled me gently into his arms. "Tell me everything."

I filled him in and he nodded, but didn't say anything as he walked me to Niall's chair, guiding me into it. I pulled my knees up to my chin and sighed. "He's hurting, love."

"I don't give one fuck, Maisie." Hatch shook his head. "He doesn't come here guilt tripping you like that. You didn't do anything wrong. His wife tried to kill you! How does he expect you to react?"

"I hear you, but it wasn't Ryan who tried to kill me," I countered. "They were there for me when I needed them. I feel like I should be doing something for them."

Hatch scowled. "I know you think you know Ryan, Maisie, but I've seen men do a lot of stupid shit for their women. This one has a badge and you don't know what he's capable of."

"Hatch—"

"Stop fuckin' minimizin' this!" he bellowed.

"Stop yelling at me!" I returned.

He dragged his hands down his face and studied me for a few tense seconds. "I'm gonna make some calls, Sunshine. You need anything?"

"I'm due for some meds," I said, my tone clipped.

"I'll grab 'em." Hatch pulled his phone out of his pocket as he headed to the kitchen, putting the phone to his ear. "Jax, Hatch. Ryan Lundy showed up at Maisie's place. Shut him the fuck down, man, or the Dogs will. I don't give a flyin' fuck why, just take care of it. This is your courtesy call. You won't get another one." He sighed. "Yeah. Bye." Hatch brought me water and a dose of pills which I readily took. "What do you want for lunch?"

"Whatever."

He gripped each arm of the chair and leaned down. "Baby."

"What?"

"Look at me."

I met his eyes and all my anger left me. I could see his hurt and fear, and knew he was worried. "When I heard you scream and saw the psychopath...," he shook his head, "...then, I couldn't get to you fast enough—"

"I know, love. I'm sorry." I wrapped my arms around his neck and let him lift me out of the chair.

Hatch buried his face in my neck. "I get that you have history with these people, but I don't, and I'll be damned if I'm gonna let one of them fuckin' hurt you again, you hear me?"

"Okay, love. I can give you that for a little while."

He kissed me and I couldn't help but whimper with need. God, I felt like I was drowning and he was my breath. He'd been sleeping on the sofa because of my injuries, and well, let's be honest; we weren't quite at the sleeping together stage of our relationship, especially because of Poppy. He could have slept in the spare bedroom, but Hatch said he wanted to be between me and the front door.

He broke the frantic kiss and settled his lips gently on my forehead. "If I'm not with you, one of my guys is."

"No."

"Not up for discussion."

"Connor, I really like my privacy. I'm the classic definition of an introvert," I argued. "I don't like people I don't know in my space. I'm weird like that."

"Cricket, then." He cocked his head. "She knows how to check a fuckin' peephole before openin' a door."

"I thought you'd forgotten I gave you keys," I defended, tugging gently on his beard.

He raised an eyebrow.

"*Fine.* I can handle Cricket," I conceded, dropping my hand. "Does this mean you're okay with me offering her a job?"

"You think she's a right fit?"

"If her résumé came across my desk randomly, I would put it in the 'yes' pile."

"Then, yeah, let's see how it works."

"Oh, can we, gentle, wise, and benevolent one?" I replied, cheekily.

"Can't wait to kiss the sass right off that mouth, Sunshine."

"Something to look forward to."

He closed his eyes briefly and whispered, "Fuck me."

"Mmm, something else to look forward to."

"Holy shit, Maisie."

"I can't believe I just said that," I whispered, my face heating.

"Me neither, baby." He kissed me. "I like it, even if it makes me crazy. But know that it's gonna happen soon and when it does, it's gonna be good."

I shivered. "Promise?"

"Yeah, baby, I promise."

"I can't wait."

And I meant it. I really *couldn't* wait.

Hatch put his phone to his ear again and walked back to the kitchen as I sat back down in the chair. "Flea, need someone on my woman's kid's school. You on mornings, Train on afternoons. Yeah. Need you to meet her first, yeah?"

"Hatch," I called.

"Yeah, good, okay. Talk to you soon." He hung up and faced me. "Yeah, babe."

"My twelve-year-old's not getting in a car with a man alone, unless it's you, and there's no way in hell she's getting on the back of a bike with any man, ever, so this idea you have of—"

"Maisie, hush." He raised his hand, cutting me off.

"Well, you've got a bloody cheek!"

Hatch chuckled. "Babe, simmer down. I just want one of my guys on her while she's headin' inside and when she's headin' out. I want them to meet her so she knows who's watchin' her and havin' men outside her school doesn't freak her out. Once you start takin' her again, they'll be watchin' you too."

"Oh."

He raised an eyebrow. "You good?"

"I'm not sure yet."

He grinned. "How about I get some food in ya and you can decide then?"

I bit the inside of my cheek to keep from smiling. "That'd be good."

"Someone's hangry."

"You should probably feed me, then."

He leaned down and gripped the arms of my chair, getting close enough to kiss me gently. "Want you both safe, Sunshine. You're mine, which means, you've got the protection of my brothers... blood and patch. It's time you start meetin' them so you know who you can trust. They'll have your back."

"I never expected that I'd be in a situation where I might need someone to have my back."

"I'm pickin' up on that, baby." He gave me a gentle smile. "Got your back on that as well."

The house phone rang and I sighed. I kind of wanted more kissing time, but since it was probably the lobby, I figured I should answer it. "Maisie Mann."

"Mrs. Mann, I have a Beckett Wickham here. He seems quite agitated."

I frowned. "Ah, that's my brother. You can let him up, Tom. Thank you." I hung up and pushed myself out of the chair.

Hatch slid an arm around my waist. "What are you doin'?"

"My brother appears to have flown all the way here from London unannounced. Apparently, someone's told him what happened, and I'd like to be standing when he lowers the hammer."

"You really think he's gonna fuckin' lower the hammer?"

"I was hurt a week ago, love, and I didn't ring to tell him."

"Babe," he admonished. "Why not?"

"Because then he'd tell Mum and Dad... he's probably already told Kenna, and they'd all come, and I'm in too much pain to deal with them. Mum and Dad are in their seventies,

Hatch. Them seeing me bruised up like this would be too much for them. I was planning on ringing this week. I just needed a minute. My family can be overwhelming. They're lovely, don't get me wrong, but they're a lot to take in sometimes. They weren't happy Niall took me away and it doesn't matter how old I get, they remind me constantly of the heartbreak I've caused."

Hatch kissed my temple. "Okay, baby. I'll stick around, but you really gotta eat."

"I can stand on my own."

"Not takin' that chance, Maisie. You just took Oxy."

"I won't feel it if I pass out, then," I retorted.

"Sit down," he ordered. "I'll deal with your brother. What's his name?"

"Beckett," I said, as I lowered myself back into the chair.

"Of course it is," Hatch grumbled, and headed out of the room and toward the door just as the bell sounded.

"Hey, Beckett, come on in," Hatch said.

I held my breath a little as I listened in. I wished I could see my brother's face.

"Who the hell are you?" Beckett demanded, his voice extra British. I could imagine his chin going up and him straightening to his six-foot-two height. My brother might be as straight-laced as they came, but he was also handsome and an imposing figure when he wanted to be.

"I'm Maisie's man, Hatch."

"Excuse me?"

"Maisie's in the other room. You wanna come in? Maybe set your bag inside?"

Bloody hell, Beckett brought a bag. That he meant he planned on staying with me and Poppy. Shit.

"Where's my sister?"

"Like I said, she's in the other room," Hatch repeated.

I smiled. Hatch was being extraordinarily patient with Beckett, but I wondered how long that would last. I should call out. I really should, but honestly, the evil part of me was enjoying this. It served Beckett right for showing up unannounced to "handle" his big sister.

"Yes, I heard you," Beckett continued. "What I don't understand is why you're here answering the door, not her."

"She just took some meds, so I told her to stay off her feet."

"Margaret Gretchen Wickham Mann!" Beckett bellowed.

Bloody hell! He's using my full name, this isn't good.

"Oh, stop your belly aching, Becks," I snapped. "You know where 'the other room' is, just come in already!"

A minute or so later, my brother stalked into the room, his face softening when he saw me. My irritation left my body as he rushed to my side and hugged me gently.

"How did you find out?" I asked.

"Ryan."

I sighed. Of course he did. Ryan and Beckett had been friends for a while, so that made perfect sense.

"Why didn't you ring me, Sausage?" he asked.

"It's only been a week, Becks. Everything happened so fast and we've been dealing with so much, I didn't want to drag you into the drama." I frowned. "Please tell me you didn't tell Mum and Dad."

"No, I didn't tell Mum and Dad, but that doesn't mean I'm not going to," he warned.

"Kenna?"

"I told Kenna. She said you suck and as soon as she sees you, she's going to give you a hiding the likes of which you've never seen. Now, fill me in."

"Babe, I'm gonna pick up a few things," Hatch said, stepping into the room. He set a sandwich and a glass of milk on the table next to me with a smile. "Made you a PB&J. You need to eat it quick, so it'll absorb your meds." I wrinkled my nose, but before I could object, he shook his head. "Just try it, Sunshine, you'll like it."

"I don't think I will."

"Have you ever tried one?"

"No."

"Then how do you know you won't like it?"

"It just sounds revolting," I explained.

"Isn't that something Americans make for their kids?"

Beckett asked.

"It's a staple, yeah," Hatch said.

I stared at the plate. "Well, I'm not six, Connor."

He smirked. "Kinda actin' like it right now, *Margaret.*"

"Cheeky bastard."

Hatch chuckled. "Take a bite."

"Hatch—"

Crossing his arms, he nodded at the sandwich. "One bite. If you don't like it, I'll grab the saltines."

I rolled my eyes and took a bite.

"You don't like it?" he asked.

"It's fine, Hatch. Food is fuel."

"I'll get the crackers."

"No, don't. Go do whatever you need to do," I insisted. "I'm quite capable of finding food or making my brother do it."

"You sure?"

I nodded. "Yes."

"You want me to bring you something back?"

"No," I said. "Are you still planning on picking Poppy up?"

"Yeah, but I can swing back here first," Hatch offered.

"No, it's okay. We'll be fine here."

Hatch nodded. "I'll see you soon."

"Thanks, love."

He left (without kissing me, which bugged the crap out of me) and Beckett sat on the sofa. As soon as I heard the door close, I bit deep into the sandwich and made a noise that I was sure sounded far too much like an orgasm (totally inappropriate in front of my brother, but I just didn't care). "Oh my *God*, Becks, this is the most amazing thing. Ever." I thrust it toward him. "Try it."

He took a bite and shook his head. "You're on your own on that one."

I sighed and inhaled the rest of the sandwich, gulping down the milk, feeling just as good as I did, if not better, after enjoying a meal at a five-star restaurant.

My satiated bliss was interrupted, however, when my

brother leaned toward me and said, "I need to know every-thing about the crash, Maisie, then you're going to fill me in on this Hatch person."

THIRTEEN

Hatch

I FIGURED MAISIE would be stuck dealing with her brother for a while, so I swung by my place on the way to the compound. My brothers were essentially running the shop for me for the next few weeks while Maisie got back on her feet. Cade still had to run his construction crew, but I had guys I trusted who needed the work, whereas he only trusted our family. So, for the moment, Cullen and Cameron could run the shop since Cricket would be moving on, and I would check in when I could.

Flea was finishing up school, but he was a great addition to my shop, plus, the Dogs had a couple of recruits I wanted to train up, but they wouldn't start until the beginning of next month, so I had a little breathing room.

I walked through one of the roll-up doors and saw legs poking out from under a red Toyota sedan. "Cam?"

"Yeah, brother?" Cameron slid out from under the car.

"Why don't you have the car lifted?"

"Because this takes less time." He jumped to his feet with a grin. "It's done and now I don't have to bring it down from the lift."

"Safer on the lift. Use it," I said as I shook my head, and walked into the front office. Cricket was helping an older female customer with her paperwork, so I slipped through the door into my private office.

A few minutes later, Cricket knocked and pushed open my door. "Hey, everything okay with Maisie?"

"Yeah." I thumbed through invoices as I powered up my computer. "Her brother showed up, so I need to check in on a few things before I head up to the club and then pick up Poppy."

"Where does her brother live?"

"London."

"Wait. He just showed up all the way from England?"

"Yeah."

"Is she okay with that?"

"You'd have to ask her."

"Well, did she *seem* okay with it?" Cricket continued.

"Cricket, what's with the twenty questions?" I ground out. "Got shit to do."

"You didn't ask her any of this?"

"Why would I? It's her business."

She threw her arms in the air. "You are *such* a guy!"

"You're fired, by the way."

"What the hell, Connor!"

I gave her a slight smile. "You're gonna be workin' for Maisie startin' tomorrow."

She grinned and punched my arm. "Ohmigod, you're such a dick!"

"You're welcome."

"You did this?" she said, her face dropping.

"No. *She* did this. I acquiesced because I need you to

watch out for her. Alison's husband showed up at her place today unannounced and she opened the door, thinkin' I'd forgotten my key."

"Holy shit," Cricket hissed. "Isn't he a cop?"

"Yeah. And he used that fact to get upstairs without a phone call, which I fuckin' don't like. Jax is handlin' that part of it for the moment, but only because I'm not interested in landin' my ass in jail while Maisie needs me."

Cricket scowled. "You're not interested in landing your ass in jail even if she doesn't need you."

I sighed. "Yeah, Cricket, I'm not gonna do anything stupid."

She relaxed. "Okay, I'll be there tomorrow at eight."

"Ten. I'll tell her you're not comin' 'til then," I said.

"I've got class tomorrow afternoon."

"Ten will still work."

"How about I text my new boss and find out what time *she* wants me to come?" she countered, her sass front and center. "In the meantime, I just checked out our last customer for the morning, so I'm going to get some lunch and then I'm going to go shopping, so I'm not coming back unless you really, really need me."

"No, Cullen can handle the afternoon." I grinned. "He smiles more than you anyway."

"Jackass," she retorted, albeit with a grin. "Thanks for not being a total douchebag about this. I love you, big brother." She kissed my cheek before walking out the door.

After looping in with Cullen about the schedule changes, I checked on a couple of parts orders and invoices, then walked back out to the shop floor. "I'm headin' out, in case anyone cares."

"No one cares," Cameron called.

"You gonna be home tonight?" Cullen leaned out from under the hood of an Impala.

"Why?" I asked. "You wanna spoon?"

Cullen laughed. "Can we?"

"Yeah, I should be home tonight. Maisie's brother's in town."

"Okay, got a lead on a place. Wanna show it to you."

"Sounds good." I left and headed to the Club.

Pulling up to the front of Big Ernie's Body Shop, I parked my truck and headed into the compound.

Ace and Knight's bikes were both in the lot, as was a large black SUV which had all the markings of an FBI vehicle. Shit. That meant Jaxon. So, either he was here to shoot the shit with his brothers, or he had news I didn't want to hear.

I entered the two outer doors, then walked through the small lobby and into the great room, relaxing slightly at the scene. Jaxon sat on one of the bar stools, an acoustic guitar balanced on his knee, playing quietly while Cambry danced around him and did her best to get her cousin Liam to join in. Liam, however, wanted to play pool with his dad, so Ace lifted him up high enough to maneuver the pool cue and helped him aim.

Knight caught my eye and gave me a chin lift. "Hey, man."

Jaxon stopped playing and set the guitar down.

"More unca Jax," Cambry demanded.

Jaxon lifted her and smiled. "In a bit, sweetness. I gotta have a word with Hatch."

"Come here, baby," Knight said, and held his arms out. "Hang out with Dad for a bit."

Jaxon handed Cambry off to Knight, and I led Jaxon down to the conference room in the back. Jaxon closed the door and leaned against the table. "Took care of the Ryan issue."

"'Preciate it."

"Got a bigger one."

"Shit," I breathed out, crossing my arms.

"Alison's out."

"What the fuck?" I snapped. "I thought psychiatric holds were irreversible? And what happened to the bitch bein' under arrest?"

"She made bail and convinced her therapist she'd take her meds and stay away from Maisie and Poppy until the trial details are decided."

"That's not fuckin' good enough," I roared. "Poppy and Grace go to the same fuckin' school, Jaxon, there's no way for them to avoid each other."

"We'll put a car on the school. Make sure she complies."

"I'm done with you fuckin' doin' anything, Jax. We'll take care of it from here. This is bullshit."

I ripped open the door and stormed out to my truck. I didn't stop, even when Knight called my name and I heard heavy footsteps following. I felt an urgent need to get to Poppy before Alison could. I didn't know why, there was no reason to believe Alison would even be there today, but I refused to let that crazy bitch anywhere near her.

"Hatch!" Knight called again, slamming his hand against the hood of my truck. "Hold up, man."

"Gotta pick up Poppy. We'll talk later."

"Brother, just take a beat."

"She's fuckin' out, Knight."

"Yeah, man, I get it. But Flea's on the school, so's Brock. No one's gettin' close to Poppy. So don't go drivin' off half-cocked," he said. "Just take a beat."

"It's been a beat." I pulled open the door. "I'll talk to you later."

Knight nodded and backed away, so I could back out of the parking space. I debated whether or not I should call Maisie, but I figured she would have gotten notice already. Just as I hit the freeway, my phone rang, so I hit the hands free. "Hatch."

"Honey?"

Fuck, she'd been crying.

"You heard?" I asked.

"Yes," she sniffed. "How did you hear?"

"Jaxon just told me," I said. "I'm on my way to the school now."

"How could they possibly let her out?" Maisie demanded.

I sighed. "I don't know, baby. But you're safe, yeah?"

"I am so *sick* of being stuck in the bloody flat, Connor. I want out."

"I know, Sunshine, but you—"

"Need to heal. I fucking know that!" she snapped.

I was so surprised to hear her drop the f-bomb, I couldn't help the laugh that escaped. Damn, her foul mouth was surprisingly sexy.

"Stop laughing at me."

"Sorry, baby. It just took me by surprise. Look, I'm pulling up to the school now. Jaxon's got his guy watchin' the south entrance and we've got guys watchin' too. Poppy's covered."

"I'm not worried, Connor, I'm pissed," she clarified. "She's sick! She needs help. What if she hurts someone else? Because her husband's a cop and she has money, she's out? It's unfair."

"You have money too, baby. Fight it."

"I fully intend to! But that's not the point."

I really had no idea what the point was now, and I wasn't sure I wanted to ask, but I was curious, so, "Wanna fill me in, beautiful?"

"What about the people who don't have money?"

Well, that kind of went in a different direction.

"They aren't currently your problem, baby."

"Well, maybe they should be!" She burst into tears. "There are people who get stuck with medical bills because someone else has intentionally hurt them and then gotten off because they had money to buy their way through the system. Who's fighting for the injured people who don't have money, huh? Who?"

"I don't know, baby."

"They're just hard-working people, Connor. Trying to do the right thing," she continued.

"I get it, Sunshine," I said. "When did you last take your meds?"

"About an hour ago."

I frowned. "Just how much Oxy did you take?"

"I'm out of Oxy."

Shit. "So you took the Vicodin?"

"Yes."

I found a parking space right out front of the school and parked. "You're not out of Oxy, remember? I picked up the refill this morning. It's up next to the spices. You can't take the Vicodin because it makes you really sad."

"It doesn't make me *that* sad," she sniffed.

I shook my head. She had enough emotional shit going on without the pills adding to the stress. "Baby, no more Vicodin."

"But what about the people who can't pay their medical bills?"

"We'll find out how you can help them, okay?" He climbed out of the truck. "But let's give it a day or two."

"Okay," she conceded. "Can we help Sarah McLachlan's puppies too?"

Fuck me. I dropped my head back. "Sure, Sunshine. Whatever you want to do."

"Thanks, Hatch."

"You good, baby?"

"Yes," she whispered. "I'm good."

"Don't take anything else until I can monitor your meds, okay?"

"Okay."

"I'm gonna hang up and get your girl now, yeah?"

"Okay, darling." She sighed. "Thank you."

I smiled. "You got it."

I slid my phone into my pocket and headed to the school entrance to wait for Poppy.

FOURTEEN

Maisie

AFTER HANGING UP with Hatch, I washed my face and rejoined my brother in the family room.

"You okay, Sausage?" he asked.

"Yes, I'm okay. I just can't believe they let Alison out."

"How does that work exactly?"

I sat in Niall's chair and sighed. "Money and privilege."

Beckett raised an eyebrow. "*We* have money and privilege, Maisie."

"Well, I suppose if *I* tried to kill my best friend and her daughter because I went on a bi-polar frenzy, then I'd get out too," I said a little more ungraciously than I intended. I burst into tears again and Beckett handed me a tissue. "Thanks." I blew my nose. "I'm warring with these feelings of frustration because she's my best friend and I love her, but she tried to hurt us—"

"Kill you," he corrected.

"Becks, she's not well."

He pinched the bridge of his nose.

"Well, she's not," I stressed.

"Forgive me, Maisie, if I'm a bit biased and a little less willing to give the woman who tried to murder my sister the benefit of the doubt!" He roared the last bit and I blinked as I watched him try to bring his emotions under control.

"Sorry," I whispered.

"No, I'm sorry," he said immediately. "I want to be sensitive to what you're going through, but I can't forgive her. Not yet, anyway."

"I understand, Becks."

Before anymore could be said on the subject, Hatch and Poppy walked into the flat and Poppy flew at her uncle with an excited squeal. Hatch, on the other hand, made his way to me and pulled me up for a gentle kiss.

"You didn't tell her he was here?" I asked as he wrapped an arm around me.

"Figured she'd like the surprise," Hatch said. "You doin' okay?"

I shrugged, snuggling against him. "I really wish you and I could go somewhere, just the two of us. I want to shut out the world for a while."

"I know, baby."

I lifted my head and whispered, "I really need you to make that happen. As in now."

His eyes got soft and he smiled gently. "Yeah?"

"Please."

"Okay, baby. I'll make it happen." He turned to face Poppy and Beckett. "Poppy, say hi to your Mom, I need to talk to her privately for a minute."

"About...?" Poppy asked.

"Yeah," Hatch said.

Poppy nodded and hugged me, then Hatch took my hand and led me into my bedroom.

"Tell me what's going on," I demanded.

He looked away.

"Hatch, you're all tense. What happened?"

He let out a breath. "Alison was at the school today. She didn't go anywhere near Poppy, but Poppy was confused... no surprise there. I filled her in, but she said Grace is scared to be at home, so now Poppy's also scared for Grace and she wants me to fix it."

I raised an eyebrow.

"The cryin', the stompin' of the foot, that kind of shit."

"She *didn't!*"

"Not sayin' she isn't valid in what's she's feelin', Sunshine, but I've been there. I raised Cricket. It's not fun. Poppy's a little miffed that I'm not rushin' in to rescue Grace from her "abusive" home."

"Oh dear," I breathed out.

"So, this now falls to you."

"Yes, I suppose it does."

"Not sayin' I don't have your back. Just sayin' I'm not gonna tell you how to parent your kid."

"I appreciate that." I dropped my forehead to his chest. "Let's just run away together. Beckett can finish raising Poppy. He can take her back to England. Kenna has kids, she can help. My parents would love it."

Hatch chuckled and wove his fingers into my hair. "You're obviously feelin' better."

"I always feel better when you're here."

"Yeah?"

"Yes," I whispered. Hatch sighed and I leaned back to catch his eye. "What?"

"Gotta head home tonight after church, Sunshine."

Church was what his club called their weekly Wednesday meeting.

"Oh." I swallowed back tears with a nod, dropping my head back to his chest. "Okay."

"I fuckin' hate the Vicodin."

"It's not the Vicodin."

"Really? The thought of me leavin' you for a night brings

137

you to tears?" he challenged.

"I'm not crying," I lied.

He tilted my head back and kissed me gently. "I'll be back first thing in the morning."

"You're leaving *now*?" I sounded far too desperate, even to my own ears. "I mean, if you need to go…"

Hatch chuckled. "I just figured you'd want time with your brother. I'm not on a clock, so I can stay for a while if you want me to."

"It's fine, love. I know you have a life outside of me and I can't expect you to be at my beck and call every minute of the day and night…" I ran my good hand up his chest. "Even if I've come to really like it."

He slid his hand to my neck. "You want me to stay, Sunshine?"

I nodded.

"Then I'll stay."

I smiled. "Thank you."

"Wanna make out a little?"

"Ohmigod, yes please."

He grinned and locked my door, taking my hand, leading me to the bed, and pulling me down beside him.

That was as far as we got because my gorgeous, sweet, kind, lovely, generous, pain in the ass child began knocking on my door, jiggling the doorknob, calling through the door, and wondering out loud why the door was locked.

"I'm gonna find a place we can be alone together soon, Sunshine," Hatch promised.

"That would be really good." I slid off the bed and pulled open the door. "Poppy, we're trying to have a private conversation."

She glanced at me and then Hatch. "You never lock your door."

"Well, it's because we didn't want to be interrupted."

"So are you going to get Grace?"

"We can't go and get Grace, Poppy," I said.

"Why not?" she demanded.

"Because it would be illegal, sweetheart." I sighed. "We

don't have any cause to take her from her home. Her father has to protect her from Ali, love. I can't."

"Hatch can."

"Baby girl, I can't," he said.

"Why not?" she demanded as tears welled up in her eyes. I felt Hatch at my back and leaned against him.

"Baby girl, Grace is not—"

"Club business," she interrupted. "You said that."

"What exactly does *that* mean?" I asked.

"I don't really know," Poppy admitted. "But somehow we're club business but she's not."

"I'll explain another time," Hatch said.

"Look, we can't do anything about Grace, love."

"But she's *scared.*"

"Fuck me," Hatch whispered for my ears only.

I stared at Poppy. "You're really serious, aren't you?"

Alison had never threatened her kids and there had never been any indication that she would harm one of them, but Poppy seemed genuinely concerned, so I took notice.

"Yes, Mum. This isn't like the time she and I did our drama pact to get matching iPhones, I promise."

"I'll call Jax and see if he can do anything," Hatch said.

"Is he the FBI man?" Poppy asked.

"Yes."

"Okay, thanks, Hatch." Poppy smiled as she turned and walked away.

I faced Hatch and groaned. "Don't let her strong arm you into anything you don't feel comfortable doing."

"She's not. I already asked Jaxon to see if he could find something. If he does, he may have some sway over child protective services or getting her in with family."

I sighed. "I need to watch out for you, huh?"

"Can't get anything by me," he said. "Keep that in mind."

"I'd never try to get anything by you," I retorted. "Keep *that* in mind."

"Love that, Sunshine."

I stared up at him. "I don't think it's a good idea for Poppy to think she can manipulate you, though."

"Baby, let her have this one. She's been dealt a shit sand-wich. We can work on her attitude at a future time, but for now, just let her do her thing and once the trial is over, you're fully healed, and we're in a normal schedule with whatever we're doin' relationship-wise, we can lower the hammer. She needs to feel like she's in control of something. I'm fine with her "controlling" me for the moment."

I poked at his chest. "Do *not* let her hear you say that."

"Okay, baby." Hatch chuckled. "She's worried about her friend and if we can help, we will. From what you've told me, it's not always a good situation, so if Jax can step in, he will."

"Okay." I hugged him tighter. "Did you thank him for his help today?"

"Why would I?"

I frowned up at him. "Really?"

"Babe, just drop it. He and I know where we stand."

"Well, then if I write him a thank you note, will you de-liver it?"

He dropped his head back and swore.

"Hatch."

He continued to mutter to the ceiling.

"Will you deliver the note?" I pressed.

"Yeah, Sunshine, I'll deliver it."

"Thanks." I kissed him again and he smiled.

"Let's figure out what I'm cookin' for dinner."

"You're going to cook for us?" I asked, my stomach rum-bling.

"Unless you want to make your brother go grab take-out."

"Is it too soon in this relationship to tell you I love you?" As soon as I said it, I gasped, slapping my hand over my mouth. "Sorry. That was really dumb."

Hatch's arms came gently around me and he kissed my forehead. "Don't do that, Maisie. Don't censor your thoughts. Nothing you say is dumb."

"It's the Vicodin."

"Okay, baby, it's the Vicodin."

But it wasn't the Vicodin and I knew it as I settled my cheek against his chest. I was falling in love with him. Maybe it was too soon to confirm that earnestly out loud, but this man, this man who dropped everything to take care of me and my daughter when he hardly knew me, was everything to me, and the thought of him not being near me even for a night bothered me. If that wasn't love, I didn't know what was.

"You could always show me how to make one of those jam things," I said to his chest.

"PB&J?"

I nodded.

"So you liked it?"

I grinned.

"So all that drama before was just ball bustin'?" he accused.

"I really had never had one before," I said. "But I couldn't very well tell you I loved it right off the bat, could I? You would have won."

"What exactly would I have won, Sunshine?"

"I don't know. Something."

"You're a fuckin' nut, baby."

"Guilty," I agreed, kissing him gently.

"Did you and Cricket coordinate tomorrow?" Hatch asked, breaking our moment.

"Yes." I pulled away. "She's going to be here at ten."

"I'll swing by and pick up Poppy at the normal time, then give you the day."

I followed him out to the family room. "That works."

He smiled at me over his shoulder. "You *can* call me, you know."

"Oh, stop. I *will* survive without you for one night, Connor Wallace."

We walked into the family room to find Beckett with his laptop settled in front of him and Poppy sitting cross-legged on the sofa watching television.

"Homework status?" I asked.

"Done," she said.

"Great," I said. "Let me have a look at it while you help Hatch with dinner."

"Do you need a third?" Beckett asked.

My mouth dropped open. "Since when do you do anything domestic?"

He set his computer aside and rose to his feet. "You've been gone a long time, big sister. Lots of things have changed."

My heart hurt. "Direct hit, Becks."

He frowned. "Sorry, Sausage. I didn't mean for that to be a dig."

"Poppy, why don't you grab your homework and take it out to the island for your mom?" Hatch suggested, and ushered Poppy out of the room.

Hatch and Poppy left the room and I slid into my brother's hug. "I've been really slack in keeping you in the loop."

"Yeah, you have," he confirmed. "I miss you, Maisie."

"I miss you, too. I'll be better, I promise."

"You need to come home," he whispered. "Not forever, but for a little while. It's like Niall died and you disappeared, physically and emotionally."

I sighed. "I know."

"Lecture over, Saus. Love you."

"I love you too." I smiled up at him. "I really do."

Feeling more settled than I had in a while, I followed Beckett to the kitchen and joined in in the domestic bliss of homework and dinner and all around joking amongst ourselves as we bonded closer together. By the time Hatch left, my cheeks hurt from smiling so much, but I also felt the pit in my stomach knowing he wasn't going to be close in the middle of the night. It didn't matter that he'd been sleeping on the sofa. Now that I was back in my own bed, he'd been within shouting distance and I'd come to cherish it.

With one final kiss, he walked away, and I locked my door and joined my family, settling in to watch a movie and call it an early night.

* * *

Hatch

I walked through my front door to find Cade sitting at the

kitchen table, beer bottle lifted to his mouth, computer open in front of him, and some weird-ass furball thing sittin' on his lap. "What the hell is that?"

Cade set the beer down and grinned. "This is a dog."

"That is not a dog."

The furball yipped at me and I frowned. "Seriously, Cade, what the fuck?"

"Got out to the site this morning to find them dumped—"

"Them?"

"Dad!" Devon called.

Cade turned in his chair. "Yeah, bud?"

"I can't keep them in the box." He rushed into the room, carrying three matching puppies. "They keep escaping."

"Fuck me," I ground out. "You brought them *here*?"

"We couldn't leave them there to die," Cade said.

I felt something on my leg and looked down to see a little white fluff of fur tugging with its teeth on the hem of my jeans. The furball growled, baring its teeth. I dropped my head back and took a deep breath, only to be brought out of my attempted trance by a little bark. I looked down again at the fuckin' cutest pair of puppy eyes looking up at me and begging to be picked up.

Well, shit.

I bent down and scooped the little guy up, receiving a face full of puppy tongue for my efforts.

"Can't resist the little fucker, huh?" Cade said.

I held the puppy closer. It really was cute. "Some asshole just dumped five puppies?"

"In a paper bag, yeah, but there should be six." Cade rose to his feet. "Cullen, you got one?"

"Yeah, man," he called back. "Little shit just pissed on me."

I chuckled. "Like 'em already."

"Dev and I stopped by the pet store and grabbed food and bowls for 'em, but we'll probably need to take 'em to a shelter or somethin' tomorrow."

"Knight can look 'em over," I said. Knight was a vet and would be able to hook us up with an adoption service as well.

143

"He'll probably be able to take care of their shots, then get them farmed out or whatever."

"We're not keeping them?" Devon asked.

"What are we going to do with a fru-fru dog, Dev?" Cade asked.

He pulled his three close to his chin. "I don't know, Dad, love it?" he replied, sarcastically.

"We'll talk about gettin' a dog when we have a place of our own, sound good?"

Devon frowned. "Whatever."

I dropped my keys on the counter and carried my puppy out to the backyard where I set it down. My brothers and nephew followed, and six little cotton balls waddled around marking their territory.

"I'm gonna go change," Cullen said, and walked back in the house.

"Where's Cam?" I asked.

"Chick," Cade answered. "What about you? Seems like you're gettin' in deep."

I nodded.

"Does that mean we're gonna meet this Maisie woman?"

"Yeah, man. Soon."

Cade grinned. "Like that, Con."

Over the next few hours, I caught up with my brothers, checked out the house Cullen was lookin' to buy, and took a longer than normal shower to release some of the tension created by Maisie and her mouth. The mouth I wanted wrapped around my cock. Fuck! I needed to find a way for us to be alone. I was pretty sure this was the longest I'd ever gone without sex since I'd hit puberty.

My phone buzzed just as I stepped out of the shower, so I wrapped a towel around my waist and answered it. "Hey, Sunshine."

"Hi honey. Is this a bad time?"

"Just got out of the shower. It's all good."

"Bloody hell," she whispered. "Does that mean you're all wet?"

I grinned, my cock hardening. "Yeah, baby."

"Not fair, Connor." She whimpered. "I miss you already and it's only been a few hours."

"Miss you too." I chuckled.

"I have something to talk to you about."

I stretched out on the mattress. "That doesn't sound good."

"I need to go home." She sighed. "Home, home."

"Okay," I said slowly. "Like for good?"

"No. Nothing like that. But I am going to have to go for a while. Maybe a month. Probably over Poppy's school holidays. Mum's birthday's in August, as is Poppy's, so we were thinking we might go then."

Maisie's arm would probably be good to go by then.

"What about the trial?" I asked.

"I'm hoping there won't be one, but if I'm gone and can't be here to testify, maybe I can force her getting a reduced sentence."

I sighed. I didn't like that.

"Anyway," she continued, "I... um... I'll be gone for a while... so, I... I'm not sure... well, if..."

Fuck, she was ending it. "Just fuckin' spit it out, Maisie," I snapped.

"Why are you mad?"

"If you're gonna dump me, just do it."

"Dump you? I'm not going to dump you! I want you to come with us."

"Come again?" I sat up.

"It's too soon. You're right. It was dumb," she said. "You also have a job you can't just up and leave. I just assumed you'd... that... God, that was so insensitive. You know what? Forget I said anything. I'm sorry, Hatch. I'll see you tomorrow."

She hung up.

FIFTEEN

Maisie

WHAT THE HELL *is wrong with me?* I'd known Hatch for less than a month; of course, he wasn't going to fly all the way to England with me! Granted, we'd be going on several months by the time we'd be heading there, but still, it was a lot to expect from someone.

God, I'm such an idiot.

Feeling totally embarrassed and dejected, I climbed into bed and turned off the light. Poppy had helped me take a shower and wash my hair earlier, which had been easier than expected. She'd even gone so far as to blow dry and braid it for me which was probably why I had the false sense of confidence to call up my boyfriend—or whatever the hell he was—and ask him to come home with me. Idiot.

I probably shouldn't have hung up on him, but then again, he didn't try to call me back. Feeling remorseful and wondering if I could still salvage the situation, I'd tried to ring him one more time but no luck. I squeezed my eyes shut and tried not to overanalyze, waffling between ringing him back again and digging myself a hole so I could avoid him until I felt like less of an idiot. It was past eleven and I knew he was with his family, and since I'd already interrupted him... Gah! This was driving me nuts. I hoped he wasn't mad at me. He'd done so much for me and the thought of doing anything that might offend him, gutted me.

The door to my bedroom opened and I craned my head and whispered, "Poppy, you okay, love?"

"It's not Poppy," Hatch whispered back, and closed the door.

I heard the lock click and then he stretched out beside me and gently pulled me into his arms. I sighed as he covered my mouth with his and kissed me until I was sure I might melt.

"I'm sorry I hung up on you," I whispered against his lips. "And I'm sorry I asked you to come home with me. It's too soon—"

His mouth covered mine again and he stroked my cheek. "I'd love to come home with you, Sunshine."

"You would?"

"Yeah. And if you call yourself dumb or stupid one more time, I'm gonna get a little pissed off." His hand slid over my cami, around my back, and down, cupping my bottom.

I scooted closer to him. "You didn't need to come all the way over here, love. You could have called to growl at me."

His hand dipped under the waistline of my knickers. "Not as much fun, though."

"My brother and daughter aren't far away," I warned.

"Then we're gonna have to be really, really quiet," he whispered.

I bit my lip and nodded, gasping as his fingers slid between my legs.

"*Really* quiet, Sunshine," he whispered close to my ear. "Can you do that?"

"I don't know," I admitted.

He grinned and pushed himself off the bed, turning on the side lamp.

"What are you doing?" I hissed, reaching to turn it off again.

"No. I want to see you, Maisie." He flicked the light back on, then reached behind him and pulled off his T-shirt and I swallowed at the sight of his bare chest. Good lord it was delicious. He was muscular with very little hair and his pecs were covered in tattoos. As were his upper arms. I couldn't wait to play trace the lines with my tongue.

"Roll on your back, baby," he directed.

I did as he instructed, and he cradled my bad arm on a pillow. "You feel pain, you tell me to stop, yeah? I'm gonna go as easy as I can."

I nodded and he slid my undies down over my hips, grinning as he threw them in the corner. I squeezed my eyes shut as I felt heat flood my face. God, I couldn't believe we were doing this with the lights on. Niall and I never did it this way.

"Eyes, Maisie," he ordered.

I looked at him, but my hand flew to the stretchmarks on my belly. He quickly moved my hand away with a shake of his head and I swallowed convulsively. He leaned over me and kissed one stretchmark, then another, then another, running his tongue down my belly and to my very private area.

His arms wrapped around my upper thighs and pushed them apart, then he leaned down and covered my core with his mouth. I arched into him as my body came apart. His tongue swirled around my clit and then he sucked gently, and I bit my fist to keep from crying out. I lost his mouth and stared down my body to see him removing his jeans. I shivered as he knelt between my legs, slid on a condom, and then hovered over me with a grin. "You okay?"

I nodded because I couldn't speak.

"You in pain?"

I shook my head.

"Why aren't you saying anything?" he demanded

"Because I just had the most incredible orgasm of my life.

I need a minute to process," I hissed.

"Of your life?" Hatch grinned. "Really?"

"Oh, stop it," I sassed. "Wait. No, don't stop. Keep going. More of that. Whatever that was."

He chuckled quietly, sliding my cami up over my breasts and drawing a nipple into his mouth, sucking it into a tight pebble. "Your body's fuckin' beautiful, Sunshine."

"Yours is too." I reached up and slid my hand along his jaw. "I can't believe you're here."

"You're mine, Maisie. You get that right? After tonight, no one else's. Forever mine."

I blinked back tears. "I'm super okay with that, Connor."

"Yeah?"

"Yes. I like you here. In my space, in my life. In Poppy's life. I want to take you home to meet my family and show them that I'm finally okay." I stroked his cheek. "I never thought I'd ever feel peace again. Never thought I'd feel joy. It was my new normal to just exist and live within that existence. You walk into a room and my stomach flutters and I'm so excited to see you even if you just came from the kitchen." I smiled, running my thumb along his lips. "I think about you when you're dropping Poppy off at school and can't wait to see you when you go to pick her up. I wonder what it would be like to…" I bit off my sentence.

"To what, Sunshine?"

I took a deep breath. "To have your babies."

His breath hitched.

"Is that stu—?"

He frowned.

"Sorry," I rushed to say. "It just all feels so alien to me, you know? I'm almost thirty-six and before you, I had no interest in more children, but I keep having these dreams of little boys in tiny leather vests running around terrorizing Poppy and it makes me feel excited." I giggled. "God, I'm *such* a girl."

His mouth crashed down on mine and our conversation was over. His hand slid between us and he guided himself inside me before shifting so I could wrap my legs around him.

He cupped my breast and slammed into me and the bed let out a loud squeak. I forced back a giggle as he tried again, and we got the same result.

"Fuck!" he whispered, lifting me. "Keep your legs around me."

I nodded as he carried me out of the bedroom and into my bathroom. Hatch settled me on the vanity, guiding me to the edge. He was tall enough that I could loop my good arm around his neck, and he could anchor me firmly to the granite. Despite the cold, I relished the feel of him sliding deeper into me, but I couldn't help a shiver.

Hatch tugged my cami completely off and pulled me closer to him, his body heat warming me as he moved again. "You're so tight."

I smiled. "Um, it's kind of been a while."

"You okay?"

"So much better than okay."

His hands cupped my bottom and he held tight as he slammed into me over and over again. I whimpered and, when I knew I couldn't wait, I bit down on his shoulder to keep from crying out as my orgasm exploded around me.

"Fuck," he rasped, and I felt his cock pulsate inside of me.

I dropped my forehead to his shoulder, but found my head lifted and Hatch peppering kisses along my jaw. "Fuckin' beautiful, Sunshine."

"I'm so sorry, Connor."

"What the fuck?" He leaned back with a frown. "Why are you apologizing?"

I nodded to his shoulder. "I kind of left a mark."

Keeping an arm around me, he leaned toward the mirror and chuckled. "Yeah you did."

"Does it hurt?"

He nodded. "So bad, baby. I think you may have given me rabies."

I gasped. "Rude!"

Hatch chuckled and pulled out of me, wrapping the condom in toilet paper and chucking it in the rubbish bin. He lifted me off the vanity and leaned down to kiss me. "You doin' okay?"

"At the risk of being really inappropriate, I've never had two orgasms back-to-back in my life." I bit my lip. "I loved Niall, but he wasn't the most creative when it came to sex." I groaned. "God, I'm a horrible person. I should never speak ill of the dead, especially someone I loved."

Hatch pulled me closer to him. "First, never apologize for having an orgasm. Second, Niall's dead, baby. It's okay for you to move on. And third, we're not done."

"Really? What's your plan, handsome?"

"You're gonna have another orgasm or twelve."

I shivered. "Twelve, Connor, seriously?"

"I'm always serious about orgasms, Sunshine."

"I'm very impressed by the focus you've given your task, darling." I slid my hand to his cock. "Now, I'd love to see if I can get you to rise to the occasion so I might also have a little fun." I grinned as his breathing grew shallow. "Mmm, nicely done, Connor." With his help, I knelt in front of him and wrapped my mouth around him. I really wish I had use of both hands, but for the moment, I'd have to make do. I couldn't keep myself from comparing, considering he was only the second man I'd seen naked... at least up close and personal.

I enjoyed oral sex, but I typically preferred giving more than receiving. Tonight, however, I'd enjoyed receiving it immensely and I knew that was because Hatch knew what he was doing. I took his cock in as far as I could and used my hand to pump, adding a little pressure as I slid up and down his shaft. I knew he was into it the second he slid his fingers into my hair and anchored me against him.

His body moved against me and I took him all the way, grabbing his ass to steady myself as his legs locked. "Baby, I'm gonna come."

I nodded.

"You sure?" he rasped.

I nodded again and swallowed as he came inside my mouth. I honestly couldn't think of anything sexier than taking his cum inside of me. I sucked and kissed until I felt he was done and then his hands were under my armpits and I was lifted to my feet. "Fuck, Maisie."

I grinned. "Was it as good for you as it was for me?"

He kissed me gently and stroked my cheek. "This was really supposed to be all about you tonight."

"Well, that worked."

"How's your arm?"

"It's a little sore," I admitted.

"How long ago did you take your pills?"

"Right after you left."

He frowned. "Babe, that was like seven hours ago."

"I'm trying to wean myself off."

"Do you have any in here?"

I shook my head.

"You okay with me getting some from the kitchen?"

"Not naked, I'm not."

He grinned and walked into the bedroom, pulling on his jeans and buttoning them. He left the bedroom and I took a minute to clean up.

* * *

Hatch

I walked out to the kitchen and grabbed the Oxy and a couple of bottled waters. I'd just closed the refrigerator when Beckett walked up to the island. "I thought you left."

"Maisie was havin' a rough night, so I came back," I said.

Beckett cocked his head. "What exactly do you want with my sister?"

"What do you mean?"

"I can't quite get a handle on you," he continued not really answering my question.

"What you see is what you get, man. I got nothin' to hide. I care about your sister and Poppy. Where it goes from there's really none of your business."

"Do you want money?"

"What the fuck?"

"From my sister. Do you want her money?"

"I get that you don't know me, but you askin' me that question is the same thing as challengin' me to a duel in your country, so I'd suggest you fuckin' walk away before I say or do somethin' I can't take back."

"We don't challenge people to duels anymore."

"No shit?" I droned, because I didn't really give a fuck. "Well, whatever you consider to be the biggest insult, that's what you just delivered." I leaned against the counter. "Maisie's fragile, so I'm not gonna burden her with this and I'm gonna let it go. But when we get to the point to make this permanent, and I believe we will, I'll make sure her money's protected. I don't need it, I don't want it. You got questions or concerns outside of that; you need to bring those up to her, or to her and me together. I'm not gonna talk about her behind her back or make back room deals that involve her." I nodded toward the bedroom. "Now, I gotta get Maisie some pain meds."

I forced down my irritation as I headed back to Maisie's bedroom, locking the door behind me.

Maisie walked out of the bathroom her smile fading quickly. "What's wrong?"

"Nothing, baby."

"Connor," she admonished.

"Your brother's concerned."

"Bloody hell," she snapped. "What did he say? Tell me everything."

"No."

"Yes."

"No, baby. If you want to know what he said, you can ask him." She moved to leave the room, but I stopped her. "But not tonight." I grinned at her huff. "Look, he's your brother. It's his job to look out for you and I don't fault him for that. I said my piece. He either accepts that or he doesn't."

"Well, it's none of his bloody business and I'm going to make sure he knows that."

"*Not* tonight." I dropped the waters on the bed and slid my arm around her waist. "I'm not done with you."

"Hatch."

"Maisie, you're naked and smokin' hot and you just gave me two incredible orgasms. I want a couple more of those before I have to get up and leave your bed." I kissed her neck. "I don't want to talk about your brother anymore."

She sighed. "Me neither."

"Except, what's up with the 'sausage' shit?"

She giggled. "Dame Edna. I'll show you some clips tomorrow. We all call each other Sausage."

"And I thought it was somethin' weird," I retorted. "Let's get some meds in you and then I'm gonna soothe other hurts, okay?"

Maisie nodded, and I kissed her again before we spent the night making love as quietly as we could.

SIXTEEN

Maisie

I AWOKE THE next morning to an empty bed and turned my head to see my clock said nine a.m. I sat up with a gasp and shook my head. Hatch must have turned off my alarm. I saw a bottled water and a pill sitting on top of a post-it note.

Take this when you wake up. I told Cricket to come at eleven and turned off your alarm. See you after I drop Poppy off – H.

I'd just taken the Oxy when my bedroom door opened, and Hatch walked in. "You're awake."

"Just. I can't believe you turned off my alarm," I complained. "I have work to do."

He chuckled and closed the distance between us. "You

155

needed to sleep."

"I get it, but your sister has class this afternoon and we have limited time."

"You'll work better if you're not exhausted," he countered.

"You did kind of wear me out."

Hatch kissed me gently. "I grabbed bagels and coffee, and got the mail while I was out. You need help gettin' dressed?"

"I might. But you have to promise you'll actually dress me... no getting sidetracked." I heard a quiet yip and frowned. "What was that?"

Hatch stretched his arm out toward me. "That was Little Fucker."

"Excuse me?"

Opening his hand, the tiniest little puppy rested its head on Hatch's fingers before trying to chew one of them off. Hatch gave it a little cuddle then handed it to me. "Some asshole dumped six puppies at Cade's site yesterday. I was taking them to the Club and Poppy begged to keep one. I told her I'd talk to you. So, I'm talkin' to you. Yay or nay to Little Fucker?"

"Honey, I can't deal with a puppy." I slid out of bed as I hugged the furball to me. "You and I both work full-time, Poppy's in school, we're heading to London in a few months... no. No to..."

Hatch grinned again. "Little Fucker."

"You can*not* call him that, Hatch." I held the puppy to me. "Can he? No, he can't. You're not a little fucker, are you? At least you won't be when your tiny little balls get chopped off. We need to come up with something better."

Hatch chuckled. "You name him, you keep him, Sunshine. That's the law."

"What the heck are we going to do with a dog when we're out of the country?"

Hatch slid his arm around my waist. "Got a family who can watch him while we're gone, honey. He can come to work with me as well. He'll be good in the office and I bet the customers will love him."

I smiled slowly, my heart racing. "Does that mean you're really coming with us?" I asked hopefully.

"Said that already, right? Gotta get a passport, but yeah, baby, I'm comin' with you."

I jumped a little and let out a squeak. "I wish I could clap my hands."

Hatch dropped his head back and laughed. "Fuck you're cute."

"Glad you think so." I kissed Hatch's chin. "Because you're potty training Little Fucker."

"Yeah?"

"Yeah," I retorted. "We'll let Poppy rename him."

Hatch shook his head. "Like hearin' Little Fucker outta your mouth, Sunshine. Gonna miss it."

I batted my eyelashes. "I'll call your cock that next time I blow you."

Hatch laughed so hard he started coughing. "Holy shit, baby, warn me when you're gonna be funny."

"No way. This is way more fun for me."

The puppy started to squirm, and I handed it off to Hatch. "Looks like he needs to pee. I think I'm good to get dressed on my own, so I'll meet you in the kitchen."

Hatch took the puppy and left my room and I got dressed as best I could and headed for the food source.

I walked out just as Beckett arrived wheeling his bag past me. "You're leaving?"

"My job here's done. I'll report back to Kenna that you're better than expected," he said. "But I'm coming back if you're not at the table for Mum's birthday."

I rolled my eyes. "I'll be there. And I'll ring them soon."

"I already said good-bye to Poppy." He pulled me in for a gentle hug. "I love you, sis. Don't ever doubt that."

"I don't Becks. I love you, too." I grabbed his arm. "But if you ever disrespect my man again, I may do something nasty to you in your sleep."

With a chuckle, he kissed my cheek and then walked out the door.

Hatch walked in a few minutes later and locked the door.

"Saw your brother. All good?"

I nodded. "I think so."

"Did you know he was leaving?"

I shook my head. "My brother does his own thing. No one knows what he's doing unless he wants you to know." I raised an eyebrow. "A lot like someone else I know."

Hatch handed me the dog. "Coffee?"

"Yes, love, that would be great." I snuggled close to the furball. "Thanks."

"What time's your brother's flight?" Hatch asked, and handed me a cup of coffee and a bagel.

"No idea. I'd imagine his pilot filed the flight plan a while ago if Becks just left."

"Come again?"

"Beckett has his own plane, Connor."

"No shit?"

I shivered at his tone. It was flat. This was not good.

"Just how much money do you have?" he asked.

"Not enough to have my own plane," I assured him. "Beckett's loaded, Connor. I'm comfortable. And you haven't met Kenna. She's in between me and Beckett, age-wise. She's a total nut. You will *love* her."

Hatch's knuckles were white as he gripped the island.

"Don't shut down on me, Hatch."

"Just give me a second here, Maisie."

Growing up the way I did, I learned pretty quickly that money separated you from the real people. Moving to America evened the playing field a little bit, but if Hatch knew just how much money my family had, he might run before he knew how little I cared about it. "Please don't think this changes us."

"Changes us, how?"

I shrugged. "I don't know. You're freaking me out a little because you look like you just swallowed poison."

He took a deep breath. "I grew up rough. Poor. Poorer than poor. Mom died when I was barely twenty, Dad went to prison the same year. I was left to raise myself and my siblings, including Cricket who was three. I was makin' minimum wage. We had nothin', so I have no concept of flyin' anywhere, let alone overseas and in my own plane. You gotta give me a minute."

I blinked back tears. "You raised—"

He shook his head. "Not havin' this conversation right now, Maisie. Don't want your pity."

"I'm not giving you my pity," I snapped.

"Yeah?" he challenged. "Why you cryin'?"

"Because sometimes I cry for no reason!"

Hatch's expression went blank and my heart raced.

"Forget it." I slid off the stool. "Your sister's going to be here soon, and we have a lot to do. I'd just like to say that I can't help that I have money and if you come with us to England, you're going to have to gird up your loins because you're going to meet other people with money. You may even meet the queen."

"You're shittin' me."

"Yes, I am. You won't meet the queen," I confirmed.

I heard some unintelligible muttering as I headed into the bathroom and brushed my teeth.

* * *

Cricket arrived just before eleven. Hatch and I were at a stand-off, and Cricket gave her brother a pretty forceful glare when she walked into the condo. "What did you do to Maisie?"

"I'm headin' to the club," Hatch said not answering her question. "Am I takin' Little Fucker?"

"Yes," I said, my tone clipped.

Hatch scooped the puppy off of my lap, turned on his heel, and left the apartment, barely managing *not* to slam the door.

"You okay?" Cricket asked.

"Yep." I opened my laptop and pulled up my email.

"Whatever he said or did, let it roll off your back," she instructed. "My brother can be a dick. He'll calm down. He probably won't say he's sorry, but he'll realize he's wrong and apologize another way."

159

I sighed. "We come from two completely different worlds, Cricket. I don't know if he'll be able to get past that."

"Well, there *is* that."

"It's hard when he won't talk to me about his past. *Your* past," I confessed. "He just shuts me out."

"What do you want to know?" Cricket asked.

"Nothing." I grimaced. "I don't want to betray his confidence."

"You aren't. It's my life. I can share *my* life."

This was true. "It's not even so much that I need to know, to be honest. I just want him to *want* to tell me, you know?"

Cricket chuckled. "Well, don't hold your breath. He won't talk about it to anyone."

"That's sad."

She shrugged. "It's the biker way."

"Which is *sad*," I reiterated.

"Then you're going to have to adjust your expectations. If you want a man who'll share his thoughts and feelings, you need to hook up with Cullen. Connor's not that guy."

I smiled. "Oh, I don't doubt Connor's my guy. We just have to figure out how to communicate with each other."

"Good luck with that."

"Tell me about your brothers," I said. "I know their names, but that's about it."

Cricket filled me in on Cade, Cullen, and Cameron, but I got sidetracked by Cullen's story. "Wait. So, Cullen was only married for two years?"

Cricket nodded. "Ohmigod, Maisie, Elizabeth was so beautiful. Inside and out. They totally fell in love fast and hard. She got cancer. A brain tumor. It was devastating. As much as Jana totally fucked with Connor and as bitter as he is, Cullen is still so happy and sweet and sees the good in humanity. But he swears he'll never date or marry again."

"Never?"

"Nope. Says he'll be celibate until the day he dies."

"Wow," I breathed out. "What about Cade?"

"Cade's dealing with a crazy ex. She likes money and Devon's in the way right now, so he's staying with Cade.

160

Cade's going to try and get him permanently."

"Is that why Hatch is so anti money?"

"It's probably one of the reasons." Cricket grimaced. "We've never really known a whole lot of people with money who weren't assholes. Except Kim. But everyone else in her family are total dicks, so it's kind of a miracle she's not."

"Well, I'm not a dick, so either your brother pulls his head out or he needs to keep his opinions to himself." I sighed. "What's with all the 'C' names?"

"Mom's thing, I think." Cricket smiled. "Dad said he'd give her anything she wanted, and she wanted all her kids to have 'C' names, so that's what we had."

"Sweet," I said. "How did your brother end up raising you?"

"My dad lost his mind when Mom died. He killed some guy at an underground, illegal open fist fight. He got caught. They used him as an example and we didn't have the money for a decent defense, so he got the max. Dad died in jail a couple of years ago. When Dad got locked up, CPS was gonna farm us out to foster homes, but Connor fought for us. He made it work."

I forced back tears. "See? This is why he's *totally* my guy."

Cricket opened her mouth to say something... just as Hatch walked back in.

He didn't say a word. Just dropped Little Fucker next to his sister, lifted my laptop off my lap, and pulled me gently from my chair. "Be back, Cricket."

He wrapped an arm around my waist and guided me into my bedroom, closing the door behind us. I faced him, but didn't speak, figuring he had something he needed to get off his chest, so I'd let him do it in his own time.

He studied me for a few seconds and then sighed.

"Spit it out, Hatch."

"Just thinkin', while we're in London, maybe you should hang with your family and I should stick with the Dogs."

I felt like I'd been slapped. "Meaning, you're not going to come with me?"

"We got a chapter in London, Sunshine."

I scowled. "So you're going to come with me, but you're going to "stick" with your friends while I "hang" with my family?"

"You can come hang at the club, babe."

"And you can come hang with my family."

He snorted and I realized pretty quickly what this was all about.

"No," I snapped. "Unless you are going to come with us and stay with me and my family, Connor, then you're uninvited."

"I'm not staying with your family, Maisie."

"Then you're uninvited."

His head dropped back and he stared at the ceiling. "Fuck me."

"I would have done that in London, Connor. Several times. But you're uninvited," I said. "A whole month, darling... without me." I bit my lip. "I guess you could partake of that club whore pussy I read about, but then I'd have to kill you."

"Maisie." His voice sounded irritated.

I forced a smile. "My family's going to love you and if they don't, then we'll leave and never speak to them again."

"I don't really care one way or another what they think of me, but I don't want them thinkin' differently of you."

"They won't think differently of me. Don't judge my family on what you saw of Beckett. Please," I begged. "His overprotective meter's broken, and that's something even my father says."

Hatch slid his hand to my neck. "Unfamiliar territory here, baby."

"Me too, *baby*," I pointed out, and I dropped my head to his chest. "Will you just apologize already so we can make out a little and I can get back to work?" He stared down at me and I stood on my tiptoes and kissed him. "You know I see you, Connor Wallace."

"Yeah?"

"Yeah," I whispered. "You're a good man. Even when

162

you bury it under that thick skin of yours, your eyes show me what you're feeling, and I will always honor that."

"God, you're beautiful."

"So are you."

His arms clamped around me and he lifted me enough, so I could wrap my legs around his waist. He carried me to my bed and settled me gently on the mattress.

"We don't have time, darling," I whispered.

He slid off his cut and unbuckled his belt. "We'll be quick."

Tugging off my yoga pants, undies and all, he buried his face between my thighs and I immediately lost my ability to breathe, let alone worry about time constraints. I slid my ankles over his shoulders and arched my hips as he sucked my clit and slid two fingers inside of me, but I lost my control when he was suddenly slamming into me and his mouth covered mine to stifle my scream.

One orgasm followed another and I somehow managed to whack my arm against my headboard, so my blissful climax was quickly followed by agonizing pain.

"Fuck, baby, I'm sorry," he rasped as he yanked his jeans back up and rushed to the bathroom. He returned with water and pills and sat beside me on the bed. "Big ibuprofen or Oxy?"

"I'm going to start with the ibuprofen, I think. I really do have a lot of work to do." I took the pill from him, his expression tortured. "Don't worry about it, love, it's my fault."

"How's it *your* fault?"

"Um, because you drive me crazy enough to flail my arms like a mental person," I said.

"I should be more careful."

I shook my head. "I don't want you to be more careful. I like you just like this. Now, help me get dressed. I really hope your sister put headphones on or something."

Hatch chuckled. "She's been around bikers her whole life, Sunshine. None of this fazes her."

"Well, it fazes me!" I hissed. "Good lord, I've never had sex with someone in the next room before."

"You'll get used to it." He helped me back into my clothes and kissed me gently.

"Don't think I will."

"I'll get you there, baby, 'cause the alternative is abstainin' and that ain't happenin'."

I bit my lip. "Well, there is that. Abstaining would suck."

He kissed me again and I shook my head, pushing him away. "No. You will *not* get me riled up again."

Hatch chuckled, advancing on me. "But I like gettin' you riled up."

"I'm figuring that out," I said. "And when this arm is healed and I don't need a modern-day scribe, I will match your riling with some of my own. But right now, I have work to do."

He grinned, leaning down to kiss me gently. "I'm sorry I stormed off."

"Thank you. Please trust that you're perfect just the way you are, and I don't expect you to be anything different, okay? You might get some looks and pushback from the "crowd" I'm forced to associate with on occasion, but it won't be from my family, and it sure as hell won't be from me or Poppy."

"Looks and pushback I'm used to, Sunshine."

"Don't like that," I admitted.

He cupped my face. "Like that you don't like that."

I let out a frustrated groan. "You need to stop looking at me like that. I have work to do."

He chuckled, kissing me again and then pulling the door open. "Have a good day, honey."

I giggled and headed back out to the family room. Cricket wasn't there so Hatch followed me into the kitchen and we went about making another pot of coffee, making out as we waited for it to brew. I picked up the mail and found a card from Lonnie, my hairdresser. "What the heck?"

I opened it and a Visa gift card fell out of an apology card.

Maisie, I'm so sorry that I didn't assist you with

your car. I hope this gift card will compensate you for any inconvenience I may have caused. I hope you'll give me another chance. I'll be happy to give you fifty percent off. Sincerely, Lonnie.

I glanced at Hatch who sipped his coffee, his expression entirely too innocent to not know something about the card. "What did you do?"

"I didn't do anything."

"*Hatch.*"

"I may have deflated her tires and when she came in for help, explained the correct way to treat my woman."

"You threatened her?"

"Would never threaten a woman, Sunshine," he said. "I just explained I didn't appreciate her leaving you stranded. I helped her with her car, and she went on her way."

I picked up the gift card. "This is twice what I paid for the hair appointment."

"Good."

"You promise you didn't make her feel like crap?"

"Babe, it was all good."

I wrapped my arms around him and kissed him gently. "Well, thank you for defending my honor, even if it was a little overkill."

"You gonna take your man to dinner with your newfound wealth?"

"Absolutely."

The doorbell pealed and Hatch went to answer the door, leading Cricket in a few seconds later. Hatch held the puppy who appeared just as happy to see him as I was every time the man walked into a room.

"I took Little Fucker out for a walk," Cricket explained. "I figured you needed some privacy."

Heat infused my face. "Thanks."

Hatch chuckled. "I'm gonna head to the shop. Am I taking the dog?"

"No," Cricket and I said in stereo.

Hatch handed the puppy to his sister and then kissed me

thoroughly. I patted his chest. "No riling," I ordered.

He smiled against my lips. "No promises."

"Save it for later."

"That I can do." He kissed me again. "I'll plan on picking Poppy up after school."

"Thanks, love."

Hatch walked out the door and I glanced at Cricket to find her staring at me with open interest. "What?"

"What the hell have you done to my brother?"

I frowned. "What do you mean?"

"He's being nice."

"He is?"

"Yes," she said. "He actually pulled me aside and *thanked* me for taking Little Fucker for a walk and for helping you out."

I chuckled. We really need to change the dog's name... pronto.

"And he smiles. *Smiles*, Maisie! My brother doesn't smile."

My heart felt squishy. "I like that, Cricket. Your brother deserves to smile. He makes me really happy."

She kissed the dog. "Well, you're doing everything right, so keep doing it. I like him this way."

"Me too."

Cricket and I got to work and by the time Cricket had to leave for class, we'd caught up on everything I'd missed since the accident. I finally felt like I could breathe and I didn't dread the phone call to my parents... which went surprisingly well.

Hatch and Poppy walked in just as I hung up and, since Hatch had to get back to the shop, Poppy and I hung out and watched a movie after her homework was done while we waited for Hatch to get home with dinner. All in all, it was a pretty perfect first day back at work.

Maisie

THREE WEEKS LATER, life had settled into a regular routine. I had returned to the office, although, on a part-time basis since I still couldn't use my hand for long periods of time. I was slowly getting back to normal, but it was frustrating at times. I was now the owner of a shiny new Volvo. I loved it and since Hatch knew how to fix them, I felt safer knowing he could check for cut brake lines and disabled airbags.

Cricket had walked into the job and owned it in less than a week. I had never seen anyone pick up a job so quickly, and I don't think I could have eased back into my day-to-day so seamlessly without her.

Alison was keeping her distance, which I fully understood

and appreciated, but through Ryan, she relayed that she didn't want her actions to affect Grace and Poppy's relationship and I agreed. So, the girls got together on a regular basis, but always at my place or somewhere public. Poppy was never allowed at their house or somewhere Alison would be. I don't think the girls really cared one way or the other, so long as they got to hang out.

I hated it. I missed my best friend. I'd see her from a distance while I was picking up Poppy from school on occasion and she'd give me a sad smile and wave. I'd wave back then I'd go home and cry privately, unless Hatch was with me, then I'd cry in his shirt.

I wanted everything back the way it was. I knew it never would be, but it didn't make me wish for it any less.

Jaxon had alerted Child Protective Services to the volatile nature of the Lundy home and they did a full investigation, but with Ryan being a decorated police officer, and Alison never having threatened her children (or anyone before me), there was no evidence to warrant them stepping in. Hatch wasn't happy with this answer and neither was Jaxon, so the Dogs and Jaxon's team were watching at a distance for any red flags. So far things were calm, and Poppy promised she'd let me know if Grace said anything to the contrary.

A little before three on Friday afternoon, my cell phone pealed on my desk. "Maisie Mann."

"Mrs. Mann, it's Anthony Miller."

Anthony Miller was the lead prosecutor on Alison's case. I really had no desire to speak with him, but I'd stupidly answered the phone. "Hello, Mr. Miller."

"I need to run something by you. Is now a good time?"

"Ah... sure."

"Mrs. Lundy has indicated she may be willing to take a plea to avoid trial."

"Well, considering I don't think she should go to trial at all, you should let her."

"Even after what she did?"

"Look, Alison has some issues with mental health, but she needs help, not jail," I said. "If there's a way she can be treated instead of doing time, I'd like that to be the priority."

"Okay, Mrs. Mann I'll see what we can do," he said.

"Thanks, Mr. Miller."

I hung up and immediately called Hatch. "Hey, Sunshine."

"Hey."

"What's wrong?"

I groaned and filled him in on my conversation with the D.A.

"Wow," he said.

"Yeah." I squeezed my eyes shut trying to ward off a headache. "I can't believe they're even going there. I'm not pressing charges, why am I even involved?"

"Because—"

"I know, I know. She totally single-white-female'd my life."

"Technically, she married-white-female'd it."

I snorted on a reluctant giggle. "Don't make me laugh. I'm too frustrated."

"It's the State versus now, Maisie, so it's really out of your hands. But be prepared for them to subpoena you to testify if it goes to trial."

"I might be conveniently out of the country."

"Rebel," he said.

"That's me. Badass to the core."

Hatch chuckled. "Got a club get together tomorrow night. Family only. You and Poppy in?"

"Um, sure." I dropped my head to the desk and stared at the carpet. "What happens at a Club get together?"

"Food, drink, communing with the brothers and their families," he explained. "Showing you off."

I smiled. "So, this is the equivalent of meeting the parents for me?"

"Pretty much."

"I like that, darling."

"Me too, Sunshine."

I sat up and turned my chair to look out the window. "I miss you today. I kind of want to blow this joint and find

169

somewhere private where we can get naked."

"Your place or mine?"

"I can't just up and leave."

"You're the boss, Maisie. That kind of ensures you *can* just up and leave."

He had a point.

"You got a meetin'?" he asked.

"Well, no. But, didn't you drop Poppy at my place?"

"Right," he said. "Why don't you meet me at the shop? We can swing by the compound."

"I can't leave Poppy at the condo, love. It's fine for an hour or two, but not forever."

"Susie's with her."

"Who's Susie?"

"Prez's old lady. She's cool. You'll love her."

"Okay, we need to have a conversation about not leaving my daughter with people I've never met before."

Hatch sighed. "I get it, baby, but it was either Susie or Flea, and I know you've met Flea, but he's young, and from what I've been told, considered hot, so I figured you'd feel better havin' the fifty-six-year-old wife of our Club president hangin' with her, rather than the twenty-two-year-old horny-as-hell recruit. Not that he'd touch her, just to be clear, but I wanted to make sure she was covered, and I made a judgment call in the moment."

"You have a point."

"I know I do, Sunshine."

"I feel weird about making Susie stay with my daughter for us to go off for an illicit sex hour."

He laughed. "Babe, believe me, she'd be all for it."

"Seriously?"

"Yeah, seriously. So, compound, yes or no?"

I bit my lip. "Will we be alone?"

"In the sense that I have a private room there, yeah. People are in and out all the time, baby, but think of it as a hotel."

I wrinkled my nose. "This isn't what I had in mind for a private—"

"I know, Maisie, and I've got somethin' planned, but that

somethin' isn't gonna get me access to your pussy in the next twenty minutes, so… meet me here?"

I shivered. Yes, I absolutely wanted him to have access to my pussy in the next twenty minutes.

"Sunshine?"

"Oh, sorry. Yes. I'll meet you at the shop in twenty minutes."

He chuckled. "Okay, baby."

I hung up, grabbed my laptop, and packed up. "Cricket," I called, and she peeked her head into my office. "I'm heading out for the weekend. If you want to finish up whatever you're working on and do the same, go for it."

"Thanks, Maisie, that'd be great."

"Will you lock up when you leave, please?"

"Sure thing."

I headed out to my car and grinned as I made my way to my man. We'd done all the things we were supposed to do when starting a new sexual relationship (according to Hatch). He got tested and I went back on the Pill.

Since I no longer had Alison to talk to, I was grateful he'd filled me in on the necessity that I demand a clean bill of health from my sexual partners. Pointing out the fact he was my *only* sexual partner, and I had no desire to look for another one, ever, had earned me a mind-blowing orgasm before we had the additional conversation about me going on the Pill so we didn't have to use condoms. Secretly, I didn't care if I got pregnant, but considering we'd been dating for just over a month, the responsible thing to do was… well, to be responsible.

Pulling up to the shop, I climbed out of my car and walked into the small customer area. Hatch was at the front counter helping a young woman who looked like she might want to devour him. Seriously, the girl was virtually panting. I got it… Hatch is pant-worthy, but I immediately wanted to scratch her pretty green eyes out. I took a deep breath and reminded myself that this was his place of business and Hatch's crazy hot body was mine. I had nothing to worry about.

"You should be all set," Hatch said, and handed over her keys.

"Thanks." She twirled her hair. "What was your name?"

"Hatch."

"Thanks, Hatch. That's my cell, you know, if you ever want to grab a drink."

My mouth dropped open and I stepped forward. *I will cut a bitch!*

Hatch grinned. "Sorry babe, I'm very, very taken."

"You sure?"

"Yes, he's sure," I snapped.

The woman turned, obviously surprised someone else was even in her space. "I take it he's taken by you?"

"Indeed," I said smugly as I closed the distance between myself and my man. My hot man. Hatch settled his hand on my lower back. *See whore? My man!*

She did a full body scan of Hatch. "Lucky."

"Very much so," I breathed out.

"Well, should anything change..."

"Are you for real? Walk away," I hissed, and Hatch hooked his arm around my waist as I lunged for her.

The woman quickened her step and headed to her car.

"Bitch-whore!"

Hatch chuckled turning me to face him. "Someone's feisty."

"How often does that happen?"

"Not goin' there, Sunshine," he said.

I growled. "The audacity!"

"Hey."

"What?"

Hatch's eyes softened and he smiled. "Hey."

I sighed, melting against him. "Hey."

"There's my girl. How was your day?"

"Other than the obvious, not bad." I looped my arms around his neck. "How about yours?"

"Good now."

I grinned and he lowered his mouth to mine. Breaking the kiss, he pulled away and headed toward the shop. "Gotta wash up. Come meet Cullen."

I followed him into the back and a tall, gorgeous, dark-haired man peeked out from under the hood of an electric blue car. Don't ask me the make or model, I have no idea, but it was a pretty color. Cullen looked like Hatch, but with much shorter hair and clean-shaven. He also smiled immediately.

"Cull, this is Maisie," Hatch said, and walked to the sink.

"Hey, Maisie," Cullen said. "I'd shake your hand, but I'm covered in oil."

"No worries. It's lovely to meet you."

Cullen glanced over his shoulder then stepped closer to me. "Whatever you're doing, keep doing it. He's really happy. We all appreciate it."

I blushed. "It goes both ways, Cullen, but thanks for saying that."

Hatch walked back our way and slid his arm around my waist. "You comin' tomorrow night?"

Cullen nodded. "Yeah, I think we all are."

"Cool. We're headin' out. Bill's not expectin' his car 'til next week, so if you want to close up for the night, feel free."

"Okay, brother." Cullen smiled. "I think I'll do that."

"See you tomorrow."

"It was nice to meet you," I said.

"You too, Maisie." Cullen shut the hood on the car and went about closing the big bay doors while Hatch grabbed his stuff.

"I'll drive, Sunshine," Hatch said.

"You don't have your truck?"

"Cullen will take it home."

"Why?" I felt heat infuse my face. "Does he know what we're doing?"

Hatch laughed. "No, but damn you're cute right now, so maybe I should tell him."

I grabbed his arm. "Don't you dare."

He kissed me as he backed me out to my car. "Need to get you naked, Sunshine, so hand me your keys."

I did so immediately, and we headed to this compound he spoke of.

We pulled into the parking lot of Big Ernie's and I was a little taken aback. I'm not sure why, really. I suppose when Hatch said "compound," I was expecting an impenetrable building like a castle with a moat, or a fortress of concrete or something.

He parked the car and we headed inside. The place was eerily quiet, and we didn't see another soul as he led me up a back stairwell and down a hallway to a door near a window to the outside. Unlocking the door, he pushed it open and stood back so I could precede him in, flipping the light on behind me.

Before I could take in the room, my purse was removed from my hand, and I was turned to face him. "You're gorgeous, you know that?" he said.

I grinned, tugging at his cut. "Why, sir, are you just saying that to get into my knickers?"

"Knickers are panties, right?"

I shuddered. "I hate that word, but, yes."

"You own a sex toy company and hate the word panties?"

"Yes. Don't judge me."

"No judging." He chuckled. "Just want into your knickers." He threw off his cut and pulled off his shirt. "Is it working?"

"Why yes, yes, it is." Licking my lips, I ran my fingers between his pecs. He reached for me, but I shook my head as I unbuttoned my blouse. "You don't get to touch."

"Come again?"

"Oh, you will, baby." I ran my tongue over my upper lip. "Again and again and again."

"Fuck me."

"Hmm-mmm, I'm gonna do that too."

He reached for me again, but I stepped away.

"Maisie," he growled.

"Yes, darling?" He crossed his arms and I smiled. "I'd like you naked and on the bed, please."

He raised an eyebrow.

"Connor," I nodded to the bed as I slipped out of my blouse, "now, please."

I bit the inside of my cheek to keep from laughing. He looked like he had no clue what the hell he was supposed to do. To be honest, I wasn't quite sure what *I* was supposed to do. I'd never been bossy in the bedroom, but it was turning me on, so I went with it.

It took him a few seconds, but he let me go with it as well, getting naked and stretching out on the bed. I removed the rest of my clothes and stepped to the bed smiling down at him. I didn't think I'd ever get sick of basking in the glory of his body. He had the words "Never Forget Catherine~1995" in flowing letters just under his heart and I leaned over and kissed it like I had several times before. He'd gotten it the day after his mother had been buried and I know he still felt her loss.

"Watch your arm, Maisie."

"I'm fine." I was putting all of my weight on my left arm in order to baby my right. "No talking."

Hatch stretched his arms behind him and settled his head on them. "Whatya gonna do, Sunshine?"

"I'm working on that."

He grinned. "I'm at your disposal."

I wrapped my fingers around his hardening length and slid my hand down, cupping him before taking his cock into my mouth. Hatch hissed, bringing his knees up and fisting his hands in my hair.

Before I could get to anything fun, I lost purchase on his dick and I was dragged up his body. "Hey!" I snapped.

"On your knees."

I wanted to bitch about not getting the chance to finish what I started, but on my knees was my absolute favorite position and I immediately went there. Hatch guided himself inside of me and I dropped my head back at the sensation.

"You wanna be the boss, Maisie?" he asked as his palm connected with my bare bottom.

I whimpered and pushed my body back against him.

"Mmm, you like that, huh?" He slammed into me again, his palm slapping me a little harder this time and the sensation overtook everything. God, it felt amazing, but when he slid one hand between my legs and fingered my clit, I came the second the palm of his other hand slapped against my bottom again, and I cried out his name as I buried my face in the mattress while he continued to thrust into me. His body locked and he wrapped his arms around me, gently rolling us to the side so we were spooning, staying connected as he kissed the back of my neck. "Just gets better."

"What does?"

"Everything."

I smiled, sliding my hand down his arm and linking my fingers with his. "Yeah, it does."

He pulled me closer. "Love you, Maisie."

I stilled for about two-point-five seconds before untangling myself and rolling over to face him. "Say that again," I demanded.

Hatch chuckled, reaching out to slide my hair away from my face. "I love you. I know it's soon and I fuckin' hate pretty much everything, but I love you. You're everything to me, baby."

I let out a ridiculous girly squeal and pushed him on his back, straddling him as I leaned down and peppered kisses all over his face. "I love you too, even though I don't hate pretty much everything."

He gripped my hips, lifting me slightly, then lowering me onto his already hard cock. I let out a quiet moan and he grinned as he sat up and kissed me. "You ever need to do research on any of your products?"

I lifted myself and then lowered slowly. "I have a research department for that."

"Don't think you're pickin' up what I'm puttin' down, Sunshine."

"Oh." I giggled. "I have never had the desire to do research before, but I will keep that in mind should something interesting come across my desk."

He buried his face in my neck. "That's my girl."

For the next blissful hour, Hatch and I explored each other until it was time to get back to reality. I had to admit, getting dressed after an hour-and-a-half of illicit sex made our time all the more exciting and I couldn't wait to do it again, but I was also happy to get home to Poppy and enjoy a Friday night just the three of us. I loved having Hatch in our space. It all felt so right.

EIGHTEEN

Maisie

SATURDAY NIGHT, HATCH arrived just before six, while I was attempting to put on a pair of earrings. Unfortunately, something so intricate was still difficult. I let out a frustrated growl and dropped the hoops on my dresser.

"Need help?" Hatch asked from the doorway.

"Hi," I said, rushing to him and kissing him deeply. "Yes."

"You okay?" he asked after breaking the kiss.

"I just missed you and I can't get my stupid earrings in."

He chuckled. "I can help with both o' those."

"Mom!" Poppy bellowed.

"Oh, and *that*." I dropped my forehead to his chest. "Can I hide, please?"

"What's going on?"

"She has her period," I whispered. "And is on the war-path."

"Don't want or need to know, Sunshine." Hatch squeezed his eyes shut. "You go deal with her. I'll grab a beer and help you with your earrings when you're done."

"Chicken."

He grinned and stalked away.

I walked into Poppy's room and found her face down on her bed. "Are you dead?"

"Yes," she mumbled into her duvet.

"What do you need, Poppet?"

"Boobs."

I bit back a giggle, but a snort escaped, and Poppy rolled over and sat up. "You're twelve, love, let's wait on boobs for a while, okay? You're already illegally pretty. It's hard enough to ward off the boys."

"Was it Devon?" She grabbed my arm. "Were you warding off Devon? Was he asking about me?"

Shit!

"Ah, no, not that I'm aware of."

"Is he going to be there tonight?"

"Probably." I stroked her hair, sliding it down her back. "Why?"

"Because he's super hot, Mum, and if Lily's there too, he won't even look at me."

"Sweetness, I don't *want* him looking at you!" I ground out. "You're twelve."

"Almost thirteen."

"Twelve," I repeated.

"*Almost thirteen.*"

"I still have well a little time until you officially hit your teens. Please don't rush me, okay?" She rolled her eyes and I smiled. "I will concede that you're growing up and it's giving me ulcers, but Devon's older than you, Poppy. He's in high school. As is Lily, so I'd really like you to just stick close to me and Hatch tonight, and try not to feel like you have to be

179

anything other than who you are, okay?"

"Can Grace come tonight?"

"We didn't really plan on that. But next time for sure, okay?"

Poppy brightened and wrapped me up in a hug. "That'd be really great, Mummy. Thank you."

"Hatch is here, so please finish getting dressed."

She nodded and I left her room. I found Hatch in the kitchen opening a beer. "All good?" he asked.

"She has a crush on Devon."

"What the fuck?"

"Devon is gorgeous, Hatch. You must know this."

Hatch frowned. "Well, he touches her, he dies."

"Whoa, that escalated quickly. He hasn't done anything. She has a little crush. It's totally innocent."

"Poppy," he called.

I grabbed his cut. "Honey, please don't embarrass her."

"I'm ready," she said, skipping into the kitchen.

"You look beautiful, baby girl."

Poppy blushed. "Thanks, Hatch."

He crossed his arms. "Which poses a problem."

She frowned. "What kind of a problem?"

"You get prettier every day and that makes things more difficult for me and your mom."

"Why does that make it more difficult?"

"Well, there'll be teenage boys with hormones ragin' and they do stupid things because of that. So, if one of them looks at you the wrong way, I need to know about it."

"What?" she squeaked.

"Seriously, Poppy. Not one of my brothers' kids comes anywhere near you tonight without you telling me, got it? Devon already knows the drill."

"You told Devon?" she asked, horrified.

"I told Devon he goes nowhere near any of the girls at the club and that includes you."

Poppy glanced at me and then back at Hatch.

"But that includes school," Hatch continued. "Guys bug you there; I need to know about it."

"Why?" she asked.

"This is part of me protecting you, Poppy, got it?"

She blushed and nodded as she lowered her head, but I didn't miss her smile and my heart lightened.

"I'm gonna help your mom with somethin' then we'll go."

"Okay, Hatch."

He moved out from behind the island and pulled her in for a hug, kissing her head. "You good?"

She hugged him back and nodded.

"Good."

I followed Hatch back into my bedroom and closed the door, wrapping my arms around his waist. "Thank you."

"For what?"

"For making her feel special."

"Is that what I did?"

"You're a shit liar, darling, and I love you for it." I leaned back and rolled my eyes. "Now help me with these earrings."

He grinned and helped me put them on, then we gathered up the dog (newly named Sparky because when Poppy had picked him up, she'd received an electric shock) and headed to the compound.

The party was in full swing when we arrived, but I saw Cricket tap the arms of three men who turned and started our way. I recognized Cullen, so I deduced the others were Cade and Cameron.

"Poppy!" a feminine squeal sounded, and Lily came rushing toward us. "Ohmigosh, you got one of the puppies? I'm Lily. I don't know if you remember me from dance class."

"Hi, I remember," Poppy said.

"What's his name?"

"Sparky."

"He's so cute," she said, scratching his chin. "I love your hair, Poppy."

Poppy smiled. "Thanks."

I could see Poppy's surprise as the beautiful young woman showed genuine interest in her. "Is it okay if she comes and hangs out with us in the back, Mrs. Mann? Mom and Dad are out there too."

"It's where the grill is and generally where the older kids hang," Hatch explained. "She'll be covered."

"Up to you, Poppy," I said.

Poppy nodded, and Lily led her and Sparky away.

"That was easy," I said.

Hatch wrapped an arm around my waist and pulled me close. "Cam, Cade... Maisie."

Cameron pulled me away from Hatch and wrapped me in a bear hug, lifting me off the ground. "Damn, Con, you said she was pretty, you didn't tell me she was sexy as hell."

"Put her the fuck down, Cam," Hatch growled. "Watch her arm."

"I'm okay." I giggled as he set me on the ground. "Nice to meet you, Cameron."

Cade was much more subdued, and I saw where Devon got his good looks from. Cade hugged me as well, but gently and he didn't linger, obviously heeding Hatch's warning quicker than Cameron. Hatch pulled me back to him again and tucked me under his arm.

"Cameron's already decided Ashley's his conquest for the night," Cricket said.

"Cricket," Cameron said on a groan.

"Who's Ashley?" I asked.

"Prez's daughter," Hatch said. "You go ahead and go for it, Cam."

"Seriously?" he asked, his face lighting up.

"Yeah, brother."

Cricket grinned and I figured something had to be up, so I waited for Cameron and Cade to walk away before I asked what that had been all about.

"Ashley will annihilate him," Cricket said.

"She's a ball-buster." Hatch chuckled. "No doubt about it."

I slapped his chest. "Don't be disrespectful."

"No, he's right," Cricket said. "She's a totally self-confessed one. She has no time for stupid men and Cameron won't be able to charm her. He won't know what to do with himself."

"You don't want to warn your poor brother?"

"No," they said in unison, and Cricket giggled.

"Come on, I'll introduce you to everyone," Hatch said.

Cricket walked away and I gripped Hatch's waist. "Or...?"

"Or, what?"

"It's not like anyone other than your family has seen us, right?" I said. "We *could* take a little detour up to your room."

Hatch grinned, leaning down to kiss me. "Looks like I've created a monster."

"Yes, yes you have." I nodded. "And your monster needs to be fed, especially if there's a little of that spanking action we had yesterday. That was fu—"

"Maisie! You're here!" a female voice called, and I dropped my head onto Hatch's chest with a groan.

Hatch slid his hand into my hair with a chuckle. "Hey, Kim."

"Hey, Hatch."

I forced a smile and raised my head. "Hi, Kim. How are you?"

She smiled. "I'm good."

"Where's Knight?" Hatch asked.

"He's out back. You should head out there. This little guy's stomping on my bladder, so I'll be out in a bit."

"Sounds good," Hatch said, squeezing my neck gently.

Kim walked away and I stared up at Hatch. "Will she notice if we're not out there?"

"Yeah, but I'm good with that, Sunshine."

"Quick before anyone else stops us."

He grabbed my hand and tugged me down the hallway toward the stairs and we made a run for his room. I was laughing so hard by the time he unlocked his bedroom door, I could barely breathe... then he was kissing me and I couldn't breathe for an entirely different reason.

"Don't mess up my hair," I ordered as he yanked my shirt over my head.

"When the hell did you get so bossy?"

I giggled, tearing at his jeans. "I don't want to meet your "brothers" looking like I've been... well, just laid."

Hatch ran his thumbs over my nipples. "You will have been just 'laid.'"

"But I don't want *them* to know that." Having unbuttoned his jeans, I slid my hand inside and cupped him. "You are a work of art."

Hatch grinned, lifting me onto the bed and divesting me of the rest of my clothes. We made our tryst a quick one since I didn't want to leave Poppy alone for long, and then we headed back to the party and out to the back where a few of the club brothers and their families milled around waiting for meat to cook.

NINETEEN

Maisie

I MET LILY'S DAD, Hawk, who was blond and gorgeous, and rocking a handlebar moustache to die for. I'd already met her mom, Payton, at the dance class, and she stopped to offer me a drink and we chatted about our kids. She and Hawk had a couple of other children in the little kids' room, apparently, which she promised to introduce me to later. I met Cassidy's husband, Ace, and their older son, Maverick, and Booker and Dani, and Mack and Darien (I think) whose kids were also in with the little ones.

I kind of lost track of names after that, relying on Hatch to fill me in on occasion, but everyone was warm and welcoming. They did treat me a bit like a unicorn, several admitting they'd been questioning my existence, but they all seemed genuinely thankful that Hatch was "less of a dick" since we'd gotten together.

Poppy loved the attention Lily lavished upon her. There didn't seem to be a mean bone in the older girl's body, and they became fast friends, exchanging phone numbers and promising to hang out more.

"What's up with that?" I asked Hatch after watching Maverick and Lily. Maverick held Lily's hand on occasion, stroked her hair, and all around appeared to worship the ground she walked on.

Hatch sat on the picnic table, and situated me on the bench between his legs, my arms over his thighs, and lowered his mouth to my ear. "He decided when he was six or so that she was his old lady."

"Shut up," I breathed out.

Hatch nuzzled my neck. "Been in love with her since the day he met her."

"How does she feel about him?"

"Don't know. Hawk keeps her pretty sheltered. They live next door to each other, but Lily goes to the art school up in Vancouver. Mav's on the football team at Skyview, so they're in two different worlds right now. Lily's all sweetness and innocence. Mav's a good kid, but he's the son of a biker and he's around women who don't have a whole lotta class, and they're starting to notice him."

I frowned. "I don't want to know."

"Didn't say he does anything with 'em, Sunshine. Cass'd kick Ace's ass if he let that happen."

"Well, these women shouldn't even think about it. He's in high school."

"I agree, but look at him... does he look like he's in high school to you?"

"Well, no," I conceded. "But, still. Ew."

"Doesn't matter. Maverick's only got eyes for Lily. If they don't get together, it'd have to be because of an act of God... or Hawk."

"Hawk would stop it?"

"Right now, hell yeah."

"Good dad."

Hatch chuckled. "Yep."

Poppy watched Devon covertly, but I noticed. He respected her space, stepping away if she got too close, but seemed to enjoy her company. He was charming, but not *too* charming, which I believed would serve him well in life.

Hatch slid my hair away from my neck and kissed me gently. "What are you thinking about?"

I craned my neck and smiled up at him. "The charm of the Wallace men."

He raised an eyebrow. "Don't typically get called charming, Sunshine."

"That's a load of crap and you know it." I turned back to watch Poppy. "Did you forget I nearly had to cut a bitch yesterday?"

Hatch dropped his head back and laughed, drawing confused looks from the rest of the brothers standing around.

I waved my hand. "Don't mind him. I just reminded him of something."

"Burger or dog, Maisie?" Knight asked.

"Burger, please," I said.

"Hatch?"

"Burger." Hatch leaned down and wrapped his arms around my chest. "Like that you think I'm charming."

"The problem is you're supposed to only be charming to me."

"I'll work on that."

"No, don't. That'll just make you more lethal."

"You like me lethal," he whispered. "Especially when I do that thing—"

"Stop," I ordered a little too loudly, and Hatch started laughing again, while I blushed profusely.

As we dressed our burgers, my phone buzzed in my pocket, so I pulled it out and glanced at the screen. Alison's name popped up and I frowned. Choosing to ignore the call, I slid my phone back and continued about my business. A few minutes later, my phone buzzed again. Handing my plate to Hatch, I sighed. "Excuse me for a minute."

I walked to a private area away from the group and answered the call. "Hello?"

"Maisie?" Alison said, sobbing into the phone. "I'm so sorry."

"Maisie! Mom has a gun!" Grace screamed in the background.

"Ali, what's going on?" I spun to face the group again and locked eyes with Hatch who stalked toward me immediately.

"I can't keep doing this," Alison rasped.

"Doing what, love?" I asked, then muted my phone and said to Hatch, "Something's going on with Alison. Gracie's screaming in the background that Ali's got a gun, she's terrified, Hatch."

"It's all too much, Maisie, you know?" Alison rasped.

I unmuted my phone as Hatch gathered up his brethren.

"What's too much, love? Where are Ryan and Merrick?" I asked Alison.

Gracie continued to scream in the background and my heart raced painfully.

"Do you remember that time we took the kids to the museum?" Alison asked.

I tried to keep my voice calm and carefree as I said, "The great pink eye incident of two-thousand-six?"

"Ohmigod, yes," she giggled, but her laugh sounded manic.

"No, Mama, please don't," Grace begged.

"Alison?" I called.

"Huh?"

"Ali, love?" I called again.

"Yes, I'm here."

"Remember, after the kids got pink eye, how Grace took care of Merrick and Poppy? She went and got her plastic stethoscope," I reminded her. "Goodness, she was the cutest little nurse, eh?"

"I forgot about that," Alison whispered. "Why don't they wash those damned toys?"

I hated it when she segued. "They probably do now, but it wasn't the greatest memory, was it, love? But remember how

Ryan watched the kids the next day so we could go to the spa? That was such a great day."

"We had such good times, didn't we?"

"We did, love."

"I'm so sorry, Maisie."

"I know, love," I whispered.

"If I could take it back, I would."

"I know, love. I forgive you."

"Goodbye Maisie."

Before I could process the meaning behind her words, a loud blast sounded. Over the ringing of my ears, I could barely hear Gracie's gut-wrenching scream.

"No! Mama! Ohmigod, why did you… you…! Mama, get up!"

The reality of what had just happened hit me as my knees slammed into the concrete and I fell to the ground. Somewhere in the background I could hear Poppy calling out to me and then strong arms lifted me and pulled me close.

Hatch grabbed my phone and I think he spoke into it, I'm not really sure. I climbed into the dark recesses of my mind and hid there.

"Goodbye Maisie."

She couldn't have killed herself, but I knew it was true even as I clung to Hatch and tried to deny it.

No, Ali. We can fix this. We'll get through it. I won't press charges. Everything will be okay.

But I was only trying to convince myself. I knew in my gut my friend was already gone.

"Mummy?" Poppy asked, her soft hand wrapping around mine.

"I'm okay, Poppet."

I was, but Alison… My eyes burned.

"Mama, get up!"

She'd done it in front of Gracie. How could she? She was getting help.

Hatch had me cradled on his lap on one of the picnic tables, my phone to his ear, his face unreadable.

"What's going on?" Poppy asked.

189

"Grace is okay," I lied. Grace was far from okay, but it was the only hope I could give Poppy. "She'll be fine. She's tough."

"Grace," Hatch said into my phone. "I need you to call 9-1-1. I know this is scary, but I need you to do that right now, can you?"

Knight walked up to us and Hatch raised his head.

"Jax is on his way out to their place," Knight provided.

"Someone's comin' to help and he'll probably beat the cops. His name's Jaxon Quinn," Hatch said. "But you still gotta dial 9-1-1, okay? Tell them who your dad is and that they need to call him." He squeezed his eyes shut. "As soon as they can, Grace, yeah? Okay."

He hung up and I swallowed convulsively. "Did Alison really...?"

"Yeah," he breathed out.

"What's going on?" Poppy demanded.

I linked my fingers with hers. "Alison..." I swallowed. "There's been a..." Another swallow. My throat was suddenly so dry. "Alison was very sick, Poppy. And she's going through a lot and..." I turned toward Hatch. "The ambulance is on the way, right? She could still pull through. We don't know for sure that she's dead."

"What?" Poppy burst into tears.

My stomach clenched. "I think I'm gonna be sick."

Lily stepped in and wrapped her arms around Poppy as Hatch led me away from the group. My knees stung, and I looked down to see blood seeping out the holes in my jeans but couldn't have cared less.

"She's dead, Hatch," I whispered. "She really... oh God." Once inside his bedroom, I stepped into his private bathroom barely making it to the toilet. After emptying my stomach of everything I'd eaten over the last year, Hatch helped me to the bed where I fell in a heap, too overwhelmed to cry.

"Let's look at those knees, Sunshine." Hatch removed my wedges, then gently pulled my jeans off, grimacing at the hamburger that used to be my skin. "Let's get some peroxide on those."

190

I rolled to my side, hugging one of his pillows to my chest and closing my eyes. My best friend was dead. Never had I ever thought this would happen. I'd lost the two people closest to me… and I wasn't even forty. Shit like this wasn't supposed to happen to young people.

"Connor?" I whispered.

"Yeah, baby?" He crawled onto the bed with me and cupped my cheek.

"Please don't die. I can't lose you too."

Readjusting me so I was on his chest, he held me close and kissed my temple. "I'm not goin' anywhere, Sunshine. You're gonna get so sick of me, you'll be that grumpy old lady who complains about her old man to the nurses at the old folks' home."

I smiled. "As long as you're in the old folks' home with me, I swear I won't complain… ever."

"Deal."

"My best friend isn't here anymore, Connor."

He stroked my hair. "I know, honey."

"I know she… she screwed up, but she was sick, and it didn't make me love her any less. She was still my family." I took a ragged breath. "I held out this stupid little hope that she'd get well, and we could maybe get back to normal." I glanced up at him. "And don't growl at me for using 'stupid.' In this instance, I think it's accurate, because she was farther gone than I thought, which was stupid. I should have seen it. I should have protected Grace. I should have protected Merrick. For God's sake, I let Poppy into that den of crazy." I burst into tears again and Hatch pulled me closer. "But I love her still. I've missed her. How bat shit crazy is *that*?" I snapped. "She tried to kill me and my child and I still *love* her. I *am* an idiot."

"Shhh, Sunshine, you're not an idiot."

"I am so."

Hatch lifted my head and thumbed my tears away. "You are a beautiful, loving mother and friend, and you want to believe the best in people. That doesn't make you an idiot. As soon as you saw the threat, you got Poppy out of the way. No

191

one would have guessed that someone like Alison would have had the know-how, let alone the desire, to mess with your car."

"You would have."

"How do you figure?"

I shrugged. "I don't know. You know everything."

He sighed. "I wouldn't have known, baby. No one could have known. And I'd venture a guess, Ryan probably didn't know either."

"Ohmigod," I said, sitting up and scrambling off the bed. "Ryan." I hissed at the pain in my knees and Hatch sat me back down and knelt in front of me.

"Let's get these knees bandaged."

"We need to find out what's going on. And Poppy needs me."

"Baby, Jaxon'll fill me in on Alison when he can. There's nothin' we can do right now, so my priority is you and Poppy. Lily has Poppy and she'll take care of her. Your knees are bleedin' again and we need to get them bandaged." He stood. "Stay put."

I stayed put. Hatch grabbed some supplies from his bathroom and gently cleaned my knees, smearing ointment on them, then sticking bandages gently over the wounds. "How's your arm?"

"It hurts."

"You got anything in your bag?"

I shook my head.

Hatch frowned. "I'll find you somethin'."

He leaned down and kissed me gently before heading back into his bathroom and I flopped back onto the bed. "My jeans are ruined, aren't they?"

"No."

"Are they torn?"

"Yeah."

"Then they're ruined," I informed him.

He returned with a bottle of ibuprofen and a bottled water. "Not ruined, babe."

I took the pills and sighed. "You just have to argue with

everything, don't you?"

"I don't argue with everything."

"Yes you—oh, I see what you did there." I rolled my eyes, and Hatch smiled. "Thanks, love."

"Your jeans are fine, Maisie. A little blood and some tearing at the knee, but totally wearable for today."

I couldn't believe I was worried about ripped jeans when my best friend had just shot herself. I squeezed my eyes shut. This is exactly what happened to me when Niall died. I'd have these moments where I'd hyper-focus on something else. I'd worry the roses by the kitchen window were getting too much light, or that the pillowcases on the guest bed weren't ironed; stupid, insignificant things like that... Alison said it was my brain trying to give me a break from the pain.

Tears slipped down my cheeks and I burrowed closer to Hatch. *God, Ali. Why?*

Hatch shifted and pulled his phone out of his pocket, putting it against his ear. "Hatch. Hey. Yeah." He dragged a hand through his hair and glanced at me. "Yeah. Shit. Yeah. Okay, Jax. Thanks, man." He slid his phone back in his pocket and faced me. "She's gone, Maisie."

The last ounce of hope I'd been holding onto exploded and I burst into tears again. Alison had done it. She'd really killed herself.

"Ryan and Merrick went to a movie, so their phones were off. Alison has had this planned for a while... she left a note."

"Ohmigod." I covered my mouth with my hand. "Why would she do that to Grace? Kill herself in front of her own daughter?"

His face darkened.

"What?"

"In the note...," he shook his head, "she was gonna kill Gracie too."

My stomach roiled. I rushed into the bathroom again, but all I could do was dry heave. It felt like my heart was trying to come up. Hatch hunkered down beside me and held my hair back as I leaned over the toilet. I couldn't wrap my mind around what Hatch said. Couldn't do it. I didn't think I even wanted to try.

My cell phone pealed in the other room and Hatch rose to his feet. "I'll get it."

"Thanks," I said into the bowl.

The phone had stopped ringing by the time Hatch walked back into the bathroom, but he handed it to me and I leaned back against the wall and checked my voicemail.

"Maisie, it's Ryan..." I squeezed my eyes shut. God, he sounded wrecked. *"Can... ah... can you... do you have... would you be able to help with Merrick and Grace? I called my Mom. I just need them somewhere safe until I can... well... fuck. Call me if you can. Please?"*

I dropped my phone on the bathroom rug and buried my face in my hands. "Ryan. He needs help with the kids."

Hatch slid down the wall, sitting beside me and wrapping a hand around my thigh. "What do you want to do, Sunshine?"

"They don't have any family here."

He waited.

"I don't know what to do, Hatch," I whispered. "I don't have room for them."

"The kids can come here," he said. "We've got plenty of food and there's nothin' planned tomorrow, so it'll be quiet, but we can have a few of the brothers around for coverage. We can stop by your place and grab a few things for you and Poppy."

"So you can make sure we're safe too," I deduced.

"Yeah, Sunshine, that'd be good."

"God," I breathed out. "I don't know if I can do this."

"You *can* say no, Maisie."

I dropped my head to the wall and closed my eyes. "I don't think I can. Those kids have no one."

"Whatever you decide, I got your back. We all do."

I gave him a sad smile. "Thanks, love."

"Mum?" Poppy called.

"She's in here." Hatch rose to his feet and stepped into his room.

"Be right out, Poppet." I didn't really want Poppy to see

me sobbing on his bathroom floor, so I picked myself up and washed my face. I found an unopened toothbrush in his medicine cabinet and used it, then peeked into the room. "Can I get my jeans, please?"

"Why don't you have your jeans on?" Poppy asked.

"I skinned my knees, so I needed to clean them."

"Are you okay?" she asked, the worry in her voice heartbreaking.

"Yes, darling. They're all good now."

Hatch handed me my jeans and I pulled them on as quickly as I could. Contrary to his opinion, they were ruined. He might be fine with wearing jeans that were ripped up (and looked good in them), I, however, was not. I shook my head.

Again! What the hell was wrong with me? Who the hell cared about jeans when my best friend had just shot herself?

I felt tears escape. *God, Alison. What the hell?*

"Baby?"

"I'm okay," I lied, and turned to face Hatch.

He took my hand and squeezed it gently, and I stepped out and pulled Poppy into my arms. I filled her in on what was going on (filtering *heavily*), then we sat down and discussed options.

Poppy settled her chin in her palm and looked at Hatch. "Is Gracie safe?"

Hatch nodded. "Yeah, baby girl, she's safe."

"If she and Merrick are here with me and Mum, everyone will be okay? I mean…"

"What, Poppet?" I pressed.

"Will Uncle Ryan let them come here?"

"He asked me to look after them, so I think he'll be okay with it," I said.

"Well, if he's not, will you make him let them come, Hatch?"

"I'm gonna do my best," he promised. "Do you feel comfortable staying here with Cricket? Your mom and I might be gone for a few hours." I whipped my head toward Hatch and he shook his head. "Grace and Merrick will want you, Sunshine. They're gonna be freaked. There's no safer place than

195

here for Poppy."

"He's right, Mum," Poppy said. Her maturity shining as it often did in surprising ways. "I'm fine."

"You'll need to take care of Sparky," I said.

"I can do that," Poppy promised.

"I'm gonna call Jax on the way," Hatch said, and we headed downstairs.

TWENTY

Maisie

"DO WE HAVE time to stop at home so I can change and pack a bag first?" I asked. "We should probably get Sparky's bed and food."

"Yeah, I think we can do that," Hatch said.

"And do we have time for me to completely freak out?"

Hatch smiled, reaching over to take my hand. "Yeah, Sunshine. We got time for that too."

I held myself together while we drove into the parking garage and parked next to my Volvo, and I even held myself together as we rode up the elevator and walked down the hallway to my door. But the second we crossed the threshold, Hatch's arms wrapped around me and I fell against him, bursting into ugly tears and sobbing into his chest.

He slid his hands into my hair and held me close. "I got ya, baby."

Bending down, he lifted me and carried me into the family room, sitting in the big chair and settling me on his lap. We didn't speak; there was nothing really to say. I just cried and Hatch held me, stroking my hair while I mourned the loss of my best friend.

I'm not sure how long I sat there, but when I felt like I could function in polite society again, I sat up and wiped my face, leaning down to kiss Hatch. "God, I love you."

"Love you too, Sunshine," he said. "You okay?"

"Not really, but I need to help those kids. I reserve the right to get snotty on your chest later this evening, however."

He smiled. "Not a problem."

I climbed off his lap and, after washing my face, changed and packed a bag for me and Poppy while Hatch got Sparky's stuff together. We then headed down to the garage, opting to take my car instead of his.

"Ali's house is the other way, love," I said, as Hatch hit the freeway.

"Jaxon said we should head to the hospital. Grace is being checked out, so Ryan and Merrick are there for the moment. Ryan wants to get back to the house, but he's waiting for you," Hatch said.

"Does he know the kids are coming back to the compound?"

Hatch shook his head. "He and I are havin' a conversation before anything happens."

"Okay."

Hatch reached over and took my hand. "You good?"

"I don't know," I admitted. "But you know when shit's coming down and you have someone beside you that you know you can face anything with, and it gives you this strange sense of calm?"

Hatch's eyes got soft. "I do now."

"Me too," I whispered.

He squeezed my hand and we continued to the hospital.

We walked in to find that Grace had been taken to the pediatric wing for observation and my name had been put on the list of approved visitors, so I was granted immediate access to her. Hatch was only allowed as far as the waiting room which he wasn't happy about. I assured him he was close enough for me to get if I needed him, before leaving him to walk into the brightly painted area.

I saw Ryan immediately, pacing outside a closed doorway, Merrick sitting in a chair his head in his hands. Ryan caught my eye and rushed toward me, stopping a few inches in front of me and looking wholly uncertain as to how he was supposed to act. I was right there with him. After a few awkward moments ticked by, I opened my arms, which he readily walked into. "I'm so sorry, Maisie."

"I know, Ry." I rubbed his back. "Me too, love."

Ryan pulled away and I reached for Merrick who'd walked slowly over after his father, his face void of emotion which concerned me.

"Hey, Mer." I reached over and stroked his hair.

"Hey, Auntie."

"You need anything?"

He shook his head.

"Is it okay if I hug you?" I asked.

He nodded.

"Okay, thanks." I gave him a squeeze. "I really need it."

He wrapped his arm around my waist and held on. Ryan seemed to relax a little bit and I saw a tiny smile, albeit a sad one.

"Where's Grace?" I asked.

"Doc's in with her now," Ryan said, nodding toward the closed room.

We started back toward Grace's room just as the door opened and a female police officer walked out. "She's all set, Lundy."

Ryan gave her a chin lift and stepped inside. I hung back with Merrick, but Ryan waved me in, indicating Merrick should stay outside. "I'll be right out, buddy, okay? You just have a seat."

Merrick nodded and sat where he had been before while I

walked into Grace's room.

I forced back tears at the sight of my sweet Gracie sitting on the oversized hospital bed, her eyes vacant, and her body shaking as medical staff poked and prodded her.

The doctor met Ryan and me at the door. "Grace has not sustained any physical trauma, however, her emotional trauma will manifest itself over the next days, weeks, months, years, as I'm sure you're aware. She's going to need some intensive counseling, but in the meantime, I can prescribe some sedatives to help her sleep over the next few days until you can get something set up. I'll be happy to recommend a few good psychiatrists, and should you need anything, please don't hesitate to call my office. She's a very brave girl."

Ryan nodded.

"Thank you, Doctor," I said.

"Maisie?" Grace whispered.

I rushed to her side and took her hands. "Hi, sweetheart."

"Mom… she…"

"I know, baby," I whispered.

"You saved me."

"What?"

"She had the gun aimed at me, but you said something to her… she turned the gun on herself… she didn't…"

"Okay, love, we don't need to talk about this right now. Do you want to take a shower?"

She nodded.

"I brought you a change of clothes," Ryan said.

"Get out," Grace hissed.

"Baby—"

"Get out!" she screamed. "Get out! Get out! Get out!"

I rushed to Ryan and pushed him out of the room, my heart breaking for him as tears streamed down his face. "I've got her, Ry. I will take care of her. Give me her clothes and I'll make sure she's okay. I will watch her like a hawk, I will love her and hold her and do my best to help her keep her sanity. I don't know when any of this will be okay, but we're going to figure it out, okay?"

He dragged his hands down his face and nodded. Merrick

stood and wrapped his arms around his dad. I cupped Merrick's face. "Thanks for being so strong, buddy, but it's okay for you to cry as well and if you need a hug, you come find me or your dad, okay? Don't bottle this up and don't try to be strong if you don't feel it."

Merrick nodded and burrowed further into his dad.

"Clothes, Ryan," I prompted, and he handed me a duffel bag. I headed back into Grace's room and found her staring at the wall again. "Gracie?"

She turned toward me, but I didn't really get any kind of acknowledgement. "Do you want a nurse to help you shower?"

"No. Just you," she rasped.

The nurses nodded and filed out (after one of them provided shampoo, soap, and towels for Grace), and I made sure the door was closed.

I helped Grace undress and then we shuffled into the bathroom.

"Okay, sweetness, I'm going to give you some privacy. I'll be right outside and once you're done, I'm going to take you to Poppy."

Grace nodded and I left the bathroom. Peeking out of the room, I saw Merrick sitting alone and frowned. "Did your dad leave?"

"Yeah. He had to get back to the house."

"Okay. I don't think we're going to be much longer. Are you hungry? Hatch is in the waiting room. I can have him take you to the cafeteria."

"Um…"

"He's a really good guy, Mer."

"Okay, that would be great, Auntie. Thank you."

I found the call button for the nurse and pressed it, grateful someone came quickly. "What do you need?"

"There's a man waiting out in the waiting room and I'm wondering if someone could bring him back. Merrick should really get something to eat."

"I can do that for you," the nurse said. "What's his name?"

"Hatch. Long hair, tall, beard, biker. You can't miss him." The nurse walked away, and I stayed where I was, straddled between Merrick and Grace, waiting for Hatch to relieve me. I took a second to text Poppy and check in, receiving a quick response letting me know she was fine and asking about Grace. I let her know we'd be there within the hour and then slid my phone back into my pocket.

Hatch arrived with the nurse and I introduced him to Merrick. "Merrick hasn't eaten in a while, so I was hoping you might be able to find him something."

"I can do that," Hatch said.

Merrick looked up at Hatch with wide eyes, no doubt taking in his badass biker appearance, but I trusted my man to win him over, just like he'd won over Poppy.

I took a second to stand on my tiptoes and kiss Hatch gently, whispering, "Thanks, love," so that Merrick could see how I felt about Hatch. Hopefully, that took some of the fear away from him.

"You got it, Sunshine," Hatch said, squeezing my hand. "Talked to Ryan. Everything's set."

"Thank you."

Hatch nodded. "Okay, Merrick, let's head to the cafeteria. I'm starvin'. How about you?"

"Yeah," Merrick said.

"Maisie?" Grace called, and I stepped back into the room.

* * *

Later that night, Hatch and I lay in his bed and I tried to calm my mind. I couldn't.

"I should check on the kids," I said, and sat up.

Hatch pulled me back down. "They're fine, Sunshine. Bunk room's across the hall, Devon said he'd come get me if Merrick needed you. Cricket's in with Poppy and Grace. You've spent the whole day takin' care of them. It's time for me to take care of you."

"Why hasn't Ryan *called*?"

"Takes a while to clear a scene like that, Sunshine."

"You think he's clearing the scene? Wouldn't someone

else do it?"

He stroked my back. "I get the feelin' Ryan's kind of a pain in the ass and is tryin' to insert himself anyway."

"Well, you got that right." I sighed, snuggling closer. "I don't know what he's going to do now. He loved her so much, Connor. She was his world. He loved her more than his kids... not to diminish his love for his kids, but she took a lot, you know?"

"I get it."

"This all seems so surreal. First the accident, now this." I squeezed my eyes shut. "I'm having a hard time associating my best friend for the past fifteen years, with the woman who cut my brake lines and was going to shoot her own daughter. I can't figure out when the switch flipped. Ryan has always been so on top of her illness, Hatch. Neither of them wanted her to become a statistic. Her mother has the same issues, but her father wasn't as patient as Ryan. They divorced after he had her institutionalized against her will. Now Phyllis is shacking up with some guy out on a farm in the mid-west and is this whacky, hippie, hopped-up on who knows what, drunk lady who looks like she should have been dead a long time ago."

"Yeah? Is she happy?"

"I have no idea. I've only met her once and she was high, so I couldn't tell you if she remembered me or not. Ali had to cut ties with her because she wasn't safe to be around the kids."

"Makes sense."

Blood-curdling screams and a dog's barking had me knifing off the bed and running for the room Grace was in. Pushing open the door, I found her thrashing on the mattress while Poppy tried to soothe her, but since Grace didn't appear to be awake, she wasn't having much luck.

Devon, Flea, and Merrick rushed into the room as well, but Hatch ushered them into the hallway, while Cricket pulled Poppy who was holding Sparky into the corner and hugged her.

I wrapped Grace up in a motherly hug and crooned to her

as calmly as I could, "Gracie, it's Maisie. I'm here. Auntie's here. Can you open your eyes, love? I've got you, sweetness." She began to relax in stages and then her eyes opened, and she buried her face in my neck and burst into tears. "It's okay."

"You need to get out of my way. I want to check on my sister," Merrick ordered.

"It's okay, Hatch," I called. "She's okay now." I turned back to Grace. "Aren't you, love?"

Grace nodded and Merrick stalked to the bed and sat on the edge of the mattress.

"I'll give you two a minute," I said.

"I'll take Sparky out," Devon offered, and Poppy handed her dog over. Flea followed Devon, obviously to give everyone some privacy.

Pulling Poppy in for a few minutes of comfort, we walked into the hallway and I lifted her face, wiping tears from her cheeks. "You okay, Poppet?"

She nodded. "That was really scary."

"I know." I hugged her again.

"Is it true that Alison was going to kill Gracie?"

I scowled at Hatch over Poppy's head and gave him a look of desperation. I really wish Gracie hadn't told her that, but I suppose I couldn't shield my daughter from everything.

"It looks that way," I confirmed.

"Oh my gosh," she breathed out.

I lifted her face again. "But you understand that Alison was deeply troubled, right? This had nothing to do with Grace, or even Alison to a certain degree. Grace didn't do anything wrong, and Alison wasn't fully in control of her actions."

"Grace said that Alison drank a big bottle of Vodka," Poppy whispered. "She had it hidden in the laundry basket."

"That must have been really scary for Gracie."

"Grace wanted to go with Uncle Ryan and Merrick to the movie, but Uncle Ryan said she should stay with Alison. He said that Alison needed some one-on-one time with Grace."

I forced tears away. This explained Grace's reaction to

204

Ryan at the hospital.

"Gracie hates her dad now, Mummy. She said it's his fault that Alison tried to kill her and that if you hadn't talked to Alison, Grace would be dead too." Poppy burst into tears and I pulled her back into my arms, the tears falling freely down my cheeks now.

Hatch moved then, wrapping us both in his protective warmth. I shifted so I could burrow against his chest, and Poppy and I each wrapped an arm around his waist.

"Need to know my girls are okay," Hatch said after a few minutes. "I know this is a shit situation, but, Poppy, you are protected, as are Grace and Merrick, so I need to know you get that."

She nodded up at him. "I know, Hatch. I'm okay."

"I'll always have your back, baby girl."

"I know."

He kissed her forehead. "Good."

Devon returned with the dog and handed him over to Poppy. "He did his business and now he wants to play. Sorry."

Poppy smiled and hugged Sparky to her chest. "It's sleepy time, puppy, not play time." He nipped at her chin with a growl. "Let's go make Gracie feel better."

I kissed Hatch gently and he released me so I could follow Poppy back into the bedroom. Merrick hugged Grace and then moved to leave the room, but I pulled him in for a squeeze and held him probably longer than he expected. "I love you, Merrick. I'm here for you too. Anything you need."

He settled his head on my shoulder and held on for a little while and we stood like this until he broke the connection, standing to his staggering five-foot-ten-inch height.

"Are you okay in the bunk room?" I asked.

"It's all good, Auntie. Devon and Flea are cool."

"Okay, if you need me, you know where I am."

He nodded and, after one more glance Gracie's way, he left the room.

"Grace, do you feel like you need something more to sleep?" I asked.

"Do I have to go to bed? Can I watch a movie or something?"

"I didn't bring any with me."

"They have movies here," Cricket said. "I don't know how many are suitable for kids, though. Hatch'll know."

I leaned into the hallway. "Honey, what are the odds of age-appropriate movies for Grace and Poppy?"

"Odds are good, Sunshine," Hatch said. "Got a movie room downstairs."

"Grab the dog, ladies, let's go watch a movie," I said. "Devon, Merrick, Flea, you coming?"

They didn't hesitate.

TWENTY-ONE

Maisie

ONE WEEK LATER, Poppy and I were back at our place dressing for Alison's funeral. Grace had been staying with us as well, refusing to go home, which Ryan had agreed to for the moment, but today she was with Ryan's mother, whom she adored, which meant she could have family time.

Ryan and Alison's home had been "cleared," on Monday, which meant the clean-up could begin. Ryan couldn't bring himself to sleep there again (I didn't blame him), so Hatch organized a few brothers from the club, and I got with a few of the women, and we helped pack up the house. Cade hired a specialty clean-up crew to erase the evidence of Alison's suicide, so Ryan could get it on the market.

Ryan and Merrick stayed in a hotel until he could find a more permanent solution.

"What's going to happen to Grace now?" Poppy asked as I braided her hair.

"I don't know, Poppet. We're going to have to sit down and have a very serious conversation. You and I are going to England in August, so—"

"She could come with us," she said, hopefully.

"You seem to forget she still has a father."

"She hates her father."

I turned her to face me. "Which isn't *right*, Poppy."

Poppy wrinkled her nose.

"Ryan didn't do anything wrong," I stressed.

"He left her with Alison," Poppy countered.

"Do you really think that if he had *any* idea that Alison was going to do what she did, he would have left Gracie with Alison?" I challenged.

"Well, no, but—"

"Look, these are all very adult situations that even us adults are having a really hard time wrapping our minds around, but Ryan loves Gracie just as much as I love you, Poppet. As much as your daddy loved you, and believe it or not, just as much as Ali loved her." I stroked her cheek. "Alison was sick, and that doesn't make any of this right, and it certainly doesn't make Gracie feel any better, I'm sure, but it also doesn't make Alison's love for her daughter any less. One day, Grace will see that. It's just going to take time. Uncle Ryan has a really long road ahead of him to get Gracie's trust back, Poppet, so I'm going to do whatever I can to help, but let's let them figure out what works for their family. We'll be there to support them however we can, okay?"

"Are you going to marry Hatch?"

"Wow, where did that come from?"

She shrugged. "I don't know. I was just wondering."

"I have no idea. I love him, sweetheart, but I don't know if we're at that stage just yet. It hasn't been very long."

"Well, if you get to that stage, will he be my new dad?"

"I guess that will all depend on whether or not that's

something both of you want. Your daddy will always be your daddy, Poppet, so I don't want you to ever worry about Hatch replacing him."

She bit her lip. "I don't worry about that."

"Well, that's good."

"But if you have other kids, I kind of want all of us to have the same last name."

I chuckled. "Gosh, you've got me married off and pregnant to the man and we haven't even hit the year mark."

Poppy rolled her eyes. "I know, but he's, like, totally in love with you, so it's going to happen."

"You think so?"

"Well, duh."

My heart fluttered. "I'll tell you what, if it happens, and it's something you want to talk to him about, then we'll do it, okay?"

She nodded. "I want to talk to him about it."

"Really? What if there's a boy you like and he stands at the door with a gun cleaning it, and embarrasses the heck out of you and tells you you can't date until you're thirty?"

"Then he'll just be acting like a real dad."

"Well, you've got me there, sweetheart." I smiled and pulled her in for a hug. "If it happens, we'll talk to him about it."

"Thanks, Mummy," she whispered.

"Okay, you look good. Now, let me finish up so I can be ready when Hatch gets here."

I grabbed my purse and walked out to the kitchen just as Hatch walked in the front door. I hadn't seen him since the afternoon before and to say I'd missed him was an understatement. I looped my arms around his neck, kissing him long and hard.

He cupped the back of my head and smiled against my lips. "Hey, Sunshine."

"Hey."

"Missed me, huh?"

"So, so much."

He chuckled. "Missed you too, baby."

"Hey Hatch." Poppy walked into the room and hugged him.

He hugged her back, kissing her head. "Hey, baby girl."

"We should probably head on over to the funeral home," I said. "I packed a bag since it's going to be a long day. I'm not going to want to stay in this dress all night."

Hatch grabbed the bag and we headed down to the garage and to my car. Arriving at the funeral home, we found Ryan already there with his mother and kids, and I saw Alison's mother immediately.

"What the hell is that?" Hatch whispered.

I leaned close. "The mutton dressed as lamb, as we say in England, is Alison's mother."

Phyllis wore a tight, neon-pink leather mini-skirt, see-through platform heels (sans goldfish surprisingly), a leopard print, low-cut cami, and a double gold belt to finish off the ensemble. She'd dyed her hair platinum blonde and had teased it up a bit like Dolly Parton in 9to5. I guess the hippie commune didn't work out.

Phyllis threw herself over the casket with a moan, revealing to the group she'd forgone undies, and cried, "My baby, my baby's dead! She's dead!"

Ryan caught my eye and gave me a look of panic.

"Time to help," I declared.

Hatch nodded. "I'm gonna—"

"Nope," I interrupted. "You're going to show everyone here you're my man."

"Yeah, not really what I was worried about, Sunshine." He stared down at me. "Just not real interested in seein' her shriveled up twat."

"Got it." I faced him, forcing back a giggle as I gripped his cut. "I love you, Hatch Wallace. Now kiss me quickly because I have a dead woman I need to save from a drunk one."

He chuckled and did as he was told. Poppy hung back with Hatch while I approached Phyllis with caution.

"Hey there, Phyllis, do you remember me?" I asked. "I'm Maisie. I met you a while ago. When Grace was born?"

She turned her head to look at me, but didn't stand up or

move away, so I did my best to block her vagina from the family. "Yes. I remember," she said.

I didn't believe her, but I went with it. "I'm so sorry for your loss."

"She hated me."

"She didn't hate you," I countered.

"She never called."

"I'm sorry," I said again, and wrapped an arm around her bony shoulders, pulling her (a little forcefully because she wouldn't let go of the damn casket) away. "That must have been difficult." I led her to the family row and sat her next to Ryan's mother who appeared mortified that I did so.

Ryan joined me and gave me a gentle hug, thanking me for my help.

"Where's her husband, or whatever he is?" I asked.

"Merrick said he saw him in the bathroom drinking from a flask. I thought about going and getting him, but, honestly, I just don't give a shit," he admitted in a whisper.

"I don't blame you." I glanced around. "Is Alison's dad here yet?"

Ryan shook his head. "I don't know if he's coming."

"Oh," I breathed out. "Okay."

"It's fine, Maisie. People are going to be arriving soon, though. Not sure what I'm going to do with her." He nodded toward Phyllis when he said "her."

"Get your cop friends to escort her out if she becomes a problem, Ryan. Seriously, don't feel bad. I'm surprised you called her."

"Her daughter's dead. I couldn't keep that from her."

"No, this is true." I sighed, feeling like a bitch. Even though I knew Alison couldn't stand her mother, Phyllis was still her mother. No one should lose their daughter. You weren't supposed to bury your children.

I joined Hatch and Poppy, close to where Grace and Merrick sat with their grandmother, and we muddled through the service, then onto the procession to the gravesite where we watched Alison lowered into the ground. The whole thing was just *wrong*.

There were less than twenty of us there, but I didn't miss the support of the Dogs and their bikes at the gravesite when we pulled up, along with several of Ryan's coworkers dressed in their finest Police Blues.

By the time Hatch wrapped his arms around me and Poppy, and we started back toward the car, I didn't know if my legs could support my weight... and we still had to head back to their grandmother's house to feed the guests.

I leaned heavily against Hatch as we walked away from the gravesite and by the time I fell into bed that night, I had nothing left, so I wrapped myself around Hatch and fell asleep almost immediately.

TWENTY-TWO

Maisie

ABOUT A MONTH later, Poppy had been out of school for a week or so and she and I were up at Kim's place for a riding lesson. Well, *she* was having a riding lesson, I was watching. As was Kim, considering she'd just given birth a week ago. Jagger Aidan Quinn was currently sleeping in the house, as was Cambry, both under the watchful eye of a nanny, so Kim could come down and check on the horses.

"Are you coming over to Payton's tonight?" Kim asked.

"I think so." I checked my watch. "Hatch should be here in about an hour. We were going to go from here."

"Perfect." She gave me a conspiratorial grin. "You know the house across from them is for sale."

I laughed. "Oh, *really*."

Poppy and I needed a proper house, and I'd been tossing around the idea of selling the business for a while, but especially now that neither Alison nor Niall were there to do it with me. It just wasn't the same. With Poppy's love of art, I liked the idea of applying for the art school in Vancouver and moving away from the memories. I'd mentioned this to Kim and it sounded like she'd said something to Payton.

"And Carter and Cassidy live right next door to Hawk and Payton," Kim continued.

"I did know that, yes."

"Payton's determined to have her own Dogs' commune."

I grinned. "That sounds perfect."

"Kimberly," an irritated growl came from behind us.

Kim smiled and turned to face Knight who was walking angrily toward us. "Hi, honey."

"What the hell are you doing on your feet?" Knight demanded.

"Checking on Fozzie, making sure Poppy got set up with Mary for her lesson, getting out of the house before I go insane," she retorted. "Oh, and giving my boobs a rest from being sucked dry by the moose I just gave birth to because his dad is a giant."

I bit back a laugh as Knight wrapped his arms around her and pulled her close. "Someone didn't get a nap today."

"Suck it," she said, lifting her head for a kiss.

"Hey Maisie," Knight said once he noticed I was there.

I smiled. "Hey Knight."

As Knight and Kim talked quietly, I turned back to watch Poppy. She slid off the horse and the instructor walked her through a few things from the ground. I was so focused on watching her, I jumped when strong arms wrapped around me from behind and a scruffy beard landed on my neck.

"Excuse me, sir, but if my man finds you here, you'll be in a world of hurt."

Hatch chuckled, kissed me in the sensitive spot behind my ear, then turned me to face him. I looped my arms behind his neck. "How was your day?"

"Good. How about yours?"

"Not bad." He'd left his hair down, so I slid my fingers into it. "I'm going to do it."

He leaned back. "Yeah?"

I didn't have to explain. I'd been bending his ear about selling the business for weeks now, and he said he'd support whatever I decided.

I nodded. "I told Bill to put the paperwork together today. Jeremy Marville made an offer... Bill's making the counter-offer to him next week."

"Does that mean you'll be at my beck and call all day?"

"For what purpose?"

"Sex slave sounds good."

I laughed. "That's kind of a win-win, darling, so sure."

He grinned, kissing me deeply. "Hawk says the house across from them's for sale."

"Kim told me."

"You wanna look at it?"

I raised an eyebrow. "Do you?"

He stroked my cheek. "Yeah."

"Are you asking me to move in with you?"

He shook his head. I frowned.

"Askin' you to marry me, Sunshine."

I gasped. "Seriously?"

"Yeah, but this is not your official proposal."

"Connor," I whispered. "I love you."

He grinned. "Is that a yes or what?"

"I can't say yes... this isn't my official proposal."

He laughed. "Fair enough."

"We do need to talk to Poppy, though."

"I already talked to her."

"I'm sorry?"

He slid my hair behind my ear. "Talked to her about how she'd feel if I made this permanent and she wanted to know if I could be her dad. So, we had a conversation that she asked I keep between her and I, and we have a plan."

"So, I don't get to know the plan?"

"Not yet."

I wrinkled my nose. "I don't think I like that."

"She's safe, Sunshine."

"I'm not worried about that. I trust you."

"Good to know."

"I just want to know what the conversation was about."

"And if she wants to tell you, she can," he said, patting my bottom.

I slid my hands under his T-shirt and up his chest. "Bet I can get it out of you tonight."

He kissed my nose. "You can try."

"Challenge accepted."

"Mum, did you see me?" Poppy asked as she rushed toward us. "I jumped the logs on the ground."

"I saw, Poppet." I pulled away from Hatch and hugged her. "You looked amazing."

"Thank you." She smiled. "Hi, Hatch."

He smiled. "Hey, baby girl."

"Your stuff is in Kim's downstairs bathroom so you can shower and change here instead of going all the way home," I said.

She handed me her helmet. "Okay."

"We'll meet you back there," I said, and she skipped off to the house.

Hatch wrapped an arm around my waist and I slid my hand in his back pocket. "So what did you guys decide?"

"Nice try."

"Damn it," I breathed out.

"Gonna do it right, baby."

"Glad to hear it, Connor."

He chuckled. "Gonna be a surprise, though."

"I'm good with that."

We walked back to the house and chatted with Knight and Kim while we waited for Poppy to finish getting ready. Once she was, everyone piled into cars and we convoyed up to Hawk and Payton's home in Vancouver.

The crowd was smaller tonight, just us, Booker and Dani, Hawk and Payton, Ace and Cassidy, and Knight and Kim. Admittedly, I was glad, because I wanted to eat, drink, then get my man home and naked.

I was in the kitchen with the other women, Poppy and Lily were in the basement playing pool with Maverick and the guys, and Kim's nanny, Emily, was watching the little kids upstairs.

Payton poured everyone another Margarita and grinned. "Elyse said you could come and look at the house tonight."

"Seriously?" I asked.

Payton nodded. "Want to? Huh, huh? Wanna? Wanna?"

I giggled. "If we can pry Hatch away from whatever he's doing, I'm open."

Payton glanced at the ladies. "Do you mind if we leave you for a little while?"

"Um, no. I want to go," Kim said.

"Yeah, me too," Dani said.

"She won't care," Cassidy said. "I've seen it, so I'm happy to hang here with Emily and the kids."

Leaving our margaritas in the kitchen, we headed downstairs and I put my finger to my lips as I approached Hatch. He was getting ready to make his shot, so I slid up behind him, but before I could grab his ass, he said, "I know you're there, Sunshine."

"Bloody hell," I snapped.

He chuckled, made his shot, sinking a stripe into the side pocket, then turning to pull me in for a quick kiss. "Give me a second here, babe, gotta take Hawk's money... again."

"Oooh, yay, we get to send Poppy to a fancy college," I retorted. "Thanks, Hawk."

Hawk laughed as he wrapped an arm around Payton and waited for Hatch to finish up the game.

"Poppy, do you want to come look at a house across the street?" I asked.

"Like to live?"

I shrugged. "Maybe."

"Sure," she said.

Game won, Hatch agreed to look at the house, but the other guys begged off, so Hatch, Poppy, and I followed the rest of the ladies across the street.

Cassidy was right, Elyse couldn't have cared less that

everyone converged upon her home. She was a lovely woman in her early fifties, and the only reason she was leaving was her husband had been relocated. The home had just been finished six months ago, so it was essentially brand new.

Hatch, Poppy, and I broke away from the rest of the women and followed Elyse around the house. I kept my expression neutral, however, I'm pretty sure I squeezed Hatch's arm black and blue.

Five bedrooms, four bathrooms, plus a den. A large kitchen and family room, and there was a basement with yet another bedroom, bathroom, movie room, and large area that could be anything. The house was ridiculously large, over four-thousand square feet, so that was a concern, but if we were going to do this, I kind of wanted to go big.

Once the tour was over, we thanked Elyse, and headed back to Payton's. "They don't want to list it with a realtor," she said. "Which is why they're offering it so low."

"It does seem really low," I said.

"Mack can help with the paperwork," Hatch said. "Make sure everything's legal."

"Do you like it?"

"Do you?" he asked.

"I love it," I whispered. "What do you think, Poppy?"

"I really like it and we'll be close to Lily." She frowned. "But we'll be really far from Grace, Mum."

Grace was now back home with Ryan and Merrick, and Poppy was missing her. I cupped her cheek. "I know, Poppet, but she's going to a different school next year anyway, so you'll still get to see her just as much if we move up here."

She chewed on her bottom lip. "Do you promise?"

"I promise."

"Then I love it, too."

"Okay, Hatch and I'll talk about it tonight and see if we can swing it."

She nodded and headed off to wherever Lily was, and Hatch pulled me down on his lap in an overstuffed chair while we watched the rest of the guys finish up their pool game.

Hatch had gone suddenly quiet... well, quiet for him... which I didn't like, but I figured he was processing the house information and next steps.

An hour later, we said our goodbyes and took off for my place. We pulled into my garage and Hatch turned to me, leaning over to kiss me. "You okay with me sleepin' at my place tonight?"

"No."

He sighed. "Babe."

I glanced at Poppy in the backseat and then focused on him again. "Come up and we'll talk." He frowned but I reached over and squeezed his knee. "*No*," I repeated.

Hatch turned off the engine and we walked up to the condo in silence.

After meeting Poppy in her bedroom and doing our nighttime ritual, I joined Hatch in the kitchen. He grabbed a beer and I cornered him by the fridge. "If you don't like the house, just tell me."

"Liked the house, Sunshine."

"Then why are you all grunty?"

He raised an eyebrow. "Grunty?"

"Connor, what the hell, love? Just talk to me."

He moved away from the fridge and leaned against the island, continuing to sip his beer. I shook my head and threw my hands in the air, but I didn't let him off the hook. "I'm not buying that house without you, Hatch."

"Yeah?"

"Yeah," I snapped.

"It's a lot of money."

"I'm aware. And I'm only paying half. So you better figure out how to come up with the other half, because I'm not paying more than that."

I saw his lip twitch and I *knew* I'd hit on what was bothering him.

"What if I can't come up with the money?" he asked.

I shrugged. "Then we don't get the house."

He took another swig of the beer. "But you love the house."

"Yes, but I love you more."

Hatch set the beer on the counter and then his mouth was on mine and I was in his arms, my legs wrapped around his waist, and we were headed to my bedroom. He kicked the door shut, locked it (somehow) and tore my clothes off, his mouth settled between my legs and he sucked my clit into his mouth, his tongue swirling as he added pressure each pass he made.

He slid his fingers inside of me and my body shivered. Then I lost his mouth and I whimpered. Hatch finished removing his clothes before he climbed up my body, linking his fingers with mine and holding them over my head, and then pushed into me. I sighed as I wrapped my legs around him and arched up. He slammed into me over and over again and it was sweeter than it had been, more emotional than it ever had been, and I didn't think I could love him more.

"Con, I... ahhh..." I came undone and Hatch kissed me, releasing one of my hands to stroke my neck as we climaxed, and anchored me to him as he rolled us to the side.

His hand cupped my bottom and he kissed my temple. "We're gonna get you that house, Sunshine."

"I know we are."

He chuckled.

"You need to stop shutting down on me, love," I admonished.

"I know, Sunshine. Workin' on it."

"Work harder."

"You always been a ball buster?" he asked, slapping my bottom.

"Yes." I shifted so I was straddling him and cupped his face. "I love you, you ridiculous prat."

"Fuckin' sexy, even when you're insultin' me, baby." He slid his hand between us and thumbed my clit. I dropped my head back and rocked against him. "Grab the headboard, Maisie."

I did as I was told and he slid down so his face was between my legs, lifting his head up so his mouth covered my core. I pressed my body down, but he gripped my hips and

220

anchored me where he wanted me. I tried to move (because I *had* to, *God*, I had to), but he was way stronger than I was, and he held firm, his tongue sliding in deeper and deeper.

"So fuckin' wet, baby," he rasped, and sucked my clit.

"Thank you, Captain Obvious," I retorted.

He chuckled and slid out from under me, shifting me so I was on all fours. "Cheek to the mattress, Maisie."

I obliged immediately and he lifted my hips, kissing the area just above the rise of my bottom. "One day, baby, I'm gonna take this." He slid his finger over my wetness and moved it to my very forbidden area. I blushed, but the feeling was so unbelievable, I whimpered with need.

"Finger your clit, baby," he ordered, and I reached back.

His cock slid inside me, slowly at first, and I worked my clit while he tortured my pussy. "Connor," I breathed out.

"Brace, baby."

I grabbed the edge of the mattress and he slammed into me, harder and harder. "I'm—"

"Don't come," he ordered.

"I have—"

He slapped my bottom, which *really* didn't help. "Hold it, Maisie."

I bit my lip and tried to keep my orgasm at bay, but then he did something he'd never done before and I was done. His finger slid into the tightness of my ass and I exploded, screaming his name into the pillow as I collapsed onto the mattress. Hatch rolled us to our sides again, staying connected as he continued to move, his hand sliding between my legs and cupping my pussy as he worked my clit. "Greedy fuckin' cunt, Sunshine."

I just nodded. I didn't have enough breath to speak.

While one hand worked my clit, his other rolled my nipple into a tight bud and he slammed into me, building yet another orgasm.

"Come, baby," he whispered, and I let go.

Hatch held me tight as we caught our breath and I closed my eyes unable to focus. "Holy... oh, my... I'm..."

He kissed my shoulder. "Fuckin' beautiful, baby."

"Back atya." I craned my neck so I could meet his eyes. "I loved everything we just did there, kind sir. I'd like that on the menu next time as well, please."

Hatch laughed, kissing me gently. "I think that can be arranged." He climbed off the bed and headed to the bathroom, returning with a warm washcloth and cleaning me up.

Slipping back under the covers, he pulled me onto his chest.

"I love you so much it hurts sometimes," I whispered.

"I'm not goin' anywhere, Sunshine."

"Promise?"

He lifted my chin and stared at me. "I promise."

"Do not *ever* threaten not to be in my bed, then."

"Momentary lapse."

I tugged on his beard. "Connor, I love you. I honor you. If you'd let me pay for that house by myself I would, but I know you, so however you want to handle it is fine with me. But once we're married, my money's your money and I need to know you won't be threatened by that fact. It's important to me. Because I swear to God, I'll give everything I have to the closest Catholic church if my money means losing you."

He closed his eyes briefly and then kissed me. "You'd really do it, wouldn't you?"

"Yes. I'd really do it."

"Fuck me, I love you."

"That's good," I said. "Because I love you, too. But do you love me enough to get over this?"

He smiled slowly. "Yeah, baby, I love you enough to get over it. It'll take a little time, but I'll get used to havin' a sugar mama."

I giggled. "Well, once I sell the business, I won't know what to do with myself, so be prepared to have a sugar mama who wants to hang out with you all day."

"Sex slave, Sunshine. Already told you."

"Will you let me have your babies, Hatch?"

"I'd be privileged, Sunshine."

I slid my hand to his pec and traced the tattoo honoring his mother. "How did you get involved with the Dogs?"

"It was right after Mom died. Met the Prez of the San Diego chapter at one of Dad's fights. Back then, the club wasn't as clean. Still not a one-percenter, but not as clean as it is now."

"What's 'one-percenter'?"

"If an MC is a one-percenter, they operate outside the law. They have their own code of conduct and, when they can, will pay off law enforcement, law makers, judges, people like that."

"Like in *Sons of Anarchy*."

"Sure."

"I've only watched a couple of episodes," I admitted. "It was way too violent for me."

"Yeah, well, that's what motorcycle clubs generally are, Sunshine. You don't fuck with 'em."

"So you were like that?"

"Not quite, but close. Again, not one-percenters. But we still did our own thing. Owned a few legitimate businesses, strip clubs, bars, places like that. I kept the peace."

I snorted. "My man was the peace maker."

"Fist or gun, baby. I got the peace."

"Oh, *that* kind of peace."

"Yeah," he confirmed. "Prez was there for me when Dad got sent up. Helped me keep the family together. Couple of the old ladies helped me with Cricket, 'cause what the fuck did I know about raisin' a girl, especially a baby?" He sighed. "Cricket found a box of band-aids in Mom's bag I think… and she sat on Mom's hospital bed and kept saying, 'Mama has owie. I gonna fix it.' And she'd stick these band-aids on Mom's arms. Fuckin' broke my dad's heart. I'd never seen him cry before, but he picked Cricket up and Mom passed a few minutes later. Dad lost his mind after that."

"That's devastating," I whispered quietly against his chest, trying desperately not to cry. "I'm so sorry, darling."

"This," he squeezed my bottom, "makes it better."

I met his eyes. "It does?"

"You give me peace, Sunshine." He kissed me gently. "Don't know if you've noticed, but I'm not big on sharin' my

223

feelins'—"

"You? No way," I quipped.

He grinned. "Thought if I didn't talk about shit, I wouldn't think about it, which is true to a certain degree, I guess. But when I talk about it with you, you heal it."

I blinked back tears. "Connor."

"Make sense?"

"Total sense."

"I love you, Maisie."

"I love you, too."

We talked quietly into the wee hours of the morning. Despite the vast divide of our worlds, they'd collided to bring us the richness of newfound peace and I drifted off to sleep knowing I'd been given a second chance at an even greater love.

I was taking that chance and I was holding on with all I had.

EPILOGUE

Maisie

A little over a year later…

"**P**OPPY, YOU'RE GOING to miss the bus!" I called up the stairs. It was the first day of school… the first day of *high* school for Poppy, and she was still fussing with her hair in the bathroom.

The doorbell pealed and, since I was right by the front door, I pulled it open.

Lily smiled, looking gorgeous as always. "Hi, Maisie."

"Hey, Lily. Come on in, love."

"Poppy Kenna Mann Wallace, get your ass down here, now," Hatch walked into the foyer and bellowed up the stairs, adding a little bass to his voice for oomph.

She appeared at the top of the stairs and I gasped. No, this was not my daughter. I leaned against Hatch and settled my hand against my chest. She was so grown up. She'd pulled her long, blonde hair to the side and braided it, and wore dark jeans, knee-high boots and a tight T-shirt, not too tight, but tight enough to show off the boobs she suddenly developed this summer... damn it.

"Fuck," Hatch whispered for my ears only. "Go change, baby girl."

Poppy's eyes widened. "What? Why?"

"Burlap sack. Garbage bag, whatever. But that's too revealing."

She rolled her eyes and giggled. "Oh, okay, Sid. Whatever."

My heart sang in my chest and I grabbed Hatch's hand. Poppy didn't notice as she let out an excited squeak and hugged Lily. They grabbed breakfast (which had been the plan... to eat at our place), then I took pictures (too many according to Poppy's copious amount of eye rolling), and then they were off, walking to the bus stop that was just at the corner of our street. Technically, Lily was old enough to get her license, but Hawk was having none of it, and she didn't seem to be in a rush, so they bussed it.

I watched them through the window and thought about everything that had happened since we bought the house. It had been a magical year, to be honest. Hatch had officially proposed to me in London in front of my entire family (after speaking with my father, who adored him... in fact, my whole family adored him), and he'd done right by me in the ring department. A beautiful two-carat princess cut diamond set in a Celtic knot woven ring. He'd bought the matching wedding band, and he'd also bought Poppy a promise ring which he presented to her on our wedding day, promising to always protect her and cherish her and be her stand-in dad for as long as he lived. I don't know which part of the ceremony I cried more during... him saying his vows... or him promising my daughter he'd always be her stand-in dad. From that moment on, she called him 'S.I.D.,' and it was just as special to her and him as 'Dad' could ever be.

Hatch also had Mack draw up adoption papers which he and I signed after Poppy agreed it was what she wanted. A judge signed the paperwork two days after Hatch and I got back from our honeymoon (Hawaii), so we started our lives in our new home a complete and official family.

Jeremy Marville had bought the company, fired Bill, but kept the rest of the employees right where they were, including Cricket. She even worked her way up to CFO in less than six months after Nicole got herself knocked up (she said it was because she and her boyfriend were always in a state of arousal having all of our products at their disposal...best endorsement ever). Nicole chose not to come back to work, so Cricket took her job and was flourishing. Another testament to the incredible woman Hatch had raised...not that he'd take any of the credit.

Ryan and the kids were doing well. Ryan had asked me if I wanted to read Alison's suicide note... I had quickly declined. I didn't want to know why, because to me the why didn't matter. She wasn't here anymore. Nothing could bring her back and my focus now was to make sure her kids were okay.

We had "family" dinner once a week, a tradition Hatch held onto with his siblings every Sunday, and we kind of rolled Ryan, Merrick, and Grace into the mix. I cherished our huge get-togethers, and they bled into holidays since our house was the biggest and no one had to go home if they drank too much... there was plenty of room to sleep it off.

"Sunshine?"

"Hmm?"

"You got somethin' you need to tell me?"

I forced myself away from the window and walked down the hall to the kitchen. Hatch was standing in front of the recycling bin, his face void of expression.

"What?" I asked.

He leaned down and held up the empty pregnancy test box I'd dumped in there two hours before.

"Oh, shit!" I exclaimed. "I totally forgot about that!"

"Come again?"

"I took a test when I woke up," I said, and headed to our bedroom, Hatch hot on my heels. "Morning pee is the best time to take it, so I took it when I woke up, but then I got distracted with you sticking your face between my legs, and then having to actually get up and be a functioning member of society."

"Are you complaining that I stuck my face between your legs?"

I ignored him as I walked to my bathroom vanity where I'd left the pregnancy test and picked it up. Spinning to face him, I squealed, "It's positive!"

"No shit?"

"We're going to have a baby, Hatch!" I threw my arms around his neck and kissed him.

He grabbed my bottom and lifted me, so I could wrap my legs around his waist, and then carried me back to bed. "You're gonna have my baby."

"Are you happy?"

He kissed me. "Yeah, baby. I'm happy. You happy?"

"Beyond happy. But you're gonna have to get busy so I can have another one," I bossed. "Us old ladies have been talking and we want lots of puppies. We're raising up the next generation of Dogs."

"No one's gonna call my kids puppies, Sunshine."

"Oh?"

"Wolf pack, yeah. Puppies, hell no."

"Then you better howl at the moon, love."

Hatch laughed as he tugged my shorts off and buried his face between my legs. I wove my fingers in his hair. "This is a good start, darling."

Eight months, three weeks later, Parker Connor Wallace arrived healthy and happy with his father's feisty bellow, dark hair, and blue eyes. He was perfect.

ABOUT PIPER

Piper Davenport writes from a place of passion and intrigue, combining elements of romance and suspense with strong modern-day heroes and heroines.

She currently resides in pseudonymia under the dutiful watch of the Writers Protection Agency.

Like Piper's FB page and get to know her!
(www.facebook.com/piperdavenport)

Twitter: @piper_davenport

Made in the USA
Middletown, DE
08 October 2022